The

Doctor's

Daughter

BY VANESSA MATTHEWS

First paperback edition, CompletelyNovel, June 2015
www.completelynovel.com

ISBN: 978-1-84914-737-8

Printed in the UK by Anthony Rowe CPI.

Cover design: Vanessa Matthews. With thanks to cover model Emma Tolley.

Twitter: @VanessaMatthews
Facebook: facebook.com/VanessaMatthewsWriter
Instagram: instagram.com/vanessamatthewswriter
Pinterest: pinterest.com/nessamatthews
Blog: ordinarylifelessordinary.wordpress.com

For Jim.

With special thanks to my children, your courage and endeavour inspires everything I do. To my ever supportive family and friends, you know who you are and how you have encouraged me. I may never have started, let alone finished, this novel without you.

CHAPTER ONE

VIENNA, 1927

Marta Rosenblit buttoned her father's white cotton shirt right up to the starched collar before adding his navy blue neck tie, fastened at her throat with a Viktoria knot. Next, she put on his waistcoat. Essential for propriety and to mask any traces of feminine form that might give her away during the experiment. Her father had ordered that she dress for her role this evening from head to toe, every inch of her to embody the look of a man. She did not want to disappoint him though failure was unlikely since her androgynous body offered few clues to her gender whatever attire she chose. 23 years old and yet she was barely recognisable as a woman by face or frame.

Marta was nothing like her mother or sisters. She was not a housewife, not a beauty, not a hostess. By this age, all five of her siblings had been married and pregnant, using their bodies exactly as their biology had intended. Most young women painted their lips cinnabar and set their hair, she achieved little more than a cold scrub and a quick rake with a fine tooth comb. Her stockings were hand me downs, the fabric of her chemise sagged emptily at her hips and breasts where it had once been generously filled by its previous occupant. She owned exactly two types of footwear – brown slip on Oxfords with a low rubber heel, and a pair of cumbersome black gardening boots. A pair of her mother's dress shoes had remained entombed under her bed for many years, two sizes too small now and in a cherry satin she considered far too lascivious.

She stopped dressing for a moment and reached for her father's cigarette case which he had left perched on his dresser earlier. She rolled her palm over the delicate white sticks inside before selecting one; its pristine paper casing highlighting the grimy appearance of the yellow stains on the knuckles of her index and middle fingers.

Upon lighting it, she tucked one unsightly hand into the darkness of her father's trouser pocket and pressed the tip of the cigarette to her lips with the other. She drew the hot smoke deep into her throat, warming her chest against the chill of the early evening air, releasing it with a slow sigh of satisfaction as it rolled back up and out of her mouth.

Her father's bedroom faced south and was usually bright but the last of the spring sunlight was fading and twilight danced on the window sill. She moved to the window, rolled her forehead against the cooling glass and surveyed the garden. A row of black pine trees stretched up from the boundary, forming sprawling silhouettes that sliced through the beauty of the violet and amber sky. His study was situated on the ground floor directly below, with a single window that offered the same view. As she smoked she remembered how she had spent much of her childhood behind that rectangle of glass as her sisters and their friends hosted teddy bear picnics and tea parties for their dolls. Even as a girl of 5 or 6 years she had watched them as one might observe museum pieces, not sure she understood the purpose of their play or how to interact with them without causing irrevocable damage.

She opened the window; forcing her smoke out into the fresh air, sucking on the cigarette until it burned its way down to her fingers. She stubbed it out in the ashtray on the nightstand then plucked the blazer from the bed, where it had been waiting since her father had set it out for her. She closed her eyes as she breathed in his scent, suspended in the threads of the fabric. Holding it out in front of her, she took a moment to admire the cut of the garment. *'Knize'* - Marta paused to trace the embroidered label with her forefinger before swinging it across her shoulders and slipping her spindly arms into its generous sleeves. Her father had always chosen the finest tailor for his suits and the ever popular gentlemen's outfitters on the Am Graben was now the only outlet he would consider. He admired their method and precision; each of the 7,000 stitches was crucial to the whole and comparable to his own ardent attention to detail. Dr. Arnold Rosenblit was a stickler for details and could not tolerate those who didn't share his exactness.

She did not appreciate the luxury of the the smooth silk lining inside the blazer as she wrapped it around her body; she enjoyed the rough scratch and prickle of the wool that peaked from the edges of its collar, cuffs and hem. A complex sensation, however uncomfortable, would always be preferable to the subtlety of ease.

Marta considered that, to many, the act of dressing like a man in order to be paraded before and questioned by a room full of her father's academic peers

8

might seem unusual. She did not see it as out of the ordinary. In fact, she saw it as training. If she wanted to become an expert on the oddities of the mind it seemed not only logical, but rather crucial to be able to move amongst the masters of such madness before attempting to understand it.

Her father had influence and power in the field of psychiatry and wanted her to support him in his own work, reluctant to push her to the fore. He could be encouraging but more often than not would dismiss her ideas as whims and plagiarism of his own work.

Taking up a teaching post at the Akademisches Gymnasium had been her first attempt at independence but she found it unfulfilling. The settled upper-class existence of her students left them with few psychological distinctions to set them apart. She could not see any opportunity to reshape their minds with her theories and so her ambition to work as a child psychiatrist remained fruitless.

The war had long since ended, social boundaries slackened all around and women of age now had the right to vote. Despite these monumental changes to society, many still refused to acknowledge female potential let alone support them in advancing it.

Unfortunately her father, whose own theories currently centred on hysteria amongst women, upheld and endorsed this attitude. Women could not cope, he wrote in a recently published paper, with their new found independence. *'It forces them away from their instinctive need to be protected by their fathers. Women were not born with the capacity to take care of themselves. The greater the independence the greater the hysteria - psychological components become deranged and the body grows frigid in response.'*

Glancing up at her parents' wedding portrait that hung above the bed she felt sure, had she been in residence, her mother Josefine would not agree with her participation this evening. She had been a vision in white lace ruffles and swathes of silk, espousing the qualities of women from a bygone age. From what she had garnered, her mother had been content to stow away any plans for her own life in favour of supporting her husband and children. Marta, however, yearned for the day she might strike out alone. Conformity had long been her adversary; even her facial features seemed to belie the standard set by her good genes.

As far as she could recall she had visited her mother once at the Kreis des Wahnsinns, an asylum on the outskirts of Vienna. Josefine had tried her best to hide her disappointment at the sight of Marta, an erratic toddler with untameable hair. She was scolded for pursing her lips and refusing to utter a single word. When she proceeded to throw a story book at her mother she was swiftly removed from the room by a nurse. The opportunity for a second visit had not been forthcoming.

Marta had always assumed that an innate sense of disgust at the delivery of such an unwieldy newborn must have been what had driven her mother to the brink. The final straw that had convinced Josefine that insanity was justifiable, preferable even, to attempting to be a mother to her. Her father though had been quite insistent that Josefine's psychosis was self-induced and the matter was not offered up for further debate. Marta had tried not to revisit the idea much throughout her childhood.

She finished dressing, pulling the dark brown leather belt on the waistband of the trousers a little tighter for security; so tight that it might stripe her skin or maybe even cause a bruise. She didn't care; she welcomed the painful sensation like an old friend, taking a moment to bask in the warm buzz that flickered through her body as she bound herself.

His shoes, like his suits, were of the highest quality. Made to measure by Mr Scheer on Braunstrausse 4. Her father had likened wearing shoes from a department store box to wearing the skin of a dead man. *'Clumsy, ill-fitting and sure to rot in no time at all.'* he said. She slid her feet into them and tugged sharply on the laces, forcing them to knit together extra tight. Then she waggled her foot to check they wouldn't fall off.

Her fawn coloured hair was already scraped from her face and combed into a taught bun, fixed at her nape with several hairpins. She smoothed it over with her father's pomade one last time, using the sharp point of her tail comb to tuck a few stray hairs out of sight.

She checked her reflection in the full-length mirror, she was unrecognisable. Her appearance was distorted into a myriad of tiny fractions shining out from the ornate mosaic style frame. She found it preferable to her normal guise.

The wall clock chimed eight. It was time to join her father in the drawing room. Marta descended the stairs, taking care not to stumble in his oversized shoes. By the time she reached the hallway she could already detect the smell of cigarettes and coffee; though her father would always have a whisky perched on the mantle and would not offer to share a drop with his guests.

She pushed open the door to the drawing room and, as rehearsed, made her way to the wooden chair positioned at the centre. She recognised many of the faces, having assisted her father at regular faculty meetings, research presentations and conferences. Sitting opposite her, Professor Hollriegl was quite brilliant and somewhat handsome though it was unusual for him to offer even a flicker of acknowledgment whenever they met. Dr Brueur and Dr Schorske flanked him on either side, well-respected psychiatrists and vocal ambassadors of her father who used their connections to secure funding for many of his projects.

Standing alone in the far corner, Dr Kaposi had an intent stare that had long had the power to make her feel uncomfortable. The man had appeared in her life from time to time for as long as she could remember and yet she did not know much about him. Last of the familiar faces was a pigeon chested man she had seen once before but knew only as Klaus. He was trying to talk to her father, who was preoccupied with a handful of his own notes.

Two other men sat just behind her right shoulder, but she could not recall having ever met either of them. The first was fiddling with his pocket watch, turning it over and over in his hand so frequently she feared he might rub out the engraving. He was young and she assumed fresh out of University, her father liked to think of himself as an inspiration to up and coming academics.

The second man was of slight build and had a curvature to his posture that was closed, stiff and reminiscent of a polio survivor, making him appear small. His expression was stern and pained.

Dr Rosenblit tucked his notes into his jacket pocket and gestured for Klaus and Dr Kaposi to sit. He stepped into the centre of the room, blocking the view of Marta, and sucked ceremoniously on his cigar. He waited until he was sure all eyes were on him, then with a congenial expression he opened the session.

'Gentlemen, thank you. As always your attendance here this evening validates the importance of my work. So,' he pronounced, raising his index finger in the air, 'allow me to get right to the task at hand. Tonight we shall examine the topic of gender. New research has come out of America that suggests one's gender identity may not be an issue of biology alone, but psychology too. I am eager to establish my own study and measure the perception of gender against the imposition of societal norms.'

He paused for effect, looking from one man to the next to gauge their reaction.

'I have chosen to take an experimental approach to gathering your thoughts this evening. Whilst I am not sure I agree with the findings, the American research could become the basis for a comprehensive and potentially more accurate piece of work.'

He continued, pacing the floor, hands now clasped behind his back. 'I am curious; what if gender is little more than a social phenomenon? I find it unlikely, but I would like to review the matter. In a moment, I want you to get up and examine the subject sitting before you and then consider this. What if our sexed bodies are not as essential to our construction of gender roles as we might believe?'

As he moved among his guests Marta sat passive, staring into the cut glass decanter that was in her eye line.

'Under your chairs you will find a copy of the report and its key findings. Take a moment to review it and then we shall begin.' He noted the time on his pocket watch as the men shuffled through their papers.

After four minutes, he decided he was ready to resume the session.

'Now, let's move along. As you examine the subject, ask yourselves what makes a man assertive and proactive and a woman prone to patience and subservience? Make your observations, record your findings and discuss collectively.' he concluded, sweeping his arm across his body and out to the side as if he was a magician unveiling his latest trick.

Marta was unresponsive as the men began to talk about her as though she wasn't there. She tried to ignore the sting in her side when one of the unknown gentlemen sniped that she had better be a man because she would make *'one plain ugly woman'* if put in a dress – *'just a man with more poke holes!'* added the second unknown man. Raucous laughter followed.

Comments and observations grew more lucid as the men passed around a small tray of white powder. A quick sniff of the substance seemed to liberate their thinking and discussion began to flow.

'As scientists of the mind we have come to appreciate the importance of neutrality and yet the nature of our sex must influence us in some way.' Dr Brueur suggested.

'Nonsense man, our own gender boundaries are irrelevant when administering treatment. The focus must never be on the self, but on the patient.' Professor Hollriegl argued.

Dr Schorske intervened, 'True, but treating a female is rarely as straightforward as treating a male. Often I find myself growing frustrated at a woman's general resistance to common sense. As a physician, I can only imagine that kind of irrationality to be biological.'

Arnold approached Marta, 'Vin Mariani?' he asked, handing her a small glass of the potent cocaine infused tonic. He would often pour her one when she joined him in the company of his colleagues, or sometimes during their one-to-one analysis sessions. She sipped at it, grateful for a more acquiescent way to drop her inhibitions and smooth any unsettlement in her nerves.

Some of the men kept a respectful distance, awkward at the exploration of their human lab rat. Others made no attempt to hide their curiosity, touching her intimately in order to confirm her actual gender, moving her face left and right to examine the precise components of the male versus female profile.

Far from upset by the experience, however, she considered it quite a windfall to be in such esteemed company whilst engaged in academic study. To eavesdrop on the musings of some of the most brilliant minds in Vienna was as intoxicating as any tonic she could sip. She had so much still to learn, how could she fail to be stimulated by the opportunity?

An hour had passed before her father spoke again, interrupting the quiet mumblings of the group. 'Klaus, you asked during your observations if ideas of our sexed bodies can be altered through our unconscious as well as conscious minds?'

The man nodded in acknowledgment. Arnold continued, 'Marta, please tell my friend here what you dream of most often.'

She spoke for the first time since she had entered the room. 'I rarely dream with much coherence father, but when I do, I most often dream of being great and noble.'

'Great and noble, of course – and do you take the shape of a man or a woman in these dreams?' he pushed.

'Oh, I perceive myself as a man.'

This was not true, but she had learned by now that her father liked nothing more than to have his theories publicly reinforced by his youngest and most articulate child. It was a fact that she did not dream often, but the dreams she did have could not be shared in public. Commonly exposing her lustful thoughts and intimate desires. A young woman could be arrested for that kind of talk.

16

'And what does it mean to be a man in your dreams?' he continued.

'I have power, I hold court with beautiful women and of course I drink whisky and wear fine suits, better even than yours.' she said, turning to face him.

This pleased her father. 'Ha ha ha! It seems you become a more brazen creature in your dreams – exactly like a man I'd say.'

Marta grew feisty at his lavishing her with such attention. 'In my dreams I indulge the joys of being a man in every sense, psychological and of course physical.'

'Physical?'

'Yes, such superior strength and phallic status would be wasted if I didn't put them to work.'

Arnold's raised eyebrow suggested she had overstepped. 'There! There gentlemen, do you hear it?! Just as I surmised; the envy that you have heard me speak of before. Cloistered in the dreams of my own daughter, ha! You'll excuse me for getting caught up in internal responses, it is, of course, my speciality; let's get back to observing matters of external appearance.' His eyes glistened with delight as he retreated to his whisky glass.

The tray of white powder was passed among the guests for a second time. As the gentlemen closed in around her Marta let her eyes wander to her father, anchoring her thoughts to his every movement. He was standing now to the right of the fireplace. His elbow rested casually on the black mantelpiece and his free arm gesticulated as he regaled Mr Schorske with tales of Marta's earliest and most vivid dreams. Arnold had been recording details of them since she was a child. There had been many, increasingly sexual and often revisited during daydreaming. Fantasising was one of her most exquisitely guilty pleasures.

She watched, admiring Arnold and the lines of his face as they performed a dance with every supposition that passed his lips. He was like a conductor, orchestrating his own opus with exquisite precision and timing and she was glad she had been able to please him in the way he had required of her. When he looked her way she felt electric, she took it as recognition that her input mattered if only for the amusement or education of others.

A muffled voice pierced her concentration and her thoughts scattered like dropped marbles. 'Tell me, why do I find you even more intriguing when dressed as a man Marta?'

'Excuse me?' She was shocked at his intrusion.

'Perhaps it's because you look so much like your father this way. Or because I still see everything you are, in spite of your disguise.'

She was unsure whether it was the effects of the Vin Mariani or the close warm breath of Dr Kaposi grazing the back of her neck but for the briefest of moments she felt the whole room and everyone else in it recede at a pace. As was his habit he had protruded her personal space, a feeling she found both loathsome and arousing. Though she had yet to be deflowered, Marta had imagined all manner of intimate liaisons with men but not once had her father's old friend ever featured.

18

However, her yearning for physical contact was so overwhelming it was difficult to discourage his attention.

Dr Kaposi whispered into her ear. 'You have such greatness in you Marta, don't you think it's time you stepped out of the chair and took the floor?'

She would never have had the confidence to say it herself so it was somewhat shocking for Marta to have it revealed to her aloud, especially by a respected doctor. But could she? Could she move out of the shadow of the captivating Arnold Rosenblit? Did she even want to? Would she have any credibility?

Most women in the city would be satisfied to spend their youth pouting for, preening for or otherwise pleasing a man. Here she was, sitting in the lap of genius and hoping to absorb enough knowledge that she could learn, grow and satiate her hunger to be a pioneer like so many great men she had read about or heard talk of. Maybe it was her time. Show them all how she had outgrown her father's teachings and developed her own theories. She would have more chutzpah than even Dorothy Parker could hope for.

'Let me help you. I could do for you, what Arnold should have done years ago. Let me help you become the woman you deserve to be Marta.'

With that Dr Kaposi slipped his hand inside the blazer, brushing his palm across her insignificant breast as he placed his business card into the internal pocket. She blushed as he lingered, locking his eyes with hers. The corners of his mouth betrayed an assured smile before he left her and returned his coffee cup to the gilded tray on the sideboard. He offered a congratulatory handshake to his host and departed.

For the rest of the evening, Marta's mind whirled and whirled until it was as busy as the rambling green and grey foliage pattern on the drawing room wallpaper. While the men flicked through their notes, her thoughts flipped between all the wondrous possibilities and the more glorious doubts she had about her own abilities. As they traded ideas around her it was all she could do to question the pitfalls of pursuing her ambitions. Acting on them alone could raise or ruin her reputation, and maybe even her father's too. As Arnold surmised the possibilities of a gender study and brought the evening to a close, she fought her desire to jump from her chair and get started. It was her habit to feel compelled to act on impulse whilst at the same time being paralysed by catastrophic thoughts of what might happen if she dared.

It was long after midnight when she made it back to her own bedroom, but she was not at all tired. She undressed as carefully as she had dressed just a few hours before, taking care to hang her father's suit on the door of her wardrobe. She unravelled the bun in her hair, straightening it out with a fine tooth comb before giving her face, hands and underarms a brisk wash with the soap and flannel on her vanity. The saliva in her mouth was still tainted by the flavour of the Vin Mariani and her tongue buzzed a little, but she did not brush her teeth. She did not want to rinse away every trace of the evening.

Feeling refreshed she pulled on a cotton camisole and pyjama trousers and climbed under the bedclothes;

however the coldness of the sheets did not satisfy her. She got up and paced the floor. Under lamp light, she opened the drawer of her dresser and took out her journal. She began to scribble.

'I am exhilarated by my own audacity. To consider myself for the first time as my own champion is as thrilling as any drug. Could I be 'me', without a 'he' to support my every thought? Dare I try? Tonight has been a monumental night but I fear that it will be followed by the worst of consequences if I take even the smallest step forward - and yet I have a greater fear of what might happen if I do nothing at all.'

She replaced the journal and extinguished the lamp before removing her night clothes and crossing the room to find her father's suit in the night. She pulled the blazer from the hanger and wrapped the oversized fabric tight around her bare skin. She got back into bed and began brushing herself with the roughness of it in the only way she knew would soothe her into a dreamless sleep.

21

CHAPTER TWO

On the surface, Dr. Leopold Kaposi could be mistaken for a respectable man of good breeding. Properly garbed from the top of his hat; a homburg in the winter and a boater in the summer; right down to his brogues and briefcase. He would hold his head high and whistle his own signature tune as he walked the streets of Vienna on his rounds.

A chief medical consultant and GP to the aristocracy, he sat on a number of professional panels that enabled him to proffer opinions, oversee practice, and even make decisions about a range of medical disciplines. His time as a young resident of a city doss house was not visible in his peacock posture. There was no trace of his ruthless determination in his bedside manner. His patients did not detect even the faintest hint of greed in his inflated fees.

Eager to escape his miserable beginnings in the slums, Leopold had talked his way into a night porter's job at a prominent Vienna hotel by the time he was sixteen. The hotel hosted regular medical conferences and his role allowed him unlimited access to the many doctors, consultants and physicians in attendance. Often found lurking at the back of the conference suite, he would listen and learn from the shadows. As Leopold saw it, these intellectuals had it all. They wore smart clothes, drove expensive cars, ate good food and owned their own houses. Most important, was their money.

Money gave them power and Leopold wanted in on the act.

He was determined to pursue his interest in medicine and did whatever he needed to do to keep company with the men. He would run errands for the attendees, the kind that went above and beyond his porter duties. Often questionable and sometimes illegal, but he did whatever it took to get ahead, greasing a palm or turning a blind eye when required. His blind eye earned him the trust of a senior member of the American Medical Association of Vienna. Leopold supplied the portly fellow with a steady stream of the young girls that he liked so much. Through this influential relationship he was able to secure a full scholarship to the Vienna School of Medicine.

His lack of foundational education was evident throughout his studies and he struggled to achieve the results that secured his doctorate, but what he lacked in intelligence he made up for through his powerful connections which enabled him to complete his degree in just four years instead of the usual six. Whether he was aware of his inadequacies or not, Leopold had an inflated ego that bordered on narcissism. It was the personality trait that saw him through when talent or academia failed him.

Keen to latch on to anyone of influence, the young doctor forced a network of professional men willing to help him on his way to the top. Women rarely proved such willing partners, but he knew he needed one at his side if he wanted to move in respectable circles.

He did not possess classic good looks. His face was long, his ears a little large and his nose significant and pointed. To add further distraction he had a mild squint in one eye. His blond hair was thinning but was still disguised with a side parting. Leopold worked hard to develop charm to get what he wanted from women until his social status was such that he could demand attention through sheer superiority.

Once the tables had turned he welcomed the advances of women seeking to benefit from his influential connections. That is how he came to meet Cecily.

Leopold's now estranged wife was an aspiring French actress and singer when they met, and almost nine years his junior. She had a soprano tone as delicate as a nightingale's song.

The couple met at the Diplomats Ball in 1898; Leopold had been entertaining a politician named Ottokar when he had spotted Cecily as she danced with the director of the Vienna Court Opera. Leopold interrupted the dance, luring her away with a confidence unknown to the inexperienced 18-year-old. In the early days of their courtship he had lavished her with attention, flattery and gifts, lots of gifts. Seats in a private box at the opera, an exquisite bottle of Extrait de Violette de Parme perfume (Parisian manufacture of course, to ensure quality and remind her of home) and a pair of the softest calve leather gloves she had ever touched.

They married seven months later and soon after Leopold began to exploit his rights as a husband. Always keen to extract as much personal benefit from his arrangements as possible, he encouraged Cecily to become more intimately acquainted with his friends and associates at regular house parties they attended. Cecily had been reluctant at first, but he had been so convincing, almost forceful in his persuasion of her, pushing promises of introductions, auditions and exposure. After a year of marriage, she was pregnant with their only daughter. He had suggested terminating the pregnancy but after much protest and persuasion allowed his wife to carry the baby to full term. Leopold was not the kind of husband or father Cecily had hoped for, often staying away from home for days at a time without explanation and becoming increasingly aggressive towards her. As the time passed the auditions dried up, her looks began to fade and hopes of a silent movie career waned with their marriage.

They had managed just five years before the relationship broke down for reasons he would never discuss, but Leopold was not concerned. On the contrary, he had been relieved. He knew where he wanted life to take him and domesticity was slowing his progress. Leopold did not like to look back and so from the final day of his marriage he kept on moving forward. Taking his pleasures wherever he found them, eradicating complications whenever they spoiled the view.

Though he had lived alone since then, he was not lonely. The extravagant parties they had once attended together became an exciting new playground for him, a place where he could explore frivolous fantasies at will. A place where he could take another man's wife as his own for as long as it suited him, and without his own wife in tow he was not obliged to share anything in return.

His house was large but sparsely furnished these days, a deliberate choice made as much to celebrate his single status as purge himself of the trappings of his marriage. Once Cecily returned to Paris he disposed of many of her belongings in order to transform the family home he had had built for her, into a bachelor's bolt hole.

He enjoyed antiques and collectibles, mostly vintage medical paraphernalia. He had recently had a walnut and glass display cabinet commissioned especially to house his most prized possessions. Amongst his favourites, a set of two black glass apothecary jars from the early 1800s, a pair of steel bone forceps and a Chinese ivory 'doctor's lady'. The latter was the topic of much interest amongst his house guests who liked to marvel at and fondle the pale curves of the reclining figurine.

Leopold ate well and favoured dining in restaurants and cafés. He preferred not to enlist the services of house staff and had no intentions of cooking for himself. Along with his good diet, he liked to keep his body in peak form and so would swim at the public pool three times a week. It was important that he took care of himself, it was good for business; patients did not want to see a bloated and unhealthy physician at their bedside. Projecting success was critical to achieving success, a tip he had picked up early on.

If he was not socialising he would spend his evenings smoking and listening to jazz music, perhaps entertaining a street girl, sometimes two. At the weekend, he would read for an hour in the mornings. He was not particularly well read, by choice his library was limited, however, he selected his titles wisely and read just enough to ensure he kept up with topical discussions. He would memorise quotes and plot lines that might impress his contemporaries, and revelled in sparking provocative discussion about some of his more controversial reading materials.

What Leopold wanted, he got. As he walked home from the Rosenblit household he knew that what he wanted most at this moment was to get closer to Marta. He needed to be alone with her, take her away from the watchful eyes and heavy influence of Arnold and see what she could do for him.

CHAPTER THREE

Marta laid out two slices of fresh bread on a plate for Arnold. She pressed her thumb to the centre of the crust on her own plate but it stayed firm to her touch. She reasoned that a little stale bread would not harm her and after all, Arnold's mouth would not tolerate the sharp edges even if she had thought it appropriate to serve it to him. The raspberry preserve was his favourite and so the remaining two spoonfuls would be added to his mid-morning snack and she would suffice with a little unsalted butter.

Since childhood she had joined Arnold in his study once a week, most often a Wednesday afternoon, to review his interpretations of their dream analysis sessions and he always insisted she bring refreshments along. Sometimes she would bring pretzels and espresso and other times Arnold enjoyed Linzer sablés followed by a glass of sparkling water dashed with elderberry syrup.

With her mother gone and receiving little attention from her sisters, she had relied on the companionship of her father. Her eldest sibling Bertha had made it clear that the arrival of her youngest sister was an annoyance at best, a sickening burden at worst. Her care for Marta was functional. Her clothes cleaned, starched, buttoned and tied. Her cleanliness maintained with a daily flannel wash from the bowl, the water usually cold and murky from cleaning the other girls first. A deep bath every Sunday, she would be plunged into the steaming metal tub for a matter of seconds as

Bertha soaped her skin and hair before a giving her a rinse. When her sister bothered to speak to her she used clipped tones.

"Arms!" Bertha would order as she scrubbed with a determination that suggested she was trying to erase her youngest sibling. Marta would offer up her right arm followed by her left.

"Legs!" She would repeat the process for her lower limbs whilst trying to hold steady on one foot then the other.

"Turn!" This signalled that Marta was to turn her back to Bertha so that her bottom, back, neck and behind her ears could be washed.

"Out!" Bertha would then lift her out onto a scratchy towel where she was to wait until moved to a space in front of the fireplace.

At least the water was not cold on Sundays; however she would have to wait until all of her sisters were clean before she was able to get her hair dry and nightdress on, so she would end up shivering anyway.

Meal times were also perfunctory. She was not consulted on food choices but served a plate of whatever was given. The girls would chatter amongst themselves, Christiane and Nora had developed their own language so that they could communicate with one another in code. Marta had presumed they used it specifically to exclude her, as she had not heard them talk that way in front of Bertha, nor Lotte or Carla. Either way, it did not seem to be too hard to fathom and by the time she turned six years old she had figured out that they would just add the nonsensical '*lala*' to the beginning of every word and the meaningless *'levlav'* somewhere in the middle of longer words.

The closest Marta would get to indulge a sense of familial acceptance was when she would listen in to the girls' stories. Told at the end of every day just before bed, they would exchange anecdotes about boys they liked, friends they had teased and dreams they held for the future. She most enjoyed hearing tales about their mother, accounts of sunny days when she had taken them swimming in the lake near to their grandmother's house; winter nights when she would part hum-part sing Schrammelmusik as she kneaded bread dough in the kitchen.

The girls would light up at the memory of watching their mother dress for nights out with Arnold. Sometimes their parents would be gone for hours and the girls would have fallen asleep in spite of their best efforts to await their return. When they hosted parties at the house lots of elegantly dressed men and women would attend but none, she was assured, were as stunning as Josefine and Arnold. But it was Bertha who offered the most intriguing recollections. She had been there since the beginning.

She had seen so many things, including the arrival of each of her siblings. She had witnessed her mother struck down with morning sickness, seen the squishy reddened faces of each newborn daughter and felt a piece of Josefine slip away with them all. She seemed to resent every one of them to some extent, but none more than Marta. All of the sisters longed for Bertha's approval and so, just like the victim of a bully might turn traitor in favour of the acceptance of their tormentor, the girls mimicked her disdain. It was almost as if Bertha led them as a pack of wolves and Marta was the weakling cub. Away from Bertha, Lotte and Christiane demonstrated some kindness but their unpredictability left Marta with a mistrust that could not be remedied.

As a result, much of her childhood was spent with her father as her main companion. She found relief in the routine of his study. It saved her from the banality of watching the girls play and listening to their repetitive squabbling. With the exception of Bertha who at least demonstrated some cunning.

Marta had participated in Arnold's dream analysis sessions from the time she was able to talk. It was quite normal for her dream states to be laid out and interpreted, often with graphic references that no longer shocked her. She did not consider it an invasion of privacy. When Marta was seven years old the family hired help and she at last had some alternative conversation that offered a refreshing connection to life outside of the Rosenblit household and schoolyard teasing.

After a few weeks she had been interested to hear her new nanny remark to the housekeeper that '...*the poor girl can't think her own thoughts or dream her own dreams. He'll take every one and make them what he wants them to be. She should be out there playing with other children, fitting in. And the girl needs a mother that's for sure; I mean would you look at the mess of her.*'

That was the first time she had ever considered that her experiences might not match that of other children her age.

Sitting on the chaise next to his desk she found herself reflecting on the words of her nanny today. Was she a motherless mess, a lost cause who would never fit in? Or had she been separated from her sisters on purpose in order to become her father's living experiment? It was possible that she had been all of those things and none of those things at various points in her life. Of course logic dictated that her mother's absence from her life was not her fault, she had been a baby and any undoing had begun to take hold on Josefine long before Marta came into the world. But if 'reject' were a signpost, it would be illuminated with lights and pointed down at her.

It was an unfortunate truth that at times she had been able to utilise her mother's abandonment to avoid all manner of punishments, turning it to her advantage.

At age nine her teacher at the Cottage Lyceum sent her to the corridor for drafting a letter to the Austrian foreign minister asking him why it had taken so long for the country to make peace with Russia. She should have been painting, or was it sewing? She couldn't remember now. It was her fourth misdemeanour in as many weeks and had followed an incident during which she had used a sharpened pencil to score the forearm of a pretty girl with ribbon-tied hair. Marta was sure she might be sent home, or worse, removed from the school permanently.

Her teacher had scolded her. 'You are a little girl; you have no place asking questions of important men.

Your behaviour is fast becoming contemptible. Why can't you just settle down and do your school work?'

Marta had replied quite matter of fact. 'That is how it is when you are raised without a mother.'

Her teacher sighed then smiled with an unexpected leniency as she said, 'Yes, quite. Well, go and sit back at your desk and please just try to concentrate as best you can.'

She used the phrase again when her sister Bertha had failed in forcing her to eat her lunch long after the other girls had left the table. For an hour, Marta refused to do more than take tiny bites which she would chew and chew, then push into the side of her cheeks or spit out if she could. Bertha was exasperated at her defiant sibling, 'If you don't eat properly right now I swear I will thump you in the stomach and send you straight to bed! Why won't you just eat?'

'That is how it is when you are raised without a mother.' she said, adding a sorrowful tone for effect.

Bertha did not sigh or smile, but she did storm out of the room leaving Marta free to throw away the leftovers on her plate and casually take herself to the bathroom to vomit the food she had been unfortunate enough to have swallowed.

There had been other times too when she had been able to use the phrase to engender sympathies or pardons for all manner of behaviours. If she disappointed her father, if she failed to wash or dress herself properly, if she spoke out of place, if she defaced an uninspiring school book. Later she had said it to defend herself against the cruel jibes of anyone who questioned the normalcy of her attitude, clothing, lifestyle, and behaviour.

The strangest truth, however, was that in spite of never having had her mother in her life Marta could not escape the constant thoughts of her; emotional preoccupations that could not be remedied cerebrally. A ghost of someone neither dead nor alive to her, Josefine had left fingerprints all over her heart even though she had never been there to touch it.

Josefine's absence had left Marta with a blind spot where she was sure predators and predicaments lay in wait – she must always expect the unexpected. Though quite what she would do when the unexpected arrived she had no idea, and that made her afraid too. Children with mothers to protect them did not have to bear such encumbrances.

Nobody had ever told Marta she was beautiful, nobody had ever plaited her hair with tenderness and care; nobody had ever enveloped her with loving arms and made her feel special. She had long been aware that she would not be able to rely on vivacity and charm in order to secure her place in society. Of course a small part of her envied her sisters for their sweet and seductive ways; she wanted to be revered too. But nature had dealt her from a deck weighted by brains rather than beauty, the two did not seem to be able to coexist within her and so she chose to run with what she had in the hope that academia would suffice. She soon learned that this was the way to capture her father's attention, but now she craved a wider audience for her one talent.

Marta poured the tea from the sterling silver teapot, her fingertips unflinching as she steadied the scalding hot lid to prevent the steaming liquid from spilling over. Her father watched eagerly and she found herself suddenly self-conscious at the sight of her bitten stub fingernails.

'You have experienced some interesting dreams this week Marta. I was excited to note some distinct symbols and I am eager to diagnose their meaning.'

'How so father?'

'Tell me more of the repeated protrusions that appeared. The mountain ranges, church spire and the coat stand. What do you think this could mean Marta?'

'"Well, I was wondering about the mountain dream you mentioned. In it I was climbing high and the weather was fierce, but up at the peak I was struck by the beauty of the vast and colourful sky.'

'Yes, yes, but how did you feel when you reached the top? Elated? Afraid?'

'At times I would say both.'

'Probably more afraid though, wouldn't you say?' a rhetorical question. 'I suggest that this dream and the others too, resulted from our experiment last week.'

'Now you mention it, yes I think I agree. The experiment did bring up a lot of feelings father.' she said, hoping to share her revelations from that night.

'You were surrounded by those men, intimidated by their intelligence. You were dressed as a man but you know it is too much for you to ever hope to be one. Am I right?'

'That is one interpretation I suppose, but what about the sky?'

'Isn't it obvious? We've been doing this for a long time now Marta, have you not learned anything from listening to me?'

She responded with a look of puzzlement.

'The vastness of the sky represents everything you lack as a woman. The colours relate to the many skills you wish you possessed, paraded before you but in a place you could never reach. Your desire to climb the mountain represents your lusting after those men Marta, a desire to soak up all that they are for your own gain. Quite riveting.' he said, rolling his pen between his thumb and forefinger.

Marta attempted to explain herself again. 'In that specific dream I had considered that the mountains and the weather might have represented my oppression. The sky filled with the opportunities that await me if I overcome the obstacles.'

'What obstacles could you mean?'

She continued. 'Of course I don't know for sure, but it could be indicative of academic or financial obstacles, emotional barriers or maybe even a person. I mean… for a long time now you have been quite…'

Arnold cut her off. His face brightened and he began to laugh 'Ha ha! You have such a charming sense of humour.'

'Obstacles, oppression, yes good, very good indeed. Your spirited tongue has always been so entertaining.' he added, still laughing and waggling his pen at her.

'But I thought that perhaps…'

He interrupted again. 'That's enough for the time being Marta, we should take our work more seriously. Come on now, we have been through dream interpretations many times. So as I was saying, the mountains are quite phallic wouldn't you agree?'

'With respect father, I'm not sure I do agree.'

'With respect? I hear little respect for anything as you speak! You know better do you? Do you think you are wiser than me now?' He was not laughing anymore.

Arnold's temper could be as flighty as fearsome, but fuelled by Dr Kaposi's recent words of encouragement Marta persisted in a bid to see how far she could push the boundaries of their relationship.

'I still have much to learn, but my eyes and ears have remained open all these years. I think I have some conclusions of my own to draw.'

'Do you indeed?' He leaned in, resting his elbows on his knees. 'Enlighten me Marta, please.'

'As I was saying, I believe that the act of scaling the mountain reflected my anxieties about unfulfilled potential. I am a woman trying to open up my own sky in the face of male oppression.'

'Oh, I see. Unfulfilled potential and a sky full of opportunities. Do I not give you ample opportunity to shine amongst my contemporaries?'

'Yes, you give me ample opportunity to prove *you* correct.' She knew that such a statement might provoke a rage in him, but the words tumbled out regardless.

'Go on.' he said, goading her.

For a moment, Marta allowed herself to believe that he was taking her seriously.

'My dreams could suggest my need to form my own opinions and ideas, to develop my own theories and command audiences eager to hear them.'

'And what would *you* do with all of that attention?'

'It wasn't for attention; it's just that I have been thinking.'

'Do you like attention Marta?' he asked, ignoring her.

'Not for attention's sake, but if it were garnered as a result of my ideas then it may prove more appealing.'

Arnold raised his chin to the air. 'Please, share your ideas with me, your most supportive audience of all.' His voice soured with sarcasm.

Marta took a breath and rolled her shoulders back to correct her posture and appear taller.

'I'm sure I have a long way to go before I could be confident but I have some thoughts about the traits that one is born with and how they might influence psychology. I wonder about the potential links between our emotional and physical health.'

Arnold removed his glasses and placed them on his desk. Using the thumb and forefinger of his right hand, he pinched the bridge of his nose before running them down his face and around his bottom lip.

She continued cautious but aware that he hadn't tried to stop her yet. 'Trauma too, I have many hypotheses about the disruptive impact of certain life events, particularly in children.'

For a moment, there was silence.

Marta persisted. 'I mean I'm not saying I should explore these things alone. Do you think we could do more work with children? Start a new research project together?'

She looked at him with anticipation.

Arnold raised his hands and linked them behind his head. As he did so, he stretched back in his chair allowing his legs to fall to either side.

'You have a brilliant mind my daughter, of that I have no doubt. However, *you* are a disciple. You are *not* a leader. Women, even intelligent ones, are not destined to lead.'

She had tried to topple his pedestal and so he retaliated in his own instinctive way. 'You will follow, and one day I will gift you with my life's work and you will carry it on in my name. I did not have a son, but I do have you and I am confident that eventually my audiences will receive you as the next best thing.'

'But I want to live my own life; I don't want to be the next best thing.' she protested.

'Sometimes you just have to accept the way things are and that, my girl, is the way things are. What I wonder at this moment is this. Is my Marta suffering from narcissism? Is she egocentric?'

She looked at him, disbelieving.

'The more I consider what you have said the more I am reminded of some of my patients. Perhaps your *ideas* are early manifestations of mental illness. Have you ever wondered if you are not in your right mind? Delusions of grandeur; yes that's what they call it, or I suppose it could be megalomania.' Arnold smirked; gratified that he had restored his superiority.

Humiliated but not surprised, Marta did not speak again.

He picked up his teacup and saucer and took a sip. 'Well, good luck to you and your flock of imaginary devotees. Now, let's get back to some proper psychiatry so that we can continue to enthral my real supporters, shall we?'

CHAPTER FOUR

Elise Saloman may have been sitting near the back of the auditorium but the lunacy of Arnold Rosenblit was evident to hear even from the cheap seats, and she was sure it must have been obvious to many others too. Yet, as she looked around at the male crowd she could see that the majority were all too ready to swallow his suggestion that women across Vienna were afflicted with some kind of madness that obligated them to a life of penis envy.

She had followed this wretched fool more out of morbid curiosity than any intention to learn from his teachings. Elise had recently qualified as a paediatrician though opportunities to practice had not been forthcoming and so she had busied herself exploring other disciplines and broadening her knowledge whilst she waited for her window. The only woman to graduate from her class at the University of Paris, she had long been aware that men dominated her chosen career but that had not deterred her. In fact, she considered it the perfect challenge.

She had overcome many obstacles to get through her education. It was unfortunate that she had to sit her *viva voce* examinations twice; modern languages did not come as easily as other subjects. She had been forced to jostle for a college place, almost losing out due to the sheer volume of students funnelling back into the system to continue studies upended by the war. At university, student newspaper headlines still whined about how female students had led to a decline in standards, and the professorial board was predominantly staffed by men of antiquated thinking.

She had ignored her mother's pleas to settle in Paris, choosing adventure and opportunity in Vienna over a steady existence in the back room of her mother's small apartment. It was true that they had once both enjoyed a more affluent lifestyle, Elise could still just about remember it, but her mother had been stupid enough to rely solely on a man to provide for her and now inevitably had little to call her own. Back then, she made a vow not to end up like her mother, lonely and regretful, mourning for a lost youth. Elise liked to move forward and preferred to travel light wherever she went.

Elise had ambitions – paediatrician, then head of department, maybe even open her own private clinic one day. So far she had been unable to make her mark in medicine through gainful employment, so she had decided to keep pushing her views and spreading her name in as many ways as she could think of until she achieved some recognition.

Publicly challenging some of the leading academics in medicine, she reasoned, could be the key to many doors. And as one of just a few women in the city's medical arena she was sure to make waves. It would have been easier for Elise to share her knowledge and potential whilst hanging off the arm of a senior doctor or a member of the Medical Council but she was determined to do it as an independent woman. She didn't want to end up just an educated accessory. Even the undeniably brilliant Marta Rosenblit was only worthy of merit when accompanied by Dr Rosenblit – a man who was clearly losing his grip. It was encouraging that she didn't warrant it by being somebody's wife or lover; however, she did have the fortune of being raised as the protégé of Rosenblit. Marta had an advantage that Elise had never been afforded and the injustice of that infuriated her more than she could reasonably explain.

Elise located the nearest empty seat at the aisle end of the back row, shrugged off her outdoor garments and settled in. As she waited for questions to be opened up to the audience she busied her nervous hands by smoothing the petal trim of her felt travelling hat. The auditorium was mediocre; she guessed it was used for amateur performances and school orchestras. The paintwork on the walls displayed the grubby shadows of audiences past and was peeling away in small patches here and there. The absence of plush carpet and smart drapery added to the air of austerity. She couldn't help but fidget in the folding wooden seat which was narrow and inhospitable despite featuring a subtle curve to embrace the back. The thighs of a rather large man in the adjoining seat were divided into fleshy sections by the armrests, protruding her space on one side.

Looking around in the dim light she could see that the audience consisted of bearded academics, neat gentleman in lab coats, eager-eyed students, some finely suited consultants and a number of recognisable professors. Dr Rosenblit delivered the final lines of a rousing speech pertaining to the connection between phallic symbolism and the dream states experienced by patients with hysteria. At last he invited comments and questions from around the auditorium.

Elise leapt to standing and waved her still gloved hand to attract attention to herself. 'Dr Rosenblit! Dr Rosenblit *I* have a question.'

The large man in the seat next to her, now alerted to her presence, let out a disgruntled sigh and edged away.

She narrowed her expression to form a determined glare, stepped to the side of her chair and into the aisle, and walked slowly but purposefully toward the podium at the front of the room. The men in the audience seemed to shuffle in awkward unison as each footstep echoed on the polished floor.

'Forgive me if I appear ignorant doctor, but what do you say to those who disregard your theories as the ramblings of a fantasist? An isolated society bore with an unhealthy infatuation with his daughter.'

A daunting silence hung over the room until it was disturbed by the large man who was now anxiously clearing his throat.

Arnold didn't answer but flashed a wry smile at her before casting a glance outward to the rows of his supporters seated behind her. Disappointed that he didn't appear more unsettled by her line of questioning, Elise pressed on.

'Doctor, it strikes me that you have little credible evidence for your ridiculous concepts. Many of your philosophies are as unreliable as your subjects, and I know of others who share my view.'

'Is that so young lady?' Arnold was intrigued.

'A number of scientists and medical professionals consider your ideas little more than masturbatory fantasies fuelled by some kind of messianic syndrome. I mean really, infantile sexuality and male castration anxiety, just some of the immoral ideas you hold without a shred of credible evidence.'

'Masturbatory eh? Quite a shocking word for such a decent woman as you to use in public.'

'Masturbatory, yes. It is just a word and I'm merely repeating what I have heard others say about you. The meaning of which can be shocking or benign depending on the mind of the person hearing it. So how is your mind these days Dr Rosenblit?'

Arnold was short of patience. 'Wait, before we continue with this entertaining exchange I should remember my gentlemanly conduct. I'm sorry, and you are Mrs...?' She had caught his interest.

'Ms Saloman.'

'Ah, Mrs Saloman. Do you have a first name?'

'It's *Ms*, and my first name is Elise.'

'Elise? It's pretty. I like it. Welcome Elise, I'm sure you don't mind if I address you by your first name do you? After all, we are all friends here. Just because we haven't been intimately acquainted, doesn't mean I shouldn't throw you a courtesy or two' Arnold looked her over from head to toe and back up again, lingering at her hips and breasts until he rested his stare back up at her face.

His eyes were the colour of the ocean. They had not appeared so dramatic from the back of the auditorium, but now, up close she found them somewhat startling. As a younger man, she imagined he must have been quite beautiful, magnetic even.

No, it was a trick of the light. She would not be charmed by him. Elise wriggled her toes and pushed down on the balls of her feet in order to plant them more firmly in the street shoes she had bought for the occasion.

'You can keep your flattery Dr Rosenblit. I will not be stifled by charisma. I ask again, what do you say to the critics who denounce you as a fantasist?'

Arnold paused, his face growing florid. Without warning, he lashed the palm of his hand down onto the lectern. The violence of the blow caused Elise to catch her breath. She kept her face rigid and her body stiff in an effort to hold her nerve which was making a valiant effort to escape out of every pore of her skin.

He rose to his feet and leant forward across the lectern. He was taller than she had realised. 'Enough of this nonsense woman!'

'No, it is not enough. You need to answer to your critics.' Elise persisted.

'And you think you are the person to make me do so? Tell me Mrs Saloman, or um Elise rather, were you molested as a child?'

'What? Well I... what in God's name does that have to do...how dare you be so presumptuous!'

'With respect madam, I ask because you appear a little hysterical today. Given that you are so well informed about my theories I am sure you are aware that one of them is based on the notion that molestation in your formative years can cause mental deficiencies in adulthood. You are not the first woman to have been led towards moments of uninhibited frenzy. Perhaps you would benefit from some of my treatment.'

Elise couldn't help but let out an unbecoming screech in response. 'Outrageous! I am not hysterical and I am not your average woman. I am of sound mind thank you.'

'Average woman? Not once did I suggest you were average, but you are a woman. Have you met my daughter? She does not consider herself average either and yet, whatever kind of women you are, I remain convinced that you are all as mad as hatters. I will be driven equally mad if I try to understand any of you.' With that, Arnold and most of the men in the auditorium roared with laughter.

Elise's face flushed with rage. 'You will not dismiss me doctor. I will not be dismissed. Not by any man, woman or child.'

'Oh, I wouldn't dream of dismissing you my dear, sweet Elise. I apologise for making fun at your expense. You are right, I should take you seriously and I should answer to my critics.'

For a moment, Elise was pleased. At last he was going to show some deference.

'I invite you to bring a whole army of scientists, physicians, consultants and whomever else you see fit to come and tell me in person all about their concerns. I wouldn't find that problematic at all, would you? Until then I think we would all prefer it if you could hurry along now so that we can get back to the business of the day.' He terminated the exchange with a flick of his hand.

Elise surveyed the room trying to decide what to do next. The audience had begun shuffling around and talking amongst themselves. Her voice was already lost in the din of rustling papers and mumbled complaints. She realised she must retreat or risk being discredited further.

She shouted to Arnold. 'I will afford you this moment as a courtesy, clearly you are ill prepared for a discussion today, but you will have to answer. Not even you can be right about everything; you would be wise not to forget that.'

Then she turned to the men in the room and, with an elevated chin, escalated her voice further. 'You may not know of me today gentlemen, but recommend that you pay me good mind. I am a woman of science, a graduate of the École de Médecine in Paris and one day I am quite certain some of you will be vying for a place on one of *my* research teams. Dr Rosenblit is an outdated fool and will make you all look like fools too if you continue in your devotion to him.'

Elise turned on her heels and walked out of the auditorium as purposefully as she had walked into the confrontation.

CHAPTER FIVE

Marta met Dr Kaposi in secret early in the morning every Tuesday and Friday through June and into July. She was now comfortable enough in his company to address him as Leopold. He had arranged use of a private office on Tannengasse just a short distance from Vienna Western Station. They would always take care to arrive separately, Leopold making his way by taxi ahead of doing his rounds or seeing patients at his office. Most often Marta would use the train and then continue on foot, but she had cycled there once or twice. Either way her short route was usually a pleasant one; well-dressed men rode past on the tram whilst fathers and sons strolled casually by in matching feathered hats and lederhosen. Sometimes the weather was overcast but more often she had benefited from the gentle temperature of morning sunshine. A number of women chose to walk under the cover of parasols, keen to maintain a fashionably pale complexion, but Marta found the warmth uplifting.

A small area of parkland dotted with spires of buttery yellow Mullein flowers was the only green space on her walk and a pleasing break in the street scene. Each time she crossed it she would slip past the same two smudge faced street traders, too busy negotiating the stony path with their heavy, stock laden wooden carts to pay her any mind.

Like many of the city's streets, Tannengasse was pretty, with pavements dappled in the shade of the linden trees that stood proudly on either side. The office building itself was unassuming, drawing little curiosity from passers-by as they entered. Her father did not have any associates in the area and so it seemed they could continue to meet without risk of discovery. Arnold would disapprove of course, but it was even more controversial for a woman of marrying age to go out with a man other than her father, brother or husband. She had heard of women being arrested for such imprudence, suspected of prostitution no less.

Keeping secrets from her father did not sit well. She would tell him of her plans soon, but first she required time and space to formalise her thinking and refine her research programme. He may not have cared much for hearing of her competencies and innovations but she felt it necessary to press on and satisfy her own curiosity rather than follow somebody else's.

Unlike Arnold, she did not believe that people made choices and reacted to life events based on libidinal instincts alone. She did not think that little boys were jealous of their fathers, or that little girls were angry at their mothers. Marta's interest was in the way children attached themselves to their parents, and the impact of disruptions to those important attachments on future relationships. Far from having maternal instincts towards her subjects she saw the young as portals, open and unguarded.

She would start small; approach the Federation of Women Academics of Austria to see if she would qualify for a grant to fund a study of orphans. Monitoring the differences between their play and that of children from secure families and experimenting with the withdrawal of an existing caregiver or introduction of a new caregiver. She would engage the older children in discussion and encourage them to diary their thoughts and feelings. If she got lucky the University of Vienna might give her access to a regular consulting room, if not then perhaps Leopold could find her a quiet corner of a hospital building.

The potential of any findings fascinated and excited her. She was sure that this was where the truth about human relationships and formation of psychological problems could be found.

In spite of her growing interests, she questioned her loyalties to Arnold with a degree of obsession. Over the course of the summer, she revisited and reassured herself of her intention to strike out alone until it was as necessary to her functioning as feeding or dressing oneself.

Leopold became insistent that she go further than developing her own theories, pushing her instead towards opening her own facility.

'I can see it now. The Marta Rosenblit Centre for Childhood Analysis. What do you say to that?'

He had looked into her eyes as he had asked. Stroking her hair from her face and distracting her from her doubts as he cupped his hand firmly at the back of her neck, pulling her closer until their lips were just a breath apart. He did not kiss her then, but she imagined a kiss was sitting on his lips. No, not imagined, she was sure she had seen it, felt it even. His touch was forceful and it intimidated and intoxicated her all at once.

The realisation that she was attracted to him had left her at odds with herself. She was not accustomed to having real sexual feelings for anyone. There had been a childish infatuation with her nanny when she was just a girl, and many fantasies about a mysterious masked man that had started in her teens and followed her into adulthood, but nothing tangible. Whatever it was, the thought of giving in to it was as uncomfortable as spending her days as a celibate spinster.

Today, Leopold was waiting for her at the entrance to the building. He was clutching a large portfolio and his briefcase. She was breathless and irritable but she forced a smile at seeing him there.

Without a word of hello he put his palm in front of her face as one might halt a bouncing dog, 'Wait here for just one minute; I have something I need to do before you come inside.' It was an abrupt welcome and not the kind she had hoped for, even if he was still smiling.

'But what if somebody sees me out here?' Marta asked, looking around cautiously.

'It's a surprise. Just wait there and I'll come back down in a moment.' His voice trailed off as he left her standing on the pavement.

If she could have stamped her feet like a child and demanded his return she would have. Hers had not been the easiest of journeys this morning, the streets had been busier than usual and the tram had been running late so she had disembarked a stop earlier and had ended up running some of the route in order to make it on time. She knew she would have to brush off her mood so as not to offend Leopold and so she distracted herself as she waited by studying the façade of the office building. They had always been in such a hurry to sneak inside that she had not had an opportunity to take in much of the detail. As she stepped back to take in the large polished wood double doors at the entrance of the whitewashed building, she found herself being spun around by a man striding along the street.

'Oh dear, I am sorry Miss.' A broad-shouldered figure stood before her, he was wearing a large Stetson hat.

She panicked when she recognised the man's face as that of Mr Beste. Everyone in Vienna knew of him and he, in turn, knew pretty much everyone in Vienna. A foreign correspondent during the war, she had heard he was now a newspaper editor; though she could never remember which publication he worked at.

'Think nothing of it.' Marta said, turning her face away in the hope he wouldn't recognise her. He walked on, leaving behind the smell of day old cigar smoke and a sweet alcohol she could not name.

Her heart began to pound in her chest; it was the first time she had seen a familiar face since coming to these secret meetings. She scanned her memory. Was he a friend of her father's? Had she ever been introduced to him? No, she couldn't recall a meeting. Marta reassured herself that there should be no reason for word to get back to her father that she was loitering outside an office building on the other side of the city.

The muted scuffle of footsteps and the squeak of a rusting latch preceded the opening of one of the wooden doors. Leopold bounded out onto the pavement like an over eager wolfhound.

'Quick, come inside and see what I have done for you.' He pulled her by the hand.

Marta cast a furtive glance over her shoulder in the direction of Mr Beste who was now about 500 yards further along the street. She breathed a sigh of relief when she saw that he was getting in his car and had his back to her.

Leopold led Marta up the stairs and in through the office door. He let go of her hand and strode into the centre of the sunny room where he stood squarely before her. 'Marta, I've found it. I've found the place and I have a contact who is interested in offering substantial funding. I will not let you hesitate any longer, we must press on.'

The light pouring in behind him from the two large arched windows showed him almost in silhouette. The golden glow highlighted his scalp under his wisp covered crown; fair strands of hair spread apart in what Marta considered an endearing attempt to fill the vacant patches.

He had already laid out a number of large sheets of paper featuring architectural sketches on the grand mahogany table to his right-hand side. Along with a selection of photographs of a grimy looking brick building in a state of disrepair. Marta looked at Leopold for some explanation.

'I've found it! I've found premises for you.' he said, his excitement intensified for reasons that she realised disappointed her.

She continued to listen attentively, trying to hide her alarm as he told her how he had secured a disused factory to the west of the city, and an architect friend from Prague was on standby ready to reconfigure the building at his expense. He pulled three folders from his briefcase marked 'LEGAL', 'FINANCIAL FORECASTS' and 'WORKS SCHEDULE'.

'What are those?' she enquired, pulling up a chair and taking a seat at the table.

'You don't need to confuse yourself with those; you just concentrate on your theories. I'll be taking care of everything else.' He placed the folders in a neat pile on top of a tall corner cabinet that was just out of her reach.

He turned to her, his face bright with expectation. 'So, what do you say?'

He was giving her everything she thought she wanted, more even than she had so far envisaged. She should have been impressed, she should have been squealing with delight at being showered with such a gift as this.

'I'm not ready Leopold, I'm not sure I can. I didn't consent to such a speedy…'

Leopold cut across her, impatient at her hesitation. 'Darling if I waited for consent every time I wanted something I would be a frustrated man indeed. Surely you don't want to let me down? Not after all of the hard work I have put into this.'

She dared to hesitate again. 'It's just that, well I don't have all of my research together yet and I had wanted to arrange my own funding. I was thinking it would have been nice to have the support of the Federation...'

She broke off. His excitement was gone, replaced by a hostility that made her feel uneasy. She tried to read his face before she spoke again, but he showed her his back, turning to pace the floor.

'And then there's father.' she continued.

At the mention of Arnold, Leopold whipped his head around, pinning her to her chair with a black stare she had not seen in his face before.

'What about your father?'

'What if word gets out? What if he hears of our plans from somebody else and disowns me?'

'What of me Marta? What of me?! Have I not treated you well? Have I not been more encouraging of your liberation than he has ever been?'

She tried to calm him. 'Yes, of course, you're right. I'm sorry, I don't mean to sound ungrateful it's just that...'

'I am beginning to think that you don't need me at all. Are you so driven by your own needs that you would neglect to consider my feelings in this? Casting me aside with such disregard is a cruel trick to play after everything I have done for you. Is that all you think I deserve? Is it?!'

Marta squirmed in her seat; the mounting pressure in his tone frightened her for a number of reasons. She began to pick at the loose skin surrounding her thumbnail, stripping away the tiny chunks of flesh in repetition until it cracked and bled, and cracked and bled some more. On some level, she knew that her ideas could be groundbreaking and could even call her father's theories into question. She had hoped to take things slow, build her confidence until she could discuss her plans with her father in a reasonable and rational way. She wanted his support, but she needed Leopold's courage too.

'You are not the only one with big ideas you know?' He was sneering now. 'Being raised a Rosenblit has left you with an inflated sense of entitlement, but you would be unwise to believe that you are alone in your desire to dissent from Arnold's notions. You are not exceptional.'

Marta was wide-eyed, 'No, that's not it at all. I am not entitled; I know I am not exceptional.' she protested.

'Many of them are more accomplished than you too. If you want to get ahead you had better move first or move out of the way.'

She didn't doubt him, but he was pushing her before she was ready. This was meant to be her opportunity, something she could own. Yet she knew that she needed Leopold. He knew it too.

She looked at him, unsure what to say without making things worse. 'I was just hoping we could slow things down, that's all.'

Leopold gathered the sketches and photographs together into a loose pile and shoved them back into his portfolio. He turned to leave, stopping just before the door.

'We'll go slow if you like, but don't be fooled into thinking you are good enough to take too much time.

Vienna is bursting with visionaries and innovators, inspirational men strong enough to handle anything the city throws at them. Need I remind you that you are a woman, one with a propensity for weakness at that? Today you have shown yourself as one of the weakest I have known.'

Marta felt ashamed of the rush of tears that flooded the rims of her eyelids. She tipped her head back a fraction to prevent them from spilling over.

'Nobody else will see the greatness in you Marta unless I point it out to them, but I am growing tired of your petulance. I'd thought it an attractive trait but now it irritates me. I've no time for it. Give me what I want or go back to Arnold where I guarantee you will rot before you've begun.'

With that he left. Marta slumped back into her chair, confused and defeated. Why was he so angry? She had never committed to a timeline, just an idea. She had not asked to have a tumbledown building refurbished in her name. Or had she? Perhaps she had implied it by going along with it all to this point. Was she being weak? Now he had observed her uselessness in all its splendour it was no surprise that he would want to dispense with her.

Leopold had been so certain that she could do this. He had seen her as a woman before she had been able to see herself that way, but her dithering had exposed her lack of substance and scared him away.

Why was she hesitating now? Leopold was right; she was being weak and irritating. She was capable of showing as much strength and determination as any man.

She would not allow herself to make such a mistake in his company again. She would show him what she was made of.

CHAPTER SIX

Marta pulled the office door shut with a firm tug. She put the key back in its envelope and pushed it into the plant pot in the corridor. It was too early for her to return home without arousing suspicion, having told her father she was taking morning tea at Hotel Erzherzog Rainer with a friend – he was willing to believe she had friends despite having never seen a shred of evidence to support their existence. The palatial building, with its striking pillars and prominent position near the Cathedral, had been a favourite of hers since childhood so that part of her tale was unsurprising and acceptable to him.

She decided to take the tram to Parliament and stroll through the Rathaus in an effort to gather her thoughts before heading back. She had not seen the newspaper for the past two days; Arnold had been quick to confine the latest editions to his study. Once on the tram, however, she had noticed the headline on the front page of the *Pilsener Tagblatt* being read by a gentleman two seats ahead.

'Murderers Declared Innocent'.

She remembered reading about the shooting of a war veteran and his nephew at Shattendorf over in Burgenland earlier in the year, but she had forgotten that the trial had reached its conclusion the previous evening. The shooting had been causing controversy for months and there had been ripples of rebellion ever since. Two men discussed the story across the carriage, it seemed that the release of all three suspects had attracted much media attention. Members of the lower classes across the city planned to down tools this morning and march in protest. The usually peaceful people of Vienna were ready for an uprising.

It was almost 10 o'clock when Marta arrived at her destination. She could already see crowds beginning to form, sweeping along in sombre unison toward the Parliament building and Palace of Justice. She followed them, out of curiosity for the most part, but also aware that it would be easy for her to blend in with them and cross the city unseen. Crowd mentality was also a point of fascination for Marta. The possibility that individual crowd members could somehow relinquish themselves from personal responsibility in favour of following the behaviours of the group was intriguing. Right now, she herself could choose to throw her protocols, loyalties and habits to the wind and do whatever the crowd led her to do. No thinking, reflecting, debating, just action without individual consequence. People herded around her, the majority of them men but a small number of women, some with children in tow. Many carried placards bearing messages of disgust at the acquittal, some joined the procession with tools in hand, and others just grumbled and griped to each other.

Marta negotiated her way through the onlookers and stragglers and into the thickening crowd. At the centre, it was cramped and the air was sticky. The crowd tightened as they approached the Schmerlingplatz, bodies pressed against each other and she could hear murmurs of debate as to the possible reasons for a delay. Then came a rumbling sound followed by a ripple of gunfire. Within seconds, the solemn protestors became an angry mob. Shouting gave way to screams as police rode into the crowds on glossy black stallions, fragmenting the throng with a rain of bullets. Marta watched as chaos erupted around her and the sense of unity disintegrated in an instant. To her left she saw two young men and a grey haired lady drop from the bobbing heads of the crowd, the first victims caught in the crossfire. Many of the protestors surged forward in retaliation; others ran in all directions, stumbling over each other to get away. Children wailed and hollered in fear, clutching at their mothers' skirts.

Without warning flashes of silver glinted in her eyes, more police filtered in, drawing their sabres and slicing into the crowd at random. A man standing at her shoulder let out a groan and fell to the floor, the clasp of one of his braces had torn loose and his rolled up shirt sleeve was changing from off-white to bright crimson before her eyes. Another body fell in front of her, this time a woman. Staring down at them in disbelief, she felt a sudden burning sensation across her left shoulder. She had been struck, her coat slashed apart by a passing police blade. Marta flinched as she clutched her shoulder. The fabric was frayed and bloodied but on first sight the wound appeared minor.

From nowhere, rage bubbled through her body until she could not stand still any longer. She scrambled on the floor in search of the iron bar the wounded man had just dropped and clutching it in her fist she pushed forward to join protestors who hurled cobbles and lumps of wood at police whilst a group of men stormed

Parliament. She felt alive as she raised her fist to the sky and moved with the swell. As she shouted her demands for justice, *'Gerechtigkeit!'*, her voice blended with the chanting and disorder.

When three baton-wielding policemen began beating a frail man into submission, she joined the small group of protestors who chased them away, shouting and lashing out at them with her bar. She was part of this now, part of the fight against the power givers and the power takers. She did not know the men on trial, but she knew enough of the trial to share the sense of abject horror at the acquittal, and so she raged and rallied on this otherwise beautiful Viennese morning.

It was approaching noon when the smell of smoke began to fill the air. Fires crackled in and around nearby buildings, thick noxious clouds billowed out from broken windows, even the Palace of Justice was being engulfed by flames. A second wave of fire crews turned out to support an earlier crew who had been pulled into the riot. Police arrived in their hundreds now, on horseback and on foot, and all of them heavily armed. Marta felt compelled to leave. This was no longer a matter of ordinary people versus the judicial system; this was criminality on a grand scale. Protocol, loyalties and habits returned. She could not contribute any longer; to stay on would lead to dire consequences. The police were taking control and the most probable outcome was that she would end up in jail or dead. She threw her iron bar to the floor and pushed against the crowd until she made it out to a more dispersed spot. The sound of bullets spraying out behind her made her look back to where she had been standing just moments before. More bodies dropped, more men and women clutched at bleeding limbs.

Marta started to run. She kept on running until she was able to pick up her route along the Bergasse. Clear of the danger, she slowed her pace and soon she was able to catch her breath again.

Walking towards her house she became aware of the wound on her shoulder which was throbbing and sore. Every muscle in her body ached from the pushing and shoving, but Marta felt revived. She removed her coat as soon as she reached her front door, putting her two fingers through the loop inside the neck and hurling it over one shoulder so as to hide her injury. As she snuck inside she could hear a commotion in the drawing room. Peering in she noticed Arnold who was pacing up and down and wearing a concerned expression. Then she recognised Leopold's lower legs and feet, his distinctive olive coloured brogues giving him away. She feared that she had been away from home too long.

Leopold leant forward in his chair, resting his forearms on his thighs. As he did, he spotted her in the doorway.

'Marta, at last! We were just talking about you.' A torrent of panic rushed through her as Leopold jumped up from his chair. 'It's good to see *you* are safe and well. Come over here and look at this. They shot me Marta, right here!' He patted at his side.

She wanted to move towards him, hold him tight, but she resisted her urges.

'Leopold had asked me to meet him for coffee on the corner by City Hall and the next thing we knew all sorts of people poured onto the streets from everywhere. We stood with a group of onlookers Marta, no harm to anyone, when all of a sudden they shot at us.' Arnold was sitting in his favourite chair, pointing his forefingers and thumb to signify the firing of a gun as he spoke.

Leopold raised the drama by lifting his shirt to display the minor graze on his torso. Marta stood rooted to the spot, dumbstruck, shocked but unable to avert her eyes from his bare skin.

'For heaven's sake Marta, will you come into the room so we don't have to strain for your attention?' Arnold asked, standing to usher her toward the mantle.

'Riots have been breaking out all over the city, at the University, Parliament, even the newspaper offices were raised to the ground. I tell you, it's such a relief that you weren't caught up in any of that kafuffle, riots are no place for a woman like you.' He added, returning to his seat.

'No place for decent gentlemen either.' Leopold added.

The three had not been in a room together since the night of her father's experiment back in the spring. She did not know how to react to either of the men before her.

'It is a relief. One should always do their best to avoid a kafuffle. You must have been terrified Dr Kaposi, and father what were you thinking choosing to go out for coffee in the middle of a riot?' She asked.

'Leopold was quite insistent; he wanted to talk to me about something imperative. As circumstance would have it we never even got started. What was it you wanted to tell me anyway?' Arnold said, moving things along.

Marta felt the colour drain from her face. She looked over at Leopold, alarmed to find he was already watching her for a reaction.

Had Leopold been planning to tell Arnold of their meetings? Was he so cruel that he could reveal all as she stood before them? Arnold was busy lighting his cigar. Her eyes widened as she did her best to send a silent plea for forgiveness. Her brain was a scramble, searching for reasons, excuses, apologies, anything that could lessen the blow she was sure to receive, but she drew blanks.

'Arnold my friend,' Leopold began.

It was too late; she wanted to run but her knees trembled, all she could do now was hold on to the mantle and steady herself.

'All I can remember at this moment is that I could use a drink. Perhaps today would be a good day for us to share a whisky, shall I pour for both of us?'

Leopold offered a discreet wink to Marta as he pulled the stopper from the decanter.

'Yes, yes, why not?' Arnold agreed, lost in his own thoughts as he puffed on his cigar.

'We had a lucky escape today. Do you know, I am most intrigued by the mentality of a crowd? The lower classes can be so animalistic with their penchant for violence and disarray. It has me wondering all sorts of things.' With that Arnold stood and raised his hand to dismiss Marta from the room. 'You should run along, I am sure you have already heard enough of this ugly topic today.'

'Yes of course.' Marta said, dutiful as ever. 'I hope you recover soon Dr Kaposi.' She added, tipping her head to Leopold as she passed.

'Oh, he'll be fine, just fine. Now off you go.' Arnold closed the drawing room door.

Marta stopped on the other side, pondering in the stillness of the sunlit hallway. Neither had noticed her tousled hair, the dusty cuffs of her blouse or even the faint smell of smoke veiling her skin from head to toe. Perhaps it was the adrenaline rush of the riot, or the sheer shock of coming home to find her co-conspirator holding court with the man they were plotting to discredit, but Marta could not move. She remained in that spot for several minutes before Pernilla the new housekeeper jolted her attention, scurrying into the lobby with a medicine tray and a coffee pot.

Pernilla paused for a moment as if awaiting instruction from the mistress of the house. 'Go on. In you go.' Marta said.

Pernilla looked her over; taking in all of the dishevelment the two men had missed. 'Can I get *you* anything?'

'Hmm? No, no I'm fine. Now go on with your business, it won't do to keep my father and Dr Kaposi waiting.' Marta stepped away from the door and took the stairs up to her bedroom.

She shut the bedroom door behind her, dropped her coat to the floor and fingered the rip in her blouse to expose the gash in her flesh. It was deeper than she had first thought. The skin around the wound had turned a deep pink and was beginning to swell. Dried blood crusted at the edges. It would have benefited from cleaning and stitching at the hospital, but she preferred to manage her own wounds and though it was sizeable it was nothing she couldn't contend with by herself.

She kept a bottle of rubbing alcohol hidden at the back of her vanity unit beneath the sink, to clean herself up on the days her self-harming habits engrossed her with voracity. The sting of first aid was often as gratifying as the harm she inflicted.

She doused her washcloth with the alcohol before pressing it firm against her shoulder, fighting the urge to flinch and instead leaning into the sensation for some catharsis. The odour was surgical, a smell of cleanliness and precision. After she had repeated the action three or four times she checked the cloth now sticky with blood and plasma. The sight pleased her. It had been some time since she had broken her own skin, but today's affliction came as welcome relief.

She let out a small giggle at first, before releasing a more raucous boom.

'They didn't even notice. I stood shoulder to shoulder, took blow after blow and held my ground through it all and they didn't even notice!' Marta leant back against the bedroom door, sliding down the polished wooden panel into a roaring heap on the floor. She pulled her legs up close to her chest, wrapping her arms around the backs of her thighs in a way that tugged at her shoulders and caused a small section of her wound to split apart and weep again.

Her laughter was uncontrollable now.

'Father and Leopold hid amid the onlookers, gawping and inactive. I ran into the trouble.'

Giddy now, her eyes had the sheen of freshwater pearls. 'I could have stayed for longer, battled harder. The violence, the noise, the chaos – none of it worthy of my fear.'

Marta realised that she did not fear physical pain or imminent danger. Secrets and lies frightened her the most. Unspoken but ever present.

CHAPTER SEVEN

Meetings with Leopold stalled for the remainder of the summer and the city scars caused by the riots, faded with the summer heat. At first Marta was unsettled by his absence, but she maintained her routine so as not to arouse suspicion. She filled the blank hours by wandering the riverside, riding her bike around the city or hiding away in the library to work on her analysis model. She had not given up hope that Leopold would return at some point and when he did she wanted him to see that she had made progress on her own.

Arnold too, continued as normal. Clients came and went, study groups flocked to his drawing room once a week to listen to his anecdotes, he took coffee breaks with friends, attended meetings and conferences and now and then he fell asleep at his desk with a whisky still in his hand.

By the time the crisp air and longer shadows of autumn arrived Leopold had made contact and the pair resumed regular meetings. He did not offer an explanation for his absence and she did not feel entitled to ask. She was glad to have him back in her life. Their plans moved on at a pace. Architectural drawings had been approved and legal papers exchanged on the building – a disused hat factory Marta had not yet seen. Leopold had offered to take her on two occasions, but she had not been ready to face the reality of it and so had made excuses each time.

It was late November when the first package arrived and Marta was sitting at her father's desk in the study, drafting an observation model for the research facility which would, it had been confirmed, be called the Marta Rosenblit Centre for Childhood Analysis.

Pernilla swung the door open with such force it created a whoosh of air that sent her papers fluttering all around.

As she scrambled to secure them Marta threw a sharp glance at the clumsy housekeeper who she noticed was clutching a package; an oversized brown envelope bound with household string.

'What's that?' She demanded, cross about her scattered papers.

'It's a mess. I'm so sorry; I will tidy it up immediately Ms Rosenblit.' Pernilla moved towards the desk.

'No, don't touch it! I think you have done enough. What is that, in your hand?'

'It's for you. I think.' Pernilla handed her the package.

She inspected it. No postmark and the handwritten address was almost illegible. Marta had not been expecting a delivery, and Leopold had taken charge of all documents relating to the legalities of the factory conversion so it couldn't have been that. She checked the name of the addressee for a second time. It definitely read her name and not her father's.

'Wait outside for a moment please Pernilla.' She needed some privacy whilst she investigated the contents.

She tossed the pen she had been using onto the tray of her father's porcelain inkwell, splattering it with tiny specks of cobalt liquid as she did. The tissue box was empty and there wasn't any blotting paper in the desk drawer, so she wiped it clean with her fingertips before running them along the nude female figurine that decorated it. The inkwell had always been a favourite of Arnold's, a gift from an artist friend named Moser.

Turning her attention back to the envelope she untied the string with meticulous care and concentration, wrapping it tightly around two of her fingers to create a tidy coil which she placed to one side. She pulled her letter knife out from the pocket of her house dress, pressing its pointed blade to her palm twice – a practice she had often relied upon to release her anxiety. She tucked the blade under the flap of the envelope and with one swift slash, the contents dropped onto the desk.

A photograph of a man was the first item that caught her eye, for no other reason than the face of its subject had been scratched away. On the back written in pencil – *'Posey, 1903, Karlsplatz Stadtbahn'*.

She picked up a small slip of paper and unfolded it. It was a receipt from Café Sacher for one Kapuziner and one Schwarzer. She knew the establishment well, it was a popular haunt of her father's and his society friends, but this receipt was dated many years before she had ever known of it. Another small stub from the Café Louvre just off the Ringstrasse was included, it was crumpled and worn but she could just make out two letters written on it – an uppercase J and, in different handwriting, a lowercase p. The letters linked together, at the top of the J and the bottom of the p, by a tiny sketch of a flower.

'Pernilla!' She called. 'Come, come.' Marta needed to question her and try to make sense of this.

'Yes Ms Rosenblit, do you need my assistance?' She asked with some trepidation.

'Who delivered this package?'

'I'm afraid I couldn't say. I mean, I didn't see.'

'Didn't see? It is two o'clock in the afternoon Pernilla. Explain to me how you did not see when it is bright and clear outside?'

Despite having worked in the house for months now, Pernilla was still unaccustomed to the expectations placed on her.

'Nobody was at the door... just a knock and then the package.'

'Did you not look out onto the street?'

'No. I didn't think to. Should I have?'

Marta knew it was pointless to pursue any further questioning or instruction on the matter, the girl displayed little common sense. She waved her housekeeper away without making eye contact, her attentions still on the package. All that remained within it was a copy of the Kronen Zeitung newspaper, but she could not find anything out of the ordinary contained within its pages. Somebody had circled an obituary on the back page, but the ink had bled and most of the name was obscured. Still it did not seem at all familiar.

Despite not having any idea what the information might mean to her, Marta decided at that moment that she would not share a word of the mysterious delivery with

73

anyone. Not even Leopold. It may not even be significant, it may have been addressed to her by mistake, or perhaps it was just another of her fathers' experiments. She would not react to it at all for the time being; instead she scooped up the contents and put them back into the envelope. Then she took off her reading glasses and placed them and the letter knife back in her pocket before gathering up all of her belongings to remove any trace that she had been working there. She rushed upstairs.

In her room, she pulled the bottom drawer out from her chest and laid the envelope carefully in the space underneath. It had been her secret hiding place since she was a teenager. Still unsettled by the package and its possible meaning, she felt for the reassuring edge of her letter knife.

She lifted the skirt of her house dress and rolled the left leg of her hand-me-down stockings to her knee. Starting with the side of the blade she tilted the sharp silverware into the vulnerable flesh of her inner thigh. Not enough to draw blood at first, but firm enough to cause a red score mark to appear.

The familiar warmth began to grow in her stomach, like a soothing opiate blanket that spread out and down into her groin in waves every time she increased the pressure of the metal. With a gentle twist, she broke the skin and felt an instant release. It had been a while since she had removed the knife from its hiding place; she had been so busy with her latest project. However, the need to force open the filing cabinet in the study meant that it was in her pocket today. Now she was relieved to have had it at hand.

At the sound of the front door slamming downstairs, Marta knew her father was home. She dropped the letter knife into the base of the chest and replaced the bottom drawer. She then pulled her stocking back into position, securing the thick band of rayon with a tight elastic garter. The heightened sensation as she snapped it into place sent a shock of arousal straight up between her thighs. It was not the first time a self-inflicted wound had created such a pulsing heat, but the force of it took her by surprise. If she succumbed to it now she would risk being discovered by her father but she couldn't stop. Holding the front of her skirt out of the way she turned her body to the wall, pushing her face up against the cool wallpaper. She reached her free hand up into the loose open leg of her step-ins, closing her thighs around it as she moved between pinching her delicate skin and rubbing her fingers in small circles. She had touched herself in this way since she was a child; even then she preferred a rougher touch. She had become quite adept at it, knowing when to go gently and when to push herself. Within seconds, her body was flooded with a pleasure so forceful that she felt compelled to hold herself by the crotch until the pulsing subsided. Her legs trembled as she released her hand and then her skirt.

The release of pressure was welcome. The pain, sometimes followed by erotic comfort, was a pattern she had never been able to free herself from. A respectable sense of guilt was always present of course, but that was preferable to unceasing anxiety. That would not do at all because anxiety led to a great battle inside her. The need for inclusion fought the need for withdrawal, the need to take action wrestled the overwhelming apathy, the debilitating fatigue clashed with bouts of insomnia, and the desire to feel was blanked out by the numbness. She knew it well. She had been holding it at bay for months now, but the fact that she had cut herself today was a foreboding sign. She was losing her control.

CHAPTER EIGHT

For months now Arnold had watched his youngest daughter with some trepidation as she removed her bicycle from the small dilapidated summerhouse at the foot of the garden. From the window of his study, he would observe as she pedalled in a wobbly but determined fashion across the lawn and toward the side of the house until she was out of sight. Ever obstinate, Marta had acted against her father's will when she accepted her teaching job. It wasn't that he had wanted a better career for her, teaching was a respectable job for a woman these days, he just didn't want anyone else to have control over her time or input into her thoughts.

She was not yet suited, he felt, to going out into the world alone. He had no doubt of Marta's strong will having seen her resist and rebel many a time, but she was weak in understanding the perversities of life. He had afforded her a decent education which she had eagerly supplemented by reading whole libraries worth of books, sitting in on all of his lectures and assisting at his conferences and meetings. All of which was admirable enough but it was idle folly compared to a life spent out in the real world with him, where men made sport out of one-upmanship by any means possible, often going about their business by manner of '*hintertürl*' – through the back door.

It was a relief that she had been born without the burden of prettiness but still he feared that she might be lured away from him by some pot-bellied professor;

begin fantasising about marriage and babies, never to return to his teachings. Many a good woman had been lost to the inevitability of marriage and babies, even the unattractive and intellectual types. He had not shared such concerns for Marta's siblings, finding a mate had been a necessary fortune for them, each one having matured into the personification of feminine foolishness. Whereas Marta was made of more stoical stuff, she was a bluestocking – a woman of intellect rather than glamour – her head was not filled with the woolly fluff of women, rather it had long been brimming with the gritty stuff of men, men like Arnold himself. Great men, leaders, thinkers, creators – and with Arnold giving her some credibility he was confident she could have been a real benefit to him and the future of his work.

In spite of this he still searched her face every evening when she returned from her work at the school, looking for traces of a flirtatious flush or the thrill of a kiss on her disproportionate lips. He was satisfied to see her usual scowl of discontent as she trod firm footed up the garden path and into the house for dinner. Marta was out of the house more and more lately and not just on her work days. It had not gone unnoticed that on her days off he had spotted her slipping out at dawn. Unfortunately, he was not awake and alert often enough to find a pattern in her absences, particularly if he had been working into the small hours or out dining with friends.

He assumed she was investing the time in some sort of intellectual stimulation, as was her habit. She was not forthcoming when asked of her whereabouts and he had no intention of losing hours to suspicion and mistrust. He preferred to stick to routine enquiries about her work such as, 'Did you succeed in fomenting any young minds this week Marta?'. Her response, often pre-empted by a rumpling of her heavy eyebrows as if pushing to meet in the crease of her frown, was almost always a shrug and a sigh of 'Maybe, maybe not.'

If he probed for news of her interactions with her colleagues she would change the subject, luring him off topic with questions about his clients or attempting to blind him with debate on some medical journal report or newspaper article. By his own admission, he did like to debate with his daughter. He especially enjoyed how a flash of spirit would return to her eyes just as soon as they engaged in a tug of words.

Today she had come home in a morose mood having been caught in a rain shower that had not been forecast, though even if it had she would still have insisted on riding herself there rather than taking the tram. As she removed her coat it was clear that she was soaked to the skin, her bones jutting out from behind the sodden fabric of her dress which clung to her shoulders and chest. Arnold waited until supper before tackling her about her professional choices.

'Marta, I will never understand what possesses you to go out to work at that school when you have such a rewarding path you could follow here with me.' Arnold asserted.

'I know father, you are right.' She said, dropping her chin.

'Working as a paid assistant to me is not without honour you know.' He added.

He watched as she flicked her fork around her plate of food. 'But I mustn't allow myself to assume that I will always be able to live under your providence. Such inertia wouldn't do either of us any good in the long term.'

'You worry too much about the long term. Now is the time to enjoy the world that I and my fellow academics have created for you and will continue to fuel.' He said, wagging his finger at the air.

'What if it comes to an end? What would I do then? No, I really feel that I need to learn more about independence and self-sufficiency.'

'Well pardon me but that is just cock and bull nonsense Marta.'

She looked up from her plate, aghast at his phrasing.

'It is inconceivable that a time would come where I would no longer have a hold on my profession. Businessmen, politicians, industry leaders, now I think of it, the majority of Vienna's upper-class, I've earned the respect of them all. I have stitched together a whole future for us; it seems ungrateful that you should want to forge your own way. The city can be unforgiving for a woman like you.'

A woman like you - He wasn't sure what he had meant when he said it, but Marta appeared irritated at the sentiment, her jaw clenched. She opened her mouth and let out a stutter as if to reply, but Arnold continued his monologue, 'I am the product of my own ambition, education and resilience, just as you could be too if only you'd fall in line from time to time.'

In Arnold's day it had been easier to manage the expectations of women. They wanted for much less, accepting the flattery of *'kuss die han'* (I kiss your hand), taking pride in their domestic obligations. Now it was all about rights, ambitions and independence, and quite where it might end was a thought he preferred not to venture. No wonder symptoms of hysteria were rife amongst modern women. He had written several papers on this subject in the past and whilst it wasn't popular to say so these days he had long suspected that a life of tedium was much more conducive to calming female emotional disorders. Even in the workplace, women were better off sticking to data analysis; administrative tasks that sort of thing. He had heard how inviting a group of female technicians to participate in innovative studies had caused chaos between the University of Vienna and Cambridge University over in England. From what he could ascertain, the male physicists involved had not fully considered the impact a woman's emotional state could have on her judgement and decision-making. Of course, he was forward thinking enough to value an educated woman however one must also recognise that with big ideas come even bigger responsibilities. He was not convinced that women, even well-educated ones like Marta, could cope with consequences and accountability.

Some might consider him archaic, but he had experienced first-hand how an increasing number of his female clients were gripped by the fear of not having enough in a have-it-all society. Women of status, in particular, were quite manic about it. Cases of aphonia, multiple personality disorder and even chronic constipation had increased in great numbers since the women got their rights. His female patients were literally scared to release their voices, their own personalities and even their bowels to it.

His own mother had suffered repeatedly with 'the vapours' and that was long before suffrage, even she had felt overwhelmed by her relatively simple existence in the home. And as for Josefine, well he preferred not to think about that.

Quite what would become of women if things continued to degenerate he did not care to fancy, but he would be damned if he was going to give in to Marta's yearning for independence. He had invested too heavily in her and besides, as her father it was his role to protect her. It would have been nice to have had a son, simpler he imagined.

CHAPTER NINE

Marta and Leopold stood in the street with his architect friend Jakub surveying the ivy-covered brick block that would soon house orphaned infants and children as part of her analysis work. The factory was to become the first ever child analysis facility of its kind. The building was imposing and dreary, especially on such a bleak day. An uninspiring multi-storey mass that jarred with the neighbouring baroque and renaissance buildings contributing to the whipped cream skyline.

Jakub had arrived that morning from Prague, his overcoat bore the creases of travel and he chattered with a tremble in his voice that suggested he was surviving on caffeine and amphetamines. A small case rested at his feet and the leather holder tucked under his armpit bulged with papers. His hands moved in exaggerated swirls as he hurried to reassure her that all of this could be improved upon with some exterior cladding.

'It will be a fine building with just a little wořk.' He said noting the look of dread on her face. 'The inteřioř too, will be homely enough with a few decořative details.'

She was less interested in what he was saying and more interested in the misplaced roll of his R's that exposed the melodic inflection of his native language.

'Yes Jakub, of course. Now let's get Marta inside before she freezes right through to her liver.' Leopold was keen to hurry proceedings along.

He took out a fistful of keys, there must have been at least a dozen, and tried two before he found the right one to gain access. The once black paint on the substantial door was peeling and faded, and it was rotting away at the corners. Leopold pushed hard and it creaked as it opened.

Inside, dust covered blocking machines and crown irons lay abandoned in dark corners. Marta did her best to hide her dismay as they wandered through the lower rooms and Jakub explained his plans as best he could. Leopold led them back to the lobby area where they made their way to the staircase on the left-hand side. They followed it to the upper level which opened out onto what was once a vast factory floor.

'The řubbish will be gone. This level will be split to create a boys dořmitořy on the řight side and a giřl's dořmitořy on the left.' Jakub revealed.

'Oh, we forgot, Jakub, tell Marta about the nursery.' Leopold insisted.

'Yes of couřse. Foř the little ones theře will be a modest nuřseřy situated to the řeař of the gřound flooř.' He added.

The plan was for Marta to take temporary guardianship of the children and arrange care for their basic needs. A nanny and nurse would cater to the children's practical and physical needs, whilst kitchen staff and a housekeeper would maintain sustenance and hygiene standards. A governess would provide age appropriate education, whilst Marta and a wider research team she had yet to appoint would observe their behaviours and attachment patterns, study their habits and arising disorders and record them. Time would be made for the children to reflect on and talk about their own behaviour and feelings, even the little ones. If they could verbalise, they would be heard. If they could not, then time would be set aside to monitor body language and engage the children in non-verbal communication such as she had heard was being used in America.

Leopold and Jakub made it all sound so possible they steered her along the corridors and staircases that connected the spaces. This austere building was to represent her stepping out from her father's shadow, her statement to the world of psychotherapy. Yet she felt quite detached from it. She didn't like the cold damp walls and she was sure she could hear the faint hum of white noise still reverberating from the busy machines once in motion here. The rust coloured brickwork and the black iron pipes that crept up to and along the ceilings gave the facility the appearance of an institution rather than a substitute home. The windows rattled on every floor. This was not her vision at all.

The expectation that she could fill such a domineering space engulfed her. The two men walked ahead seemingly unaware of her reluctance to follow. Marta paused at an open window in a corridor; she had lost her bearings and was no longer sure of her position in the building now. She pushed her face out into the biting winter air and drew a deep breath that made her throat and lungs constrict until it felt like the air might never be able to move in and out of her again. She forced herself to exhale, closed her eyes and reached for that impossibly icy breath again, then for a third-time longer and deeper until her lips were dry and numb. She opened her eyes to the cold and cast a downward glance to the courtyard below. As she did, the ground appeared to sway and move in her view until she thought she might topple over. She gripped at the metal window frame in an attempt to steady herself.

'This is not my vision. This is not mine.' The words slipped as a low whisper from her mouth entirely without her permission.

Marta turned to see Leopold and Jakub in the doorway. Jakub was gesturing towards the iron pillars that supported the ceiling, but Leopold was looking right at her. She was sure he must have read her lips or at least taken his lead from her pallid complexion. He studied her for a moment. She was embarrassed at herself in the face of him. She had wanted so much to impress him, to be everything he had told her she could be.

'Let's call it a day Jakub. I think Marta needs some time to think about everything you have shown us. I can see I have some convincing to do. Give us a few days will you?'

'Suře. It takes the ladies a long time to decide what they want, am I řight?' Jakub asked, with a schoolboy smirk and a nudge.

Leopold put his hand on Jakub's shoulder, but his eyes were fixed on Marta. 'Let me walk you down to the lobby.'

The two men descended the stairs. Marta felt panicked about his return. He had looked angry and though she trusted him, she feared his unpredictability. She turned toward the window again. Without warning, thoughts of leaping from it rushed into her mind. She wouldn't do it, her need to escape was not as great as her need to show strength and courage to Leopold, but she could not deny that the impulse existed. It was a bad day that was all. She had known it as soon as she had opened her eyes in bed this morning. She would go home, return to the safety and control of her letter knife and release some tension. Tomorrow would feel better.

The atmosphere in the quiet factory was suspended with anticipation as she waited for Leopold to return. Her skin jumped when she felt his firm grip on her upper arm. Where had he come from? She had not heard him return but he made his presence clear now, the smile on his face not mirroring the tension in his body.

Marta wanted him to say something soothing, or perhaps to start shouting, at least then she could read him. Instead he looked straight at her, silent. His words had not been enough to force her hand so far. Leopold decided it was time for action.

He tossed his hat to the floor and squeezed her shoulders as he turned her away from the window. Then, using his strong grip he rushed her backwards several paces until she bumped against one of the iron pipes. Still his face offered an indication of a smile, but still she did not feel any kindness behind his projection. He forced his body against hers until she was trapped between him and the pipe.

She could hear a heartbeat thudding in her ears. Was it hers? Leopold's? They were so close now she couldn't tell.

'Leopold, what are you doing?'

He did not reply. His hands moved roughly over the top of her coat and blouse as he searched for the lines of her body. She felt embarrassed at her lack of curves. She was as disgusted by herself as she was by his behaviour.

Searching for some explanation or reassurance that this was not what she feared it might be, Marta looked intently into Leopold's eyes, which appeared a darker brown than she had recalled. He did not return her gaze but pushed on in spite of her resistance.

He did not make any attempt to kiss her as she had once hoped he might, instead he rubbed one hand across her breastbone and up to her throat, whilst the other roamed down towards the hem of her skirt. He breathed into her ear as he pushed the wool fabric higher until the bare flesh above her stocking tops was nipped by the chilly air. The sweet smell of his breath was tainted with a hint of cigarettes and she felt as though she might vomit, yet she made no move to loosen his grip.

Marta was unsettled. She had never been held by a man before, let alone had her most intimate areas uncovered by one. Was this the seduction she had hoped for or an attack she should be fending off? She had often considered the prospect of intimacy with Leopold but this was not at all how she had imagined it.

Confusion and shame rattled through her as her body responded to his rough handling with waves of warmth and pleasure that exposed her own innate darkness. Was this coming together to result in the 'sex' act she had read about? Marta searched Leopold's face for the answers to her questions. He did not make eye contact and the faint smile was gone, changing his expression and adding tension to the moment. All he offered were pushy palms moving frantically over layers of thick wool and flimsy silk, peeling them away until her skin was invaded by his.

Then he kissed her, his lips unkind and haphazard. Kisses turned to small bites and his hard tongue left trails of saliva. Torn seams and dislodged buttons gave way to sharp scratches and rigid movements. She should fight back. This was not right, not this way, not here in this dank place. She pushed her fists into his chest, struggled and resisted but every attempt served to make him more forceful and in a second he had yanked down her underwear. She relented, unsure of what else to do.

As he thrust inside her she tried to detach herself for a moment, analyse the situation and see if she could make sense of it. In allowing him to continue, was she demonstrating the weakness he had once accused her of? Or was she proving her strength through her ability to suffer such a violation? Perhaps this was a test and she must demonstrate her capacity for endurance.

Leopold made an odd noise she had not heard before, a combination of a gasp and a grunt that startled her. Then suddenly he released his grip and withdrew from her body. Marta was alarmed to feel a gush of warm fluid trail out of her and down her thigh. Was she bleeding? There had been some pain and she was sore but she didn't think so. She looked down at herself as she replaced her underwear, the fluid was clear. It was not blood.

Unsure how else to respond she pulled as much of her clothing back together as she could. She smoothed her skirt over her shame, fastened her blouse to hide the flush of arousal, and wrapped her coat around her body to contain the guilt at her participation. Then she looked directly at Leopold and for the first time since the ordeal had begun, he looked into her eyes then kissed her tenderly on the forehead.

'You make me lose control of myself Marta.' He said, buttoning his trousers. 'You can be so deliciously defiant. Here I am trying to do all of these things for you, make your dreams come true and still you resist. It's quite desirable and yet quite infuriating. I think I could almost fall in love with you.'

I think I could almost fall in love with you. The words caught her attention like sharp stones on a window pane. Had she heard him correctly? Did he just utter the most beautiful sentence she had ever longed to hear?

It had not been an act of romance, no sweet seduction with candlelight and roses she was confident of that, but what did she know of sweetness anyway? She wouldn't recognise it even if it were offered; perhaps this was the reality of love? Brutal moments of pain combined with intense pleasure, a continual interchange of power.

Marta did not know; how could she? This was her first sexual encounter. Her only experience of being with a man she presumed she must now love and obey.

'Now, will you stop all this silly hesitation? You can be anything you want, you just have to push on if you want transformation.' Leopold brushed the dust from his homburg.

Marta wanted to say so many things but before she could form a single sentence, he spoke again. 'This building is perfect, don't think about it another minute, just do it. Now, I really must go, I have patients to see. You can lock up, might as well get used to it.' He threw her the bunch of keys and left.

CHAPTER TEN

Marta fumbled through the keys, her hands shaking, unsure of which one would fit the lock. Her legs felt weak and unsteady and her hips ached as she made her way along the corridor and down the staircase to the lobby. Shutting the door proved as difficult as opening it, and she had to make three attempts to slam it before the heavy panel fit securely back into its frame so she could lock it. It was a long walk but she decided not to take the tram home, convinced that her fellow passengers would know what she had been doing there in the old hat factory. Leopold's sweat, his spiced cologne and what she presumed was his semen clung to her skin and clothes, she was sure that anyone sitting close would sense it. No, she would walk and the cold air would cleanse her.

It was growing dark by the time she reached home. The moon, swollen and proud in the clear night sky, dropped an ambient glow onto the streets. Leopold's words rang in her ears. *'I think I could almost fall in love with you'*

Somebody was in love with her... almost.

Upstairs Marta ran herself a bath. Her skin was broken and marked in places, and it stung a little as she lowered herself into the water. Yesterday she had thought little of the sensations of bathing. She had approached the care of her body as she might any other practical chore, working meticulously with the nail brush and washcloth until every patch of skin beneath it was attended. This evening she was gentle with herself, fearing that the transformation from virgin to lover might drain away with the suds. Everything felt heightened, the warm water lapping at her nipples, the flush on her face brought about by the steam, the slither of soap on her limbs.

She soaked herself for a while as she reflected on the encounter with Leopold, unsure of how to feel but knowing that everything had changed between them now. She had not reached for his body under his clothes and had only been able to judge his shape and size through his dominant penetration of her. He had forced himself on her, of that she was sure, but in spite of her fear she'd experienced an undeniable heat. Whatever had happened she had to admit that his brutality had lit a fire that had intrigued her.

Would he want to do it again? Where could they be alone together again? She imagined that wherever it was, he would not be so hurried next time. He would undress and she would finally catch her first glimpse of a naked man. She would not remove her chemise, not yet. If he saw her he might be shocked at her sharp bones, her mottled skin and her scars. She especially did not want him to see her scars. She had always protected them from prying eyes.

Looking over her body she reprimanded herself for getting so carried away. Of course, he would not want to repeat the encounter. In reality, she was not a suitable lover for anyone. She was ravaged, imperfect, flawed inside and out. Who was she to think that such a role could ever be attributed to someone like her? Disobedient, unruly, incapable Marta. Men like Leopold did not want that kind of trouble. They wanted amiable, compliant, light-hearted lovers.

But he had wanted her and he had taken her, so she must have something to offer?

In the last few hours she had been led into a womanhood that was, in many ways, overdue. Sliding herself under the surface of the water a small voice inside her head told her it was too late to go back.

The temptation to cut herself did not return immediately. She had been so dizzied by her experience at the factory that she had waded through several days with a form of buoyancy that bordered on delirium. However this morning, weighed down under a taupe and grey sky, she awoke to find she was cloaked in a depressive mood once again. She had not planned to open the bottom drawer of her dresser and she had not intended to sit naked, letter knife in hand, ready to assault her body. In fact, she had not wanted to get out of bed at all, but here she was.

'To hurt oneself is to pre-empt the pain that others will undoubtedly cause, to strike first and take back control.' Marta rationalised as she twisted the point of her letter knife into her hip, first left and then right. It had become a mantra, a justification for a senseless act.

For Marta, the fragmentation of her mental state was a sad but identifiable truth. It would come on gently as it had done before, like the rise and fall of a sleeping breath, and she would do what she needed to do in order to despatch her depression if only for a short while.

There was an inevitability to self-inflicted pain that made it all seem so normal, logical even. As an intelligent female, she had always been drawn to the logical. Logical was cause and effect, a place where self-esteem and insecurities were little more than myth and legend. But even clever, logical people could make irrational choices.

Marta had never told anyone about her choice to self-harm; she enjoyed the privacy of it. She hadn't even considered her actions out of place until she read a report she found in a dusty old library copy of The Journal of Mental Science. It was written by an English psychiatrist named Savage and listed a number of behaviours she had considered soothing. It was at that point she vowed never to tell her father, who she was sure would have her carted off to an asylum just like her mother. Her sisters wouldn't understand it either, not that she would ever have dreamed of having a conversation with any of them that went beyond basic pleasantries.

It's true that before Leopold she had been steady enough, only reaching for her letter knife on rare occasions. On the whole she had found more subtle ways to numb her responses. Instead of talking about it she would visualise her anxiety, anger, frustration as tiny rosebuds then set about mentally nipping at them with pruning scissors, cutting them dead so they could not flourish into something more distracting. It had worked well, stemming the flow of black thoughts for weeks and sometimes months at a time. Except that she didn't want to feel numb anymore. She wanted to experience life be it laden with pain or glory. She wanted to feel everything more intensely than she had ever given herself permission to before. Or at least that's what her impulses most often urged her to do.

Growing up she had displayed minor warning signs that should have sparked the concern of her father; chewing the skin inside her mouth, biting her fingernails until they bled and sometimes scratching her arms and elbows raw in patches, but nothing that left any lasting damage. As a teenager, she had progressed to cutting herself, not so deep as to endanger her life but just enough to contrast the intensity of her emotions.

Much more regular were the days when she sought the calm wash of comfort that came with a simple pinch of skin or a tug of hair. Sometimes she would feel the urge to do it several times a day, other times she would be shocked to find she had pulled out an entire patch of hair from behind her ear without cognisance.

It the beginning her urge to self-harm was pathological, her way of unburdening herself of anxieties. But it evolved into something altogether more seductive as she progressed through puberty, out of adolescence and into womanhood. She missed the appearance of the unblemished skin of her infanthood, in the same way that she missed a clear blue sky or freshly fallen snow. But she couldn't go back. She needed it when she thought of how much she missed her mother, she needed it when she felt isolated from her sisters, she needed it when she had tried but failed to please her father and now she needed it from Leopold too. It was no longer enough to turn her blade on herself. His forceful punishment of her stirred those familiar feelings in her, but also sparked something new. Leopold saw her unworthiness, and still he found her arousing. It sent prickles up and down her spine. Leopold accepted her, and acceptance was so dangerously addictive.

She would not fight him again; she would welcome him and any distress that came along with this descent. As she washed and replaced her letter knife she tried to ignore the nagging voice inside her head telling her to be cautious. She might fall further and find herself in a darker place than she had so far been accustomed to, but she didn't care. She welcomed it.

CHAPTER ELEVEN

Ever since that first package had arrived at her door she had wondered what she should do with it. In the beginning, Marta had intended to disregard it as a mistake, or perhaps a fantasy played out by one of her fathers' patients. Yet something about the photo remained in her subconscious. And now, sitting with a second parcel in her lap she felt compelled to treat the contents of both packages more seriously.

This time the envelope was much smaller and it contained a pendant – a gift from her new lover perhaps? The oval trinket was set with tourmalines and blush pearls, but on closer inspection she could see that they were dull. It was apparent that the jewellery was not new and so she reasoned it could not be a gift, not from Leopold anyway. At the centre of the pendant was an enamel miniature bearing the image of a lady in a pink dress reclining on a chaise, flowers at her feet. The link was broken and the chain it must have been attached to at one time was missing.

Marta had discovered this package on the doorstep on her return from her morning meeting with Leopold, and again the sender had managed to escape with anonymity. She had taken it directly to her room knowing she wouldn't be disturbed. The pendant must have been an antique; its style was intricate and old fashioned.

She sat for a moment. What did this have to do with her? If the pendant was not intended as a gift what was it? Was it in any way linked to the photograph, receipts and newspaper she had received before? Could they perhaps be clues of some kind? She had no idea what mystery was, but she was motivated to follow it up. Today was a good day after all. She had spent the morning discussing her research outcomes with Leopold, he had been impressed and they had made love for the second time. The weather was bright and clear. Yes, today was a good day to head out and do something spontaneous.

Pernilla was shopping for groceries and running errands and Arnold was in his study with his regular Wednesday morning client Mrs Keisler. The woman was mad as a box of frogs and would be in there for three hours or more. So, at just past 11 o'clock, Marta was confident she had at least two hours before anyone would come looking for her.

She returned to the drawer where she had hidden the first package a couple of weeks ago and pulled out the large brown envelope she had hidden.

Once again, she laid out its contents, reviewing the picture and bits of paper to see if she could find a link between the items. Nothing. She must decide for herself where to start.

Marta picked out the stub from the Café Louvre. She would go there, this morning before the place filled with foreign journalists who frequented it in the afternoons. Her father was considered a friend by many of them, and she did not want them to see her hanging around alone.

She put the small scrap of paper into the black leather finger purse Leopold had given her as a gift, scooped the packages back into their hiding place and pulled on her grey wool wrap coat. She tucked her hair under her houndstooth cloche hat and laced her flat black garden boots. Rushing downstairs and out onto the street she noticed it was just beginning to rain. It was too late to go back for her umbrella; she would just have to duck in and out of doorways for cover if the soft spit turned into a storm.

The 30-minute walk to Café Louvre could be cut to 20 minutes if she maintained a brisk stride and cut across Volksgarten and along the Herrengasse.

Sitting on the corner of Renngasse and Wipplingerstrasse, the café was imposing, with high ceilings and around forty marble-topped coffee tables stretching along the centre of the room. Dark intricately carved wooden booths lined one wall, with the buffet tables and newspaper stands on the opposite side. Even though she had arrived after the morning rush, a gentle hum of background noise remained. Clinking cups being placed on saucers, the clatter of freshly cleaned silverware being replenished – busyness she found comforting to hide in. And was that jazz music she could hear drifting softly from the kitchen at the back?

A handful of customers sat dotted around the café. Two women at the centre of the room huddled around a copy of Record magazine, eyeing the latest sewing techniques and fashions they hoped to recreate. A man in the far corner was smoking a cigarette whilst scribbling in his notebook, she noticed that he was wearing two pairs of spectacles – one on the bridge of his nose and another perched on top of his head. In the corner booth, Marta could see a rotund figure she instantly recognised as Mr Beste. He lifted the broad brim of his Stetson hat and wiped his brow with a napkin before settling back down to his newspaper. It shouldn't have been surprising to see him there, local people and indeed the café staff called him a *wirthausbruder* – a café brother, using his regular table as an extension of his home and office. Every politician, diplomat, socialite or other informant in the city knew to find him there whenever they had a story for the paper. By mid-afternoon, they would come streaming in, offering a steady flow of leads, gossip, policy debate and more.

He seemed engrossed in the day's news stories and so was unlikely to notice her. She stepped back cautiously and slid herself into the nearest booth. As she did so, she failed to notice that somebody was already sitting in it. A bright-eyed young woman let out a squeal as Marta's clumpy boots trampled her foot under the table.

'Oh, I'm so sorry. I didn't realise anyone was sitting here.' Marta glanced around the café, hoping that her clumsiness had not attracted too much attention.

'It's okay, don't worry I still have five toes intact on my other foot so I'll be fine. I'm Elise. Elise Saloman.'

Relieved at the good humoured response and not wanting to make any more fuss, she introduced herself. 'Marta Rosenblit. Do you mind if I sit here?'

'It's a little snug for strangers but why not?' She said.

Marta blushed and manoeuvred herself around to the seat on the opposite side of the booth.

'Relax, it's fine I'm just teasing you. I was just thinking it would have been nice to have a friend today. Coffee?' Elise smiled again, revealing a small gap between her two front teeth.

Marta's relief was visible in the drop of her shoulders. 'I find coffee quite bitter.' She admitted, not quite knowing what made her say so.

'I agree! Tea is much more suited to my palette, but I've just finished a cup so I thought I'd have a change. Let's see, what shall I have next?' Elise picked up the menu.

Marta watched as she prattled through the drink choices. She was in awe of this confident creature with the ash blonde crop and contrasting burgundy lips. The features of her heart shaped face benefited from an agreeable symmetry and though she was not predictably pretty, she was beguiling all the same.

'Do you know Marta, I've been sitting here moping for almost an hour now and I have no idea why I am so melancholy. How about you, may I ask what brought you here today?' Elise queried.

She thought fast. 'That's a good question. Honestly, I don't know. I headed out of the door without a plan and here I am.'

Elise clicked her fingers to summon the attention of a waiter then turned to face Marta. 'I admire your spontaneity. Seeing as neither of us has so far been convinced of the pleasures of the black stuff, let's experiment to see if we can find a way to enjoy it more shall we? Perhaps we've just been doing it wrong, after all almost all of the people in Vienna are mad about it!' She paused to review the menu for a second time.

'Waiter, please bring us both a Kapuziner.'

'Of course madam. Would you like any pastries with that?'

Elise looked to Marta who was observing the exchange with the fascination of a visitor at a zoo. 'Do you have a sweet tooth?'

'Hmm?' Her concentration broken. 'Oh, I'm not sure I have a preference, but I will take something sweet if you will.'

'Two slices of your most delicious strudel please, and' holding up her forefingers in case she wasn't clear, 'two slices of dobostorte. Let's give those coffees something to work with shall we?' Elise turned to her new friend.

Still a little stunned at her unexpected companion Marta felt her cheeks glow pink as she became aware that it was her turn to say something. She struggled for words; the warmth from her cheeks was now flushing her face and décolletage.

Sensing her discomfort, Elise moved things along. 'So Marta, now we have got ourselves settled in we might as well get to know each other a little. I'll start. I moved to Vienna about four months ago after completing my medical education at the University of Paris. I'd planned to work in paediatrics but I admit I'm not finding it as easy as I'd like to get a break. Tell me about yourself.' She leaned forward and clasped her hands together with interest.

Marta was not accustomed to having such a forthright female companion. She was even less accustomed to being in control of the information she revealed about herself.

'Well, most people know me because of my father Dr Arnold Rosenblit. He's a psychiatrist.' She tugged at a lock of stray hair in habitual motion.

'Ah yes, of course, quite a prolific one at that!' Elise patted her hands on the table. 'That's where I have heard your name before. I have studied your Dr Rosenblit's work.'

Marta was surprised. 'Then you will most likely know that I have been the subject of many of his research papers. You will have learned more of me from those than I could share about myself.'

'Tell me, how do you feel about being used like that?' Elise was direct in her enquiries.

'Used?' Marta was offended. 'I don't think I would describe my participation in that way. I have always been happy and willing to assist with his research in whatever way he sees fit. It is my privilege. Did you say you know my father or just that you know his work?'

'I knew him for his work at first but I must confess I recently had an opportunity to come face to face with him. I'm afraid we did not part on favourable terms.' Elise blushed.

'Really? Tell me more.' Whilst she was aware of some rumblings of discontent emerging in the psychiatric community, Marta had never met anyone who did not adore her father.

The waiter intervened, placing the two coffees, the strudels and two generous portions of dobostorte at the centre of the table. The women watched in silence as he lifted two small china plates, bearing hand painted hyacinth blooms, from his tray and laid them out. Then he dropped napkins embroidered with the café's insignia alongside the plates and topped them with dessert forks. Finally, he left a cup of brown sugar lumps and a set of sterling silver tongs. 'Enjoy.' He nodded and then left them to resume their conversation.

Using the tongs, Elise dropped two sugar lumps into Marta's cup without consultation. 'It's a little embarrassing, but I took it upon myself to heckle the doctor during a recent talk he was giving.'

'You heckled him?'

'Mm hmm.' Elise said, with an enthusiastic nod.

Marta was impressed. 'Can I ask why?'

'I don't buy it.'

'Buy what?'

'His ludicrous theory on phallic symbolism and a number of other theories too since you are asking.' Elise stated without apology.

'I am entertained to learn that I am not the only one to find holes in my fathers' theories.'

'He spoke highly of you.'

'He did?' Marta queried with a degree of disbelief.

'If you consider him labelling you and most other women besides, as mad as hatters, then yes.'

The two women broke into giggles. Elise continued, 'Don't *you* ever challenge him on some of the things he says?'

'It's not that I haven't tried. I have but he doesn't want to hear it. He prefers to use my inquisitive nature to highlight my shortcomings. It is a trusted tactic that enables him to overlook the questions he does not want to answer.'

'And hasn't it served him well Marta?'

'Yes indeed, at times I think it serves him too well if you ask me.' Marta felt ashamed that she had let the words slip out, and to a practical stranger. It was uncharacteristically indiscreet of her but she couldn't help it. Something about this woman made her feel less inhibited.

Elise scooped up her cup and sipped at her Kapuzinger. Marta took her lead and did the same, noting how a little sugar had softened the bitterness she had anticipated. She wondered why nobody had ever thought to offer her sugar with her coffee before.

'*Does* anybody ask you?'

Marta was unsure what Elise meant. 'Ask me what?'

'How you feel or what you want?

She pursed her lips and straightened her back in concentration. 'Those questions would not be so easy to answer. I'm not sure how I feel or what I want.'

Elise failed to stifle her irritation at such diffidence as she spoke. 'Don't be ridiculous. Whatever do you mean?'

'It often depends on how the people around me are feeling. I mean, if my father is approving and satisfied with me then I feel that I am a capable consort who could achieve so many things. Otherwise I am just a queen of calamity.' Marta flashed a smile to suggest that she was teasing but Elise was not deterred.

'Ha! Well then dear queen. If you don't want anything for yourself, what do you want for your empire?'

Marta batted the question away with a wave of her hands. 'Strudel and dobostorte for everyone!' she scoffed before she could be pushed to reveal more.

Elise backed off; she did not want to scare the admirable Marta away. She plucked her dessert fork from the table and scooped up a large chunk of dobostorte. 'Here's to getting what we want!' She shoved the sticky chocolate and buttercream cake into her mouth.

Again, Marta followed her lead prudently dissecting a smaller chunk with her own fork.

'You must find me quite unacceptable Elise.' She said, her tongue darting to remove a crumb of chocolate from the corner of her lip.

'Unacceptable? No. Intolerable? Perhaps.' Elise heckled.

'I might not be able to explain it right now but I do think I am on the verge of discovering new things about myself.'

'How so?' Elise asked, her brown eyes widening.

'I have a friend, Leopold, who is trying to help me figure out what I want. Under his tutelage, I think I will soon be ready to try out some ideas for myself.'

Marta returned her attention to the contents of her plate, measuring her next bite with precision.

'We have just met and already I can tell you are smart, curious and observant, and I'm certain you are a much more rounded soul than your father. Therefore, it is intolerable to me that you don't seem able to recognise that in yourself.' Elise feared she had transgressed as Marta's expression shifted from coy to humiliated. 'Anyway, enough of that; tell me more of Leopold and these ideas of yours.'

'I don't mean to be rude but we are still strangers. I'm not sure it would be appropriate to share details of either today. What I will say, however, is that I am interested in the psychological development of children. I have little maternal instinct but I am passionate about understanding the concerns of young minds.'

Elise's face illuminated. 'Then we'd make a great team! As part of my education, I spent time on placement at the Hôpital des Enfants Malades, one of the finest teaching hospitals in France. I know little of young minds, but I am familiar with the physical ailments of children and I'm quite positive of the links between the two.'

'That is impressive Elise, but I'm not sure such links can be established without further investigation and supporting evidence.' Marta lectured.

'Well, my own experiences are evidence enough for me and have taught me this much - where the head meets the heart, *that* is where you'll find the root of both magic and misery. Hey, we could go into partnership!'

'I'm not ready for a partner; I am really just getting started.'

'Oh, rubbish. Everybody has to have somebody who believes in them.'

'Leopold believes in me. He sees something that I am not even sure I see for myself. I am positive that he will teach me some valuable lessons about myself and maybe I can teach him and others like him, something new in return.'

'I don't doubt it,' Elise tried not to sound put out. 'Well, if I can offer any kind of counsel in future then I'd be glad to participate. Us girls should stick together you know.'

'Thank you Elise, I might take you up on that someday.'

Marta checked the clock hanging on the wall above the servery, an hour had passed easily in Elise's company. Her father would soon be finished with his client and would come looking for her in her room.

A waiter hovered at the next table, no doubt he was anxious to move them along and make room for the lunch customers. She nodded her approval at him and in a beat he was at the table and clearing the remnants of their coffee break.

Pulling the tiny portion of paper from her finger purse she turned to Elise.

'Can I ask *you* something now?'

'It would seem fair.'

Marta used her fingertips to flatten the crinkled stub out on the table. An hour ago she would have been embarrassed at her bitten nails and protuberant knuckles but in the company of Elise she felt quite adequate.

'If you received an anonymous package in the post, what would you do?'

'I would hope it was stuffed with Krone, and I would spend it as quick as I could.' She joked.

'I'm serious. I came to the Café Louvre today because of this small piece of paper. It is one of a few items I have received anonymously in the post over the past few weeks. If there had been one single delivery I could have dismissed it as a mistake, but then a second package arrived and I just felt compelled to follow it up.'

'Always do what you feel compelled to do Marta. Compulsion is instinct whispering in your ear.' Elise picked up the piece of paper. 'What is it?' She held it up to the light to get a better look.

'It's part of a stub, probably from a waiter's order book or a receipt book. It features this café's logo and some writing, but that is so worn that I can only make out some of the letters. I thought it would help to come here, but now I'm here it doesn't make any more sense. I am not sure what to do next.'

'What do Arnold and Leopold make of all this, no doubt they have an opinion?'

'I haven't told them and I don't intend to. If I did they'd just dismiss it anyway. I want to work this one out for myself.'

'But you told me.' Elise didn't understand why this guarded woman would choose a random stranger as a confidante.

'Yes, I did. It's nice to seek a second opinion from someone who is disconnected from my life. Would you like to join me in straightening out my little mystery?'

'Sure, why not. If we don't find anything, well at least we could have some fun together. Who knows, we might even become friends Marta Rosenblit! Though I am not sure I can agree to meet your father again, we may have to separate our friendship from the rest of your life.' She laughed.

'It wouldn't hurt to get a little separation, Vienna can be so incestuous. Let's make a pact that we will only exchange the most crucial of personal information in the pursuit of the solution to the clues. When we are not figuring things out, we can work to support each other's ambition.'

'We could be friends too you know?'

'Er, yes, well, I mean, yes of course if you'd like?' Marta was taken aback.

'Then you've got yourself a deal!'

Marta and Elise shook on it.

'Now it really is time for me to get back to my father. I will have to run if I leave it much longer, and I don't want to arrive home panting and unkempt or I might be forced to explain myself.'

'I understand. It was nice to meet you Marta. Here, take my details and get in touch again as soon as you are ready. I've waited a long time to have cause for mischief.' Elise pulled a pen and a notebook from her bag and jotted down her address and a contact telephone number.

'Hooray for mischief Elise, and thank you for everything.' She concluded, laying down payment for her portion of the bill as she spoke.

Elise tore the paper from the notebook and handed it to Marta. 'The phone number is for the bakery beneath my apartment. You can leave a message with them; they know how to reach me.'

Marta grabbed her coat and purse and peeked out from the cover of the booth, scanning the café again for familiar faces. Mr Beste was no longer sitting at his table, but his hat still had pride of place on the marble top so no doubt he would return any moment. Confident she could extract herself unnoticed she twisted her hips until she was free from her seat and made her way to the door.

Elise watched Marta leave the cafe. Intrigued by the exchange, she was already looking forward to their next meeting.

CHAPTER TWELVE

Ordinarily Marta would relish the opportunity to attend one of her fathers' seminars. She cared little whether her participation was restricted to planning and organisation or whether she was able to act as hostess and mingle with the influential and articulate professionals Arnold inspired. Each event offered up an opportunity for her to marinate among the collective genius of the great men, some of whom had travelled from across the globe to meet and debate with her father.

Tonight, however, she was on edge. Just as she had done many times before Marta had drafted all of the invitations, issuing almost 200 personally addressed envelopes, but unlike before she had received a meagre 43 acceptances in reply. Without telling her father, she had resent another 112 assuming the postal service must have failed to deliver them the first time around. In a panic she had sought out 59 additional names (she had aimed to make it an even 60 but, having exhausted all her records, could not find one more credible name) to write to in the hope of filling the spaces left by the 45 invitees who had politely declined. She had even included two female academics, Louisa May Baker, an American doctor, as well as a British sociologist named Beattie Preston – a Baroness no less. Ms Baker had declined by immediate reply, but the Baroness had accepted and that in and of itself should have been a blessing. It was the first time she had ever risked inviting women to a Rosenblit seminar. Whilst he hadn't gone so far as to ban them, Arnold had made it clear that he did not like to have women in the audience, but what choice did she have?

In the week prior to the event she had made follow up calls to the non-responders and had been shocked to see guilt in her reflection as it beamed from the two gleaming brass domes of the ringer box on the wall. She could attribute this in part to her failure to make up the numbers, but the truth of the matter was that her real guilt was in recognising why support for her father was waning, and could feasibly wane further once she herself pushed for a place on the stage. She agreed with the growing murmurs of his critics, no worse than that, she applauded them for speaking out.

How horrifically disloyal she was. How close she herself was to highlighting his inadequacies. Not with harsh accusations, but with clandestine conversations and secrets poured onto paper. She was getting away with it for now, but it was only a matter of time before she revealed her hand.

She had been getting away with so many things lately, becoming a casual lover to her father's dear friend was not even the worst of it. She had dropped her inhibitions in pursuit of illicit liaisons with Leopold. Sex was squeezed into their business meetings, and as time went on she cared less and less.

Her friendship with Elise was another little secret she held close. She enjoyed courting her friend's brazen views, indulging in idle gossip and using Elise's support as a substitute for permission to proceed with her plans.

At 6.30pm, she paced the entrance of the University. It was a familiar venue to Marta; she had assisted Arnold with many lectures and conferences there and thought of it as a second home. She had a regular seat in the enormous library where she could be found reading, her only hobby when she wasn't working at the Akademisches Gymnasium, helping Arnold or making time for Leopold. Sometimes Elise would join her too. Academic volumes as well as some excellent fiction lined the walls from the floor up into the eaves. Depending on her mood, she would choose from what was available, or bring along a book of her own as an excuse to enjoy the stillness.

Guests began to arrive in small numbers and so, mildly reassured, she moved herself to the conference room. As always Marta was the genial host, handing out agendas to the line of serious-faced men as she ushered them to their seats.

The newcomers stood out amid a small pond of Arnold's most staunch supporters, ever dedicated to him. He struggled to draw in the fresh thinkers and visionaries he once did, which was unfortunate given that he could not see how much he needed an injection of creativity.

Marta never asked for the opportunity to offer her opinions on the content of any particular talk. She had become an expert at being everywhere but nowhere, an unseen cog in the wheel that carried the Arnold Rosenblit circus along.

Arnold gave a convincing performance as always, though a proportion of his audience seemed restless and disengaged at times. He was not deterred and rattled through the findings of his latest study entitled *'Psycopathy and the Ego'*, closing with a summary of his key findings.

Questions and congratulations came thick and fast just as soon as the opportunity was opened to the floor.

'How does this condition differ from Bleuler's thoughts on schizophrenia?' One of the newcomers asked.

'What about diagnosis?' It was a fair question Marta thought. Arnold hadn't addressed that.

'Rosenblit you are a genius!' Ah yes, Marta noted, Professor Hollriegl of course.

She was quite delighted to hear a female voice chime in. *'At what age might one first expect to see evidence of psychopathy?'* The Baroness queried.

'Arnold old friend, once again you have surprised and impressed me. I'm convinced.' Her father would be comforted by that, thank heaven for Dr Ingeborg.

The last question of the evening was delivered by an olive skinned young man with shiny black hair combed into a side parting.

'Are your thoughts any more than regurgitations of the ideas put forward by Schneider and Kraepelin? Birnbaum, in particular has done a lot of work on psychopathy, why should we listen to you now?' Marta thumbed through her guest list trying to find the man's name.

The man surveyed the other members of the audience as if proud of his vociferousness. Newcomers, especially the young ones, were less familiar with the etiquette. Not like the respectful old friends, but Arnold was not ruffled.

'If you don't want to listen you may leave? I don't know what they are teaching you at medical school young man, but perhaps we should revisit this conversation after you qualify?' Arnold retorted.

The audience relaxed in unison as Arnold gathered his papers and stood down from his platform.

Marta continued her search with determination. Perridge, Pudridge, Pontage, something like that. It must be here somewhere. Ah yes, Partridge. That was it. An outspoken American hot shot currently pushing his own ideas on psychopathy; quite how he had slipped into the mix was indefensible. Arnold should have been given a full briefing on him so as to prepare some kind of rebuke, but she had been so distracted with everything else that it had escaped her attention. It was troubling for things to end that way, but it was getting harder to stem the flow of ambitious psychiatrists snapping at Arnold's heels.

Finally, it was her turn to take the stage. 'Gentlemen,' she said as she met the icy gaze of the Baroness, 'and ladies. Drinks will now be served in the refectory.'

That was all she was permitted to say and she did not attempt to add any more. She was on hand to serve as doctors, consultants, physicians, psychiatry students and their professors drifted in. A number of the men did not return to the refectory at all.

Marta hadn't expected to see Leopold at this particular event; she hadn't shown him to a seat. She presumed his interest could be attributed to his involvement with patient care and procedures at a number of asylums across the city, but it didn't leave her any less shocked to see him approaching the drinks table.

'Wonderful seminar wasn't it Marta? Your father was impressive as always.' Marta felt exposed.

'Good evening, Dr Kaposi. I'm glad you enjoyed it, I will be sure to let my father know.' Her polite confidence was betrayed by her quizzical expression.

'So many of my patients straddle the border between sanity and insanity, I find it helps my practice to attend the odd seminar. I have been so close to your father for such a long time I am sure I could pose as a psychiatrist and get away with it, ha can you imagine?!' He added.

'These seminars hold little interest for you and you know it. What are you doing here?'

He lowered his voice and leaned in. 'Of course I am interested in psychopathy but if I am honest I haven't been able to focus my efforts on anything else but you all evening darling. I feel terrible, but I shan't have time for you this week lover. Shall I see you next Thursday?' He asked, biting his lower lip and eyeing her all over.

Marta's eyes flicked around the room and back to Leopold who was awaiting a response. 'Yes, of course, usual time and place.' She was giddy with a sensation she was ashamed to identify as lust. He retreated into the small crowd as swiftly as he had emerged from it.

'A woman like you should never behave in such a debasing manner.' Marta's stomach rolled over as she turned to face the Baroness.

'Marta Rosenblit isn't it?'

'Yes, yes that's right.' She confirmed mouth agape.

'Beattie Preston. I'm a sociologist, but I must also admit to dabbling in economics and history amongst other things.'

Marta eyed the slender framed woman and was at once struck by her imposing presence. 'Yes of course Lady Preston.'

'There's no need for pomp. My husband earned the title, I was fortunate enough to receive it by association. That said I take full advantage of it, I'm not one to go away quietly. How about you, will you continue to debase yourself for a man?'

Marta was embarrassed. Was her lust so obvious to this shrewd stranger? Without being aware of it, she began scratching and picking at the rough skin on her elbow. She attempted an answer. 'I'm sure you have misunderstood, Dr Kaposi is my father's…'

'Any fool can see that you are capable of more than…'

Marta tried to interject. 'I'm sorry Lady Preston if I could just…'

'For goodness sake young lady, stop apologising, and it's Beattie. As I was saying, you are capable of more than announcing the refreshments. Your father may cut a fine figure up there on the stage, but his is not the only voice of reason. From what I hear you have lots to offer as a collaborator or, may I venture, as an independent operator.' Beattie Preston said, without reservation or discretion.

Arnold was observing the two women from across the refectory. Disconcerted by his stare, Marta attempted to appear casual. She turned away from Arnold and back to Beattie.

'It's generous of you to say so Beattie but this evening is all about my father. I have no desire to run away with his limelight.'

Looking at her more closely, Marta noted that they shared a similar gangly posture and somatic features. Beattie's face, however, had a delicacy and kindness she could only dream of.

'I do not have children Marta, but I know that encouraging and enabling the successes of one's offspring should be a pleasure of the highest order. Ageing is a joyless process, but handing over the baton of wisdom when you start to run out of steam can be invigorating. Has it ever occurred to you that maybe your father would quite like to hand over to you so he can move into a period of hard-earned respite?' Beattie's impossibly high cheekbones rounded as she smiled.

'I must admit that I don't disagree with you Beattie, but I am not sure my father sees it as you do. He is pushing himself harder than ever. I would hate to antagonise him into taking action he does not seem ready for.'

'So you are a pacifist? How admirable dear. Of course you want the best for your father, but there's a fine line between pacifism and languor. Perhaps it is you, not your father, who is not ready?'

It was a statement that struck Marta in her solar plexus. She was ashamed to have her private doubts raised by a voice outside herself.

Beattie continued. 'Those who fear upset and commotion often hide straight and still on that line, but are merely masking their hatred.'

'I don't hate my father.' Marta asserted.

'I know you don't. You hate yourself, and that has to stop if you are ever to become your own woman.' She added, as if gutting a still quivering fish.

Marta was reeling. 'I don't know what I am supposed to say to that.'

'Don't say anything. Just start doing something. Now, I really must say goodnight, I have to travel back to Oxford first thing in the morning and I will be a frightful wreck if I don't get to bed soon.' She turned away from Marta and headed in the direction of Arnold.

She watched, a little shell-shocked, as Beattie offered her father a firm congratulatory handshake and thanked him for his hospitality. She could not hear any of the words exchanged as the woman bent her head to say something discreetly in his ear, but she suspected it related to her as she witnessed her father's expression change from charmed to stern. She pulled away and, rising up to full height, smoothed her hands over her hair and put on her hat. Seeing Beattie standing alongside her father, Marta was struck by her height. She was unusually tall, perhaps just shy of six foot, or was it just the way she held herself? Marta straightened her spine, pushing her shoulders back and elongating her neck. 'It wouldn't hurt anyone if I started walking a little taller.' She thought to herself.

An air of disgruntlement hung over the gathering all evening and it did not go unnoticed.

'What was the matter with them all tonight?' Arnold asked as he packed up his soft brown calfskin briefcase in readiness to leave.

He had been talking to himself, but Marta felt the need to reassure him, and maybe herself too, that he was not losing his touch. 'The topic of psychopaths is a dark one father, from what I could see they were pondering on the possibilities you presented. It must be quite disturbing for them to hear from such an expert as you, having to contemplate the possibility that undiagnosed psychopaths are everywhere.'

'Of course, you're right.' He was sulking. 'Some of us are just made of sterner matter and can stomach things others would find insufferable.'

'Few are made as stern as you father, that's for sure.' Marta offered as a verbal pat on the back.

'What about that young fellow, what was his name again?'

'Partridge.'

'Partridge yes, that's him. Thinks I'm a bloody fool that one. I mean, I know others have touched on the topic before, but I believe that I have added a perspective not yet considered by any other academic of our time.'

Marta remained quiet, understanding that her corroboration was unnecessary at this point.

'Where did he come from anyway, and where was everybody else this evening? I know that if my usual crowd had been present tonight they would have silenced him without hesitation.'

'They would have, absolutely. Many of your supporters had to send their apologies, I believe railway problems disrupted plans for some of our international visitors and a bout of throat fever affected a number of others.'

'Throat fever, really? I should get myself home then, you know how susceptible I am to trouble in that area. My voice is crucial to my public counsel and private client work.' He stroked a protective hand over his Adam's apple.

'On a positive note, it's always good to meet new and interesting people father.'

'I see you met that ungainly creature with all the opinions, Beattie was it? Why is it always the women who seem hell-bent on disturbing the order of things?' He asked, staring off into the distance as if recalling their conversation.

'Oh, the Baroness, yes.' She said, elevating Beattie's status in an effort to avoid the anticipated diatribe about the inclusion of women on the guest list.

Arnold lost track. 'And that Swedish zoologist fellow, did you notice how he cornered me in the refectory trying to cajole me into supporting his latest remedy. Are any psychiatrists made enough to think that rabbit faeces can cure mental illness? Can you imagine how many of Vienna's most prolific practitioners would be written off as fools and fraudsters if they started subscribing to that kind of nonsense?'

'That certainly sounds off centre.' Marta was unable to offer her full attention, she was busy recalling her own exchange with Beattie.

'I know you have been busy working at the school and gallivanting around the city lately Marta, but I would appreciate it if you could be more targeted with your invitations next time.' Arnold added before stretching out a yawn.

'Yes of course father, next time.'

As she followed him to the lobby and then out onto the dark street she reflected on the events of the evening. Marta could see that no real harm had been done – at least not to Arnold anyway.

CHAPTER THIRTEEN

'Do you think it's possible to become physiologically addicted to somebody?' Marta asked, removing her reading glasses and looking up from her book.

She and Elise had been paying regular visits to the University library whenever they had spare time to meet up. If they timed it right they could read for an hour or so before stopping at around four in the afternoon for *'jause'* – coffee, a snack and a gossip with a group of like-minded science students.

'What? You mean like somebody might crave opiates or cigarettes?' Elise replied.

'Exactly like that.'

'Friend or lover?'

'Either.' Marta tried to remain casual.

Elise arched a suspicious eyebrow. 'Why do you ask?'

'I was just debating it out of curiosity. You know, how much control we actually have over the people we choose to surround ourselves with. Whether or not we are, in truth, victims of our biochemical responses, perhaps free will is just a trick of the mind.'

'Does it make a difference? I mean either way, we act the way we act, the consequences happen anyway. Good or bad, right or wrong. Whatever drives us has more to do with apportioning blame or abdicating responsibility.'

Marta was unsure. 'Maybe our biology skews our judgement. Makes us behave in ways we would otherwise consider inappropriate or irrational.'

'I know I have seen people behave like they are out of their minds when it comes to their lovers. If they choose the right one everything is bliss, total satisfaction. But when it all goes wrong they fall apart, lose all self-respect, destabilise.' Elise placed the collection of Landsteiner's immunology papers she had been reading on the table in front of her.

'So do you think being addicted to somebody is good if you are happy, but bad if you're not?'

'I can't be certain, but I do know this – unhappiness in love is the motive for many a disastrous deed. Honestly, you'd be shocked at just how far some people are prepared to go to hang on to a lover, even if the lover has become the ruin of them. If that's not a symptom of addiction then I don't know what is.'

'My father thinks that if you just keep working at something eventually you will get it right, do it better.'

'As you know Marta, I have little time for what your father thinks. What about you, what is your opinion on the matter?'

'I'm just not sure I agree. Repeating patterns is just that, repetition. Where's the space for growth? Is growth even possible? Might we always be drawn to the wrong people if our internal chemistry dictates it? Maybe our hearts and minds just seek familiar conditions and if we recognise and change them then we can control our choices. Do you know what I mean?'

'You are better placed than me to judge the psychology of it, but as a woman of medicine I know that neurobiological functions are crucial in forming attachments – at least in studies on non-human primates anyway.'

'And does that happen throughout life?'

'We don't know yet, but evidence suggests that early attachment is when a lot of neurological processes come together or, fail to if that process is disrupted for some reason.'

Marta considered the impact of what Elise had just told her. Disruptions in attachment had the potential to change brain chemistry. Quite whether that could be best overcome with psychological treatment or medical treatment was intriguing.

She jumped up from her chair and tossed her book on the shelf behind her. 'I've got to go.'

'Go where? It's almost four o'clock, don't you want to eat or drink first?' Elise called out to her friend who was already pulling on her hat and walking away from the table.

'No. Thank you but I have an idea.' Marta shouted back.

She had been stumbling over her plans for the new facility for what felt like weeks, struggling to shake off her father's ideology but not forsaking his knowledge and experience. Yet the concept was so obvious to her now. Marta rushed home, inspired and eager to record her thoughts.

For the next few days, with the words of Beattie Preston and Elise ringing in her ears she repeated the same process of scribbling in her notebook, becoming wracked with insecurity, then tearing out the pages and tossing them into the fire in her bedroom. She paced and read, and paced and wrote, and paced and tore her work up again, but she was not giving up. She was beginning to believe she could do this. Perhaps it was being in her own home that was causing her block?

The following week Marta began working on her plans during class, looking up at the small window in the schoolroom door every couple of minutes to check that the principle Mr Spreckels, a chubby insignificant fellow with a tendency to over-manage his staff, wasn't carrying out his observations.

She had settled the children with instructions to work through the exercises in their textbooks. The class was quite manageable providing she took time now and then to encourage the studious with positive affirmations and a deliver a few 'Bertha' inspired reproaches for the unruly runts. It was an approach that seemed to work well for her which was good as she had no alternative method to try.

As she sketched out her ideas she reflected on how rapidly things were changing for her irrespective of her initial sluggishness and reluctance. A force much greater than her moved her along in spite of herself. Just a short time ago she was contained in isolation, embryonic. Arnold was her only companion, the one person with whom she had shared common ground and yet she also felt at odds with him much of the time. The only other consistent person in their house was Pernilla, but her inept housekeeping abilities had so far persisted, preventing even her from becoming a settled part of everyday life.

But now, now she was overwhelmed by the company of people who had given her a new perspective. New connections had sprung up from nowhere – a friend, a confidante and, she dared to admit, a lover. She had not had the privilege to use those terms in relation to herself before. Other people had friends. Of course she had seen friends before, friends of her fathers', friends of her sisters'. She had watched friendships being made and broken in the schoolyard, their boundaries repaired or redefined over and over. She had heard friends laugh at each other, scrutinised the faces of friends engaged in deep discussion. She had even wondered what it might be like to be greeted with a friendly hug, or held in the arms of a friend as you cried. Two people effortlessly turning in to each other for comfort. Although she had only known Elise for a short while she had already felt drunk with a desire to reach out and hug her. To hold her hand or link arms with her, a possibility so foreign it actually made her spine stiffen and crackle with tension. But at least Elise was interested in her; she was a woman whose intellect matched her own, whose curiosity spilled over in a way that elevated Marta's spirits. Elise made her forget her doubts about herself and the world she existed in, she was a multiplier. Someone who not only made the puzzle easier by adding her own pieces, but also showed you how your pieces fit together to complete it. She liked Elise. No, more than that, she was growing to love her friend and that was quite an unfamiliar feeling.

As for Beattie, she had felt some sense of unanimity with the woman to whom she had confessed her agreement with the idea that her father should step back. She was a solid and admirable treasure who Marta hoped one day to espouse - just as soon as she got herself and her thoughts collected together.

Leopold had her spinning. His interest in her was different to that shown by Elise, but Marta found it no less thrilling. This man, worldly and brilliant as he was, had noticed her and exposed her all at once. Time in his company was more erratic and unsettling than time with Elise or her father. Leopold was intimidating and then all at once he was reassuring. There was something else too. The way he looked at her with an intimidating passion when he spoke, so certain of every statement he made. Disarming her with his surety and disturbing her in the best of ways.

And then there was her work. Her mind, once a festering seedbed awaiting answers, was now alive with budding visions. Thoughts dispersed and toiled over until firm plans sprouted, almost ready to see the sun. Almost.

She had no doubt that had she attempted such a revolution alone she would have torn it all up and returned to the knowingness of her father. It seemed too risky to step outside the family circle, but with Elise and Leopold around, Beattie too, she had allies. Real ones, the kind that aren't blood bound and won't hold you hostage to a family history. Her father offered a steadiness, but the presence of new faces, beliefs and ideals was revitalising. She was beginning to realise just how much she had needed it. She could be sure of herself now, and so here in this classroom she began to commit.

Her plan was to shift the focus away from the symptom analysis her father had taught her, to something more inherent. She had a lot of work she wanted to do and she would have to work alone for the early years at least, so she would have to prioritise. Her analysis model featured three broad categories:

Character Studies. Marta was eager to understand if children were born with distinctive moral qualities, if their temperament and constitution were integral or imposed by caregivers.

Childhood Development. In understanding the biological and neurological development of children she hoped to pinpoint the most significant periods of change.

Trauma & Disruptive Influences. Finally, she wanted to correlate the impact of childhood trauma and other disruptive influences with the timeline of development. To understand if incidences were more or less likely to cause psychological damage depending upon the age at which they occurred, and if the potential to repair such damage was altered as a result.

The latter was one of the main reasons she had made the decision to specialise in working with orphans. There would be a control group of 'normal' children from secure two parent backgrounds, but the orphans provided the necessary diversity.

The regression work her father pursued with adults had its advantages, but she suspected memory was an unreliable resource. Memory could be adaptive, suppressible and protective of sanity. As a cognitive process, it could be manipulated to avoid or change painful recollections, or create monsters where they had never been. Children were unwittingly raw subjects less capable, she expected, of masking responses with such subterfuge. If she could capture their experiences as they happened, or soon after, she reasoned she could more accurately analyse psychological consequences. If she could follow these children throughout their most formative years she could gain unprecedented access to the real impact of childhood trauma and other life-altering disruptions.

Reviewing her ideas on paper was dizzying, so much so that she did not hear the bell that sounded the end of class. She was so lost in all of the limitless possibilities that she did not notice Tobias Gruber, one of the unruly runts, approach her desk. She finally saw him as he snatched up one of her pieces of notepaper, his mucky fingers smearing the page with an unidentifiable brown gloop. She hoped the gloop had come from the sandwich tin he was holding in his left hand.

'Can we go now? We can't sit here all day, it's lunchtime you know. Not that you look like you eat much.' Tobias said, fingering a few more papers on her desk.

She stood up and snatched the paper from his reach. 'Gruber, you will sit down this instant! Class,' she called to the rest of the children, now sitting open-mouthed and wondering what would happen next, 'the rest of you will go to lunch.'

The children packed their pencils, paper and textbooks away in their desks and hurried outside, leaving her and Tobias alone. Her flash of anger was gone and now Marta was unsure what to say to the boy.

She stared at him for a moment, and he stared right back; a stubborn reminder that no matter how revolutionary she imagined she could be, in reality she made quite a pitiful teacher so it seemed impossible to think that she could lead an entire childhood analysis project.

'You will eat your lunch in here today.' She stated with feeble conviction.

Tobias groaned, mumbled something under his breath and slammed his tin on his desk. 'I was just saying you are not round and strong looking like my mother. You look skinny like you might break in half.'

'I am well aware of how I look thank you Gruber. Now that's enough. Get on with your lunch or I will give you extra work to do.'

'I don't care.' The boy shrugged, rocking back on two legs of his chair.

'You will care when I take you to Mr Spreckels' office.' She threatened, knowing full well that if she did she would also have to explain what she had been doing at the time of her student's insubordination.

'I don't care, he won't listen to you anyway skinny woman.' He repeated, spreading some of the brown gloop onto a slice of bread with his finger and shovelling it into his mouth. She pretended to ignore him, but if truth be told she was inexplicably hurt by his childish words.

The end of the school day could not come soon enough for Marta. She left without a single word to anyone, buckling the wheel of her bike a little in her haste to remove it from its spot behind the caretakers shed. As soon as she was clear of the school gates Marta pedalled furiously until she was going so fast that everything around her was a blur. As she pushed her feet against the pedals she railed against the wind. She almost lost control as she rounded the corners, but she didn't care. In fact, part of her wished she would fall and break her back or be knocked unconscious; either would be sweet relief from the battle going on in her mind right now. Realise her potential or realise that she was incapable of becoming her own woman.

CHAPTER FOURTEEN

It was Tuesday morning and Marta could already feel the quiet hum of anticipation building to a swell in the pit of her stomach. She couldn't be sure what Leopold would have in store for her at the office but so often the thrill was in the not knowing. Intimate moments increasingly replaced formal discussions about the new facility. The table in the office repurposed as a base for sexual encounters. The door was always locked to prevent embarrassing interruptions, but the large windows offered little privacy from onlookers living in the apartment building across the street. Most had heavy drapes which obscured much of the view but the bright natural light that flooded in meant their trysts could still be witnessed by a determinedly nosey wife or inquisitive child.

In so many ways, Leopold was less careful these days, reckless even. He had gone as far as grabbing her bottom in full view of people on the street and didn't seem to consider it risky at all. Once inside she had attempted to reprimand him, but he had responded with agitation.

Nudity in front of a man did not come naturally to Marta who preferred to remain at least partially if not fully clothed during their fornications. Leopold seemed satisfied with lifting skirts, pulling knickers aside and unravelling stockings if required. Even so, she had learned to dress for their liaisons. Not in ways that made her appear more seductive, but in ways that allowed for efficient access and minimal damage to her body and the fabric. She had experimented with buttons and zippers, but they rarely held together for long. A loose rayon blouse was a common choice, offering room for roaming hands with minimal risk of a split seam. Belts proved unwise. Just two weeks previous, she had been shocked to feel the fiery heat of her own belt being used against her. A small break in the skin was still tender to the touch, but she had to admit that she had enjoyed the intensity of the experience and did little to deter it.

She had put on a new dress today, dropped waist and a hemline that hovered somewhere between her knee and calf. Leopold had been quite insistent on taking her shopping and had paid for everything. He had picked out the dress because of the indulgent silk fabric, but she had chosen the colour, charcoal grey, from her favoured muted palette. She now wore her roll garters at her knees, as was the fashion now apparently. The immaculately turned out store assistant had corrected her on that style faux pas. They were well worn, a birthday gift from her sister Christiane. Leopold was eager to replace them with new ones, but she had resisted, they were still in good enough shape so it seemed wasteful.

Kisses between them were still hurried and scant. She was not one for romance and fairy tales, but she did long for the tenderer meeting of lips sometimes. A secret connection that whispered love between the rough touches they exchanged.

Sometimes she was perplexed at how 'making love' was not a very loving an act at all. But it suited her dark thoughts and now she had entered so wholeheartedly into womanhood she must keep going. For what else was left behind but childish fantasy and loneliness?

Leopold was more vigorous with her today, not she felt, for reasons of passion but more out of spite and boredom. He pinched sharply at her most intimate places, like a boy prodding and provoking a tethered dog just to see how far he could push it. The sensation was not unpleasant, but the sense of surprise at his new technique made her gasp. Out of nowhere he slapped her hard across the face. She wanted to pull away, shout at him to stop, but she kept quiet as she had done many times before. He had been busy travelling and attending meetings in a bid to secure funding, and he was frustrated at having not yet been able to engender support from his contacts. He had done all of that for her, it would be selfish of her not to allow him a moment of misconduct.

As he pushed his mouth hard against her breast she lowered her face, now reddened and pulsing on one side, until it touched the top of his head. A trail of sandalwood filled her nostrils as she pressed her lips against the fine hair on his crown, sticky with Brilliantine pomade. Though they had made love several times now, the sensation of being penetrated still startled her at first. The experiences aroused her, at times she felt quite undone with abandon, but she did not experience the intense euphoria she could achieve at her own hands. Leopold handled her impatiently and cared little about confirming her readiness to receive him. It was disappointing but having a man desire her and hold her close was compensation enough.

When he was finished with her he tucked his white shirt into his underpants, before buttoning his trousers, grey herringbone with a fine pinstripe. Marta watched him straighten his sleeves with a gentle tug at the French cuffs of his shirt before pulling on his waistcoat. Once fastened, he turned his wrist over to check the time on his watch. It was a fine adornment, a black rectangular face with gold numbers and the name Patek Phillipe & Co in miniature script.

'Well would you look at that little lady, it's almost 11 o'clock. You held on to me a little too long this morning, we've no time to talk shop today. I should get going. You can let yourself out now can't you?' Leopold made eye contact for the first time since they had walked into the office.

'Well, I'd rather leave with you. Just give me a minute.' Using her arms, she pushed herself off the edge of the table, smoothing her dress.

'Can't. No time. You'll be fine. I'll see you next week.' And he made for the door.

'But wait, what about the financial forecasts? I thought we were spending time on those today? And I have done quite a lot of work on my analysis model; I think I am almost there now.'

'That's great Marta; but really, I can't give you any more time today. Anyway, this whole project is about you becoming more independent. The files are in the cabinet, take a look through them yourself and lock the door before you leave.' Then he was gone.

Marta looked around the empty room; it seemed much bigger now she was alone. She turned to look over her shoulder towards the windows. A shiver ran up her spine and her heart did a somersault when she thought she saw a curtain twitch in the apartment directly opposite. She turned her face away, not knowing what else to do, she dropped to her hands and knees so that she was just out of sight.

'What are you doing?' she asked herself out loud.

She would have to leave. From her position on all fours, Marta surveyed the carpet to see where her hat and coat had been strewn. She scrambled under the table to collect her small brown bag. It had fallen open, some of the contents spilled out. As she picked it up she chose not to check her reflection in the mirrored flap, but did her best to tuck everything back inside. Her silver cigarette case was a welcome sight. Still under the table, she rotated to a seated position and took out a cigarette. Pulling her enamel lighter from her bag she lit it and took a long, slow drag, breathing the hot tobacco fumes deep into her lungs. As she exhaled she crossed her arms loosely over her knees which were now drawn up toward her chest. As strange as she must have appeared, she found the confined space soothing. The more she puffed, the more the little ghosted clouds of smoke gathered under the table top that prevented them from drifting off to nothing.

As she sat she had vivid recollections of her lovemaking with Leopold on top of the table just moments before. It was surreal to her, sitting beneath the memory of herself, like having an outer body experience – only she was trapped underneath rather than viewing the situation from above. What would Elise think of her if she could see her now? What would Arnold think? Overwhelmed for a moment, she pushed the fiery end of her cigarette into her forearm, near the crease of her inner elbow. After four or five hot pokes she reached the end of the cigarette, a disappointment which left her feeling as vapid as the trail of stale smoke surrounding her. She couldn't keep hiding; she would have to come out sooner or later.

CHAPTER FIFTEEN

'Come Join the Crowds in London!' Elise read aloud from the front of the travel pamphlet. She was quite well travelled for a young woman, but most of her trips had been made for the benefit of her studies rather than for the frivolity of it and she always went alone. Never before had she considered travelling with a friend, but why not? She had already made the decision to take the year off before finding a job and settling into regular life, there really was no better time.

Marta was sitting on the sofa reading a research paper written by an Austrian-American psychiatrist named Matthias Biedermeier. He was exploring the use of insulin shock therapy on mentally ill patients. The paper had been sent to her father, but he had dismissed it as junk before he had even opened it and she had had to fish it from his waste paper basket.

'Come to London with me!'

'Whatever for?'

'For fun of course! Do you always have to have a reason for everything you do?'

'My father is unlikely to let me gallivant off to London without one, so yes, I suppose I do. I can't slip away without explanation; it's hardly a short journey.'

Elise looked at the back of the paper in Marta's hands. 'That's your reason. Right there on that paper, look!'

Marta turned it over. On the back page was an invitation to attend a seminar hosted by the psychiatrist at the Savoy Hotel on December 9th, the following week.

'Tell your father you are going to the seminar.'

'Oh he doesn't believe in alternative treatments, he'd never approve.'

'He might if you told him that you have heard this guy is trying to rubbish the Rosenblit school of thinking. Tell him you plan to find out more about what this man is saying. Your face is unknown outside of Vienna; you could fit in more discreetly than your father.'

Marta shook her head, laughed at her friend's outlandish idea and returned to her paper.

'Please Marta, please! Come with me. You'll come, I know you will.' Elise jumped around the room, her string of synthetic pearls rattling in harmony with her chanting. 'We're going to London, we're going to London, we're going to London!'

She had to admit that her new friend made her feel as though anything was possible. 'Why not?' Marta asked to the air. 'Let's do it.'

For the rest of the afternoon they chatted busily. Elise pulled out her map book from the drawer in her sideboard; there was no time to lose making the necessary travel arrangements. They planned their route by train, departing from Vienna to the Gare de Lyon in Paris before picking up a connection to London Victoria via Calais.

'This is so exciting Marta. We can dine, and dance, oh I love to dance! Do women in England do the Charleston or the Black Bottom do you know?'

'I have no idea if the women of Vienna do those things, whatever they are, let alone in England. I've never been out of Austria.' Marta was embarrassed at her lack of worldliness.

'Never?' Elise asked, clutching her friend's hands. 'Oh Marta, you have no idea what you are missing. Travelling is one of *the* most joyful pleasures. You will adore it; I will make sure of it.'

She was terrified and intimidated by the prospect of long distance train travel and English food and Lord knows the dancing too, but she was willing to give it a try.

That evening over dinner, Marta managed to convince Arnold that the trip was her idea. It would be more affordable if she travelled alone and of course it may just be a rumour that this bright young psychiatrist was snapping at his heels. Arnold agreed that he should not waste his valuable time on rumour alone. He could arrange a follow-up meeting if there was anything worthy of his concern. After his experience with his colleagues at his own recent seminar, he was certain that some unusual things were going on in the field at the moment.

It all seemed so possible that Marta could barely contain herself.

Just a few days later she was pulling her mother's old travel bag down from the attic. It had been passed along to all of her sisters, though they had used it to pack for their honeymoons.

Marta patted the dust off the embroidered floral bag. It was not the most glamorous of luggage, the pattern was gaudy and it was threadbare at the edges. The bone coloured handle was grimy and worn, but she could still make out the exquisite mother of pearl inlay. A dark stained patch near the base could be disguised if she held it in a way that it was close to her body.

She unclipped the button fastening and began to add her belongings. She had never packed for herself before and had no idea what to expect the other end, but she would only be gone for four days so she was confident she wouldn't need to pack too much. She decided to wear heavy items, such as her tweed trousers and coat, for travelling in. Both Arnold and Elise had warned her that England was prone to rain and could be cold at any time of year, but in winter it was a certainty. She would wear her hat and carry a pair gloves in her pocket just in case.

Ever organised, she listed each packed item on a page at the back of her journal so that she could check them off prior to her return.

Stockings, one pair
Undergarments (four)
Tortoiseshell comb
Reading glasses
Cigarettes
A copy of The Institute for Child Guidance
Navy blue pinstripe housedress
Charcoal shift dress
Black lace up shoes
Leather belt

She added her journal and a pencil, not only to diary her experiences and thoughts, but for noting down any useful British idioms and academic references she could call on later. She hoped she might bump into a chap named Dawson who was doing some useful work with children at the Maudsley Hospital in the city. If that happened it would not do to be fumbling for a scrap of paper in order to record his contact details. According to her books, the English appreciated formality and she would need to appear professional.

Last of all, she slipped her letter knife and a small bottle of rubbing alcohol into the inside pocket of the bag. No need to make note of that. Elise was to bring their travel documents; she was far more accustomed to travelling so it seemed logical for her to take on the responsibility.

She was ready. Marta carried the bag down to the front door and removed her coat from the stand in the hallway. Should she take an umbrella? She hesitated for a moment, her bag was already quite heavy and she was wearing her hat. No, she would leave the umbrella, far too cumbersome. She liked a little rain anyway.

The house was empty. It was Pernilla's day off and Arnold was taking lunch in the city with a colleague. She was relieved, she loathed goodbyes.

Looking back up at the staircase she felt small, almost like a child going off to school for the first time. Nerves shook her to her skeleton and adrenalin made her teeth chatter a little, even though the weather outside was mild and the house was temperate.

She looked down to check her shoes for a third time. They were clean. She opened the door and stepped over the threshold. As she did, she was startled to bump into Leopold as he rushed up to her door.

'Leopold?' Shocked, she looked all around.

He knew she was heading for England, but she had fed him the same story as Arnold, not telling him about Elise or the real reason for her trip.

'Darling Marta, I'm so glad I made it before you left for London.' He did not seem to notice that she was already standing in her coat, luggage in hand.

'I'm leaving now.' She said.

'No, no. Don't think of it. I have something much more important you have to do with me. We're leaving for Budapest this afternoon. You and I.' He looked her over. 'Oh good, you're already packed. That will save us some time.'

'But father is expecting me to go to London.'

'Good and you will tell him that you did, so as not to arouse his suspicions. Don't worry; you can say that it was just a rumour. We can work out the finer points. Now, come. I have an influential Hungarian friend I want you to meet. He is keen to find out more about your new facility, and if he likes your ideas he will provide enough funding to see us through the first five years.'

She disliked the way he held her by the forearm as he spoke.

She tried to resist. 'What are you doing, touching me like that in broad daylight?' She pulled her arm back to her side. 'It really is important that I go to London.'

'Marta, what could be more important than doing something for yourself. For your facility and all those troubled children you want to work with.'

She had been so excited to join Elise but she knew that if she wanted to be as successful as Beattie and the other Avant-garde women she had heard about, her work had to come first, she was at such a crucial stage.

'Okay, I understand. I'll come with you, but I must be home just as my father is expecting.' Her face softened in reluctant defeat and Leopold released a satisfied grin.

'Sure, we mustn't disappoint Arnold.' He swivelled on his heels and headed back down the front path, turning up his collar as a light drizzle began to shimmer against the sunlit sky.

'Wait, I just remembered I need to fetch my umbrella. Give me just a minute.'

With that, she ran back inside and shut the front door. Leaning against it, she took a deep breath and closed her eyes, trying to stop the day from overwhelming her. She had never travelled outside of Vienna before and now she was torn between two trips in the same day, and Budapest? It was less than ideal. Arnold used to make frequent visits to see a fellow psychiatrist there. Once a close associate and friend, the pair had ceased contact quite abruptly following a disagreement over psychoanalytic practices. Arnold had been so perturbed by the fall out that he had refused to set foot in the city ever since and had forbidden her from ever doing so too. Yet again, she found herself betraying him and in doing so she was deserting Elise too. This was not her proudest moment. As she picked up the telephone she hoped her friend would understand.

Fortunately, Elise was running late. Her neighbour Móric knocked on the door to deliver the details of Marta's telephone message, which he had scrawled on a brown paper bag. She and Móric shared the telephone line with the bakery downstairs. She tried her best to hide her impatience at being slowed further, thanked him for his time and closed her front door. She unfolded the paper bag and read the message.

'Marta says she is sorry but London will have to wait. She must travel to Budapest to meet an important investor. She will explain more when she returns.'

She returned to her lounge where her vanity case was propped against the wall. Elise picked it up and threw it across the room. It hit the corner of her armchair causing the clasp to pop open and all of her belongings to scatter to a heap on the floor. Next she reached for the tea cup on her side table, letting out an almighty yell as she hurled it at the kitchen doorway. The fine porcelain broke into pieces on impact, a tiny shard nicking her shin and creating a snag hole in her stockings as it flew.

She couldn't believe it. Leopold wanted Marta and nobody wanted her. She would be alone.

Elise buried herself face down on the sofa and began to cry with noisy childish sobs. After a moment she sat upright and slowed her breathing. Pulling a handkerchief and compact mirror from the pile of personal items now lying on the floor, she dried her face and fixed her make up. She smoothed her hair back into place and let out a sharp sigh.

She reprimanded herself. 'Don't lose control Elise. You're too close now. Nobody cares if you are falling apart, just keep going.'

She gathered up her things, folding her clothes back up and bagging her toiletries before placing them back inside her vanity case. Next she fetched the dustpan from the kitchen and cleaned up the broken tea cup. When she was sure she had scooped it all up, she removed the stocking from her left leg and replaced it with a flawless one.

Ready now, she looked around her small apartment with defiance. She would continue to play the good friend. She would travel to London alone and investigate the seminar for herself. That way she could report back to Marta and help her retain her cover story with Arnold. It was not how things were meant to be, but nothing in her life ever was.

CHAPTER SIXTEEN

It was around eight o'clock in the morning when they arrived at the Keleti Railway Terminal in Budapest, a spectacular structure that stood at the meeting point of three tree-lined avenues. Leopold was unmoved by the sight of a driver waiting for them on the platform. The man in the peaked cap did not offer his own name but seemed to know theirs. Marta was embarrassed as he plucked their bags from the pavement and carried them to the car which was waiting nearby. Her shabby travel bag gave her away; she was not used to receiving such courtesies. Nor was she accustomed to taking taxi rides. Arnold used them frequently but she preferred to use the tram, train or her bike for journeys that were not walkable.

The driver extended a gloved hand in assistance as she stepped into the back of the car. Inside it smelled of polished leather and two-stroke engine oil. Leopold hopped in unaided, bouncing along the back seat until he was close enough for their thighs to brush against each other. He nodded to the driver as he shut the car door for them, then turned his attentions to Marta, slipping a hand inside the neck of her coat. He traced his fingers across the back of her neck and squeezed it. A tingle ran through her at his touch. As the car moved away Leopold leaned in close to kiss her ear, taking a small chunk of it between his teeth in a teasing gesture.

'Leopold! Not in front of the driver, whatever is the matter with you?'

'What? It's fine, we can be anonymous here. Nobody knows us; we can behave in whatever way we want to. We're going to have a wild time Marta, just relax.'

'We're here for business.'

'There's nothing wrong with a little pleasure to help things along though is there? We've come all this way so we might as well enjoy ourselves.'

Marta assessed the city as it passed by the window of the taxi. The morning frost was heavy but the sky was clear and away from the shadows of the buildings the sun was already melting it. Budapest was a fine destination but not as exotic as she had envisaged. In many ways, it reminded her of Vienna though it looked tired and forgotten here and there. Homemade banners bearing anti-Trianon protests speckled the city, hanging from balconies and pasted to walls and windows, evidence of a troubled past. The wide streets were bordered by elegant architecture, and the bohemian undercurrent made her feel quite at home.

The driver, who Leopold had established was named Lajos, informed them that he was taking them meet Mr Aurel for a late breakfast. He would collect them again at midday and take them to drop off their bags at Mr Aurel's country house where they could bathe and take tea. This evening they would join him and his wife at the Opera House and stay the night before returning to Vienna.

As they drove, Leopold updated Marta on his friend's interest in their facility.

"Herzl Aurel is a well-connected politician and heir to a valuable liquor empire. He has business and philanthropic interests in Germany, Italy and France and is looking for opportunities in Austria."

"Why does he want to give us his money?' Marta was curious, she had never been exposed to funding meetings with her father so felt somewhat naïve.

'He's terribly concerned about all the prohibition nonsense in the United States. He figures if he can bolster the case for its use in medicine he can shore up his distribution lines should such prohibition reach Hungary and its neighbours.'

'Still, I am not sure what that has to do with us?'

'Here we are sir.' Lajos pulled the car in to the kerb before Leopold could explain the relevance.

This time Marta refused assistance from the outstretched hand of Lajos and stepped out of the car unaided. The Hotel Astoria was a bookend on the corner of the street, propping up a long line of townhouses, apartment buildings and shops. Leopold led them through the reception to where Herzl was waiting at a corner table in the Empire Hall. He was sitting alone and scoring the creases of his napkin as they approached. He stood to welcome them, his wiry frame quite insignificant against the dark oak panelling backdrop. She had expected a broad-shouldered and pot-bellied man, but he was frail. At first glance, she would have guessed he was more than sixty years old. His dark brown hair sprouted from an unnaturally high hair line betraying what she presumed was a toupee.

'Ah, Leopold my good man! So satisfying to see you here at last, it's been too long.' Herzl boomed, attracting the attention of other diners.

Leopold reached across Marta to shake hands with the man, almost knocking her off her feet. She waited for a few seconds but her impatience got the better of her.

'Marta Rosenblit.' She said, thrusting her open hand between the two men by way of introduction.

Herzl looked her over from head to toe and back up again until his eyes met hers. 'Yes, indeed you are my dear.'

'No need for *my dear*, Ms Rosenblit will do just fine for the time being.' She had intended to appear confident, but the look on Herzl's face suggested she may have come across as insolent.

Leopold began to laugh at her. 'You'll have to forgive Marta, she's incredibly academic but her education in manners and social graces has been somewhat limited.'

'Ha! I can quite imagine given that she has been raised by Arnold. The man never was one to follow the rules and so I should expect that this little lady is just the same.'

Had she heard him right, did he just mention her father? Marta panicked. Why hadn't Leopold told her that Herzl knew him, what if he said something?

She felt a reassuring pat on her shoulder as Leopold steered her toward her seat. 'As I mentioned on the phone Herzl, Marta is keeping lots of secrets from

Arnold at the moment. Rest assured she will keep your secrets too.'

'We're all good friends here and good friends keep confidences.' Herzl reassured her.

'Now, let's eat. I have taken the liberty of ordering for you. Whilst you are here I want you to indulge yourselves at my expense. I have arranged for you to use the spa after our meal and then you will return to my house and rest for the afternoon in preparation for our evening together.'

As he spoke, three waiters rallied around the table laying out toast, deviled eggs, kabanos sausages, a selection of cream cheeses including a spicy mound of körözött, cold steak, and a plate of mixed peppers and tomatoes. A number of sweet buns and fruit, and a bowl of bright pink sour cherry soup were also set down. With some minor rearrangement of the place settings, space was made at the centre of the table for pots of tea and coffee.

Marta had never seen so much food set out for so few people. Her relationship with food had always been a practical one so she hesitated at the idea of eating purely for pleasure. Leopold tucked into the plates with haste, spreading his toast with generous amounts of cheese. He stabbed at the eggs, putting one on her plate and another straight into his mouth.

'Eat, eat.' Herzl gestured to her with his fork. 'You must be starving after all of that travelling.'

She looked around the restaurant and back at Herzl who was sipping a black coffee. He had chosen a kabanos, some steak and was just arranging a slice of toast so it sat unobtrusively alongside the meat. He beckoned a waiter and whispered in his ear, and shortly after the man reappeared with a small crystal tumbler of plum brandy. It was barely 9.30am.

Marta reached for a slice of toast and covered it with a forkful of peppers and then tomatoes. She chose tea and was at once grateful for the familiar taste of the warm liquid as it trickled down her throat. Feeling refreshed, she was eager to talk about the reason for their visit.

'So Mr Aurel, what exactly do you find so appealing about the idea of funding my new facility?' She asked, a clumsy attempt at assertiveness.

Leopold dropped his fork with an almighty clatter, but Herzl was undeterred.

'Why are you so eager to talk business Marta? Do you not trust that we will come to that in good time?' He asked.

'I think trust is overrated.' Marta startled herself with this statement.

'Do you now? Well, as it happens I think intellect is overrated. Sometimes you just need to rely on instinct, and at this point in time my instinct tells me I need to oil some gears in Austria. You and Leopold could be just the people to help me move my business forward.'

'But what does my research have to do with your business?' Her tone had become arrogant.

Leopold interjected. 'Marta, I think you are being a little bold in the face of such hospitality. Let's not weigh down such a delightful meal with the drudgery of deal making.'

'Quite right Leopold. Don't worry your head about it Marta. Leopold and I have been working through your plans and all will be discussed in good time.' Herzl tapped his empty brandy glass on the table to indicate his need for a refill.

'Now, one more drink and I must leave you to your own business for the day. I have a meeting scheduled with Prime Minister Mr Bethlen so I will meet up with you later at the opera.'

'Damn it.' Marta thought on remembering that she had only packed her house dress and her one plain shift dress. She debated the merits of creating an excuse not to attend, but then she had never been to the opera before and whilst she was wary of his intentions, she was bright enough to know that she needed to impress Herzl if she were to secure the funding to get the facility off the ground.

After breakfast was over and Herzl had left to resume his day, the hotel concierge invited Leopold and Marta to sample the spa. Ever one to take advantage of benefits, he took up the offer whilst Marta declined, choosing instead to take a walk around the city.

'Before you go off for a stroll Marta, can I just check that you have packed something suitable to wear to the opera?' Leopold asked as she turned to leave the hotel lobby.

'I have my shift dress. That will be suitable enough.'

Leopold reached into his pocket and pulled out a money clip. 'Marta please, will you make the effort and buy yourself something pretty?' He said, flicking through the notes before sliding some out and forcing them into her palm.

'You're meant to be a lady, go and treat yourself.' He added moving away from her and toward a smiling salon girl who was eager to show him to the spa.

She wrapped her fingers around the notes and tried not to show her disappointment. Outside she returned to the car which was waiting exactly where it had dropped them off earlier. She tapped on the window, startling Lajos.

'I'd like my bag, please.'

'Wouldn't you prefer to leave it in the car until you reach the house Madam?'

'No thank you. I'll take it with me now, but I will leave my coat if I may? What time did you say we are leaving?'

'Midday Madam.'

'Thank you Lajos. If Dr Kaposi comes out before I return please inform him that I will meet him back here at midday.'

'Certainly.' Lajos exchanged her bag for her coat and got back into the driving seat.

She looked at her wristwatch, it was 10.25 and the weather had turned unseasonably fine. Marta scrunched up the money Leopold had given her and put it into a pocket in her bag. She felt boosted by the opportunity to spend an hour or two in solitude on the bustling streets of Budapest. She strolled for a while in no particular direction, studying the differing faces of the local people. Some had prominent noses and razors for cheekbones whilst others had snub noses on wide faces, and within each Hungarian face she could find traces of her own lineage. Upon reaching the Great Market Hall on the Váci Utca, she wallowed in the scent of persimmon and clementine, paprika and caraway. She marvelled at the creamy coloured juhturó, trappista and pálpusztai cheeses. She listened intently to a leather-faced old lady in a headscarf as she bartered with a stall holder over the price of yellow onions. Elise would have loved it here, she would have wanted to taste everything, she thought.

Back out on the street she bypassed the boutiques; she would not be trying on dresses no matter who was paying. Instead she made her way to Vörösmarty Square, eventually taking her place on a bench behind a monument which overlooked an impressive fountain. Once there, she chose to ignore the view in favour of pulling the child guidance book from her bag. It was a sizeable volume but one she was determined to complete. She took out her reading glasses and a pencil then pulled her knees up in front of her chest so that she could use them as a book rest. As she absorbed the contents, she made notes in the margins and circled passages of text erratically. This was where she was happiest, studying, learning, refining. Her head lost in the pages it didn't matter what she ate, how she spoke or whether or not she was dressed appropriately. She was aware of attracting curious glances from some of the women walking by but made no effort to hide her work, only pulled her hat down further over her head to obscure more of her face. It was getting hotter and it made her uncomfortable but the soft shallow brim shielded her a little from the sun whilst ensuring she could avoid having to connect with anyone.

By 11.30, the heat was becoming more intense and the text was soon spoiled by the black spots that started appearing before her eyes. Marta sat for a moment surrendering to the heat. She was tired and a thirst was drawing the moisture from her throat until it felt as though it was lined with fine sand. She removed her hat and used the sleeve of her middy blouse to eliminate the hair that was clinging to her now moist brow. Flicking the pages of the book in front of her face provided a welcome breeze which cooled her skin and helped restore her vision to normal.

She sighed in wonder at what she was doing here. Was this independence? Yes, these were new experiences, new places, and of course she could think and act without seeking approval but Leopold was still the puppet master pushing her forward and making decisions without even consulting her. She was operating under his tutelage. How would she know when she had made it? Before Leopold, she did not have even a glimmer of hope that she could do it alone. She was not a fan of superstition and prophecy, but she wished she could see into the future and gain some reassurance that the path she was choosing was the right one. Come to think of it, she wished she could see into the past too, maybe then things would come into focus. Whatever was to come next, Leopold was expecting her, they had business to do.

It was with a heavy heart that she made her way back to the car just before midday. She had little interest in resting at some dusty old country pile, but she knew she had a duty. Leopold was already sitting in the car when she arrived at the Astoria at five past twelve, and for a moment Marta was concerned that he might be cross at her tardiness. When she got in she was relieved to see that his time in the spa had satiated him sufficiently that he might leave her to her own devices for the rest of the day. She was not in the mood to give herself over to him.

CHAPTER SEVENTEEN

Herzl's house was vast and ostentatious with four storeys and ten bedrooms. His wife Anna was a pleasant and welcoming hostess but Marta did not relish the idea of being her companion and asked to be taken straight to her room. It seemed inappropriate to ask whether or not she would be sleeping in the same room as Leopold though she was curious. She had become so accustomed to sleeping alone and having privacy that she did not share well.

A stout looking housekeeper walked her up two flights of stairs and along a corridor until they arrived at a bedroom with flamingo pink walls and cream satin bed sheets. Ornamental bronze statuettes of long-limbed women posed on the window sills. A hair brush and powder puff sat on top of a huge dressing table which featured a folding mirror. The rug was deep and plush and a decorative screen stood in the corner alongside a large white gloss wardrobe.

'Scheisse! What *is* this place?' Marta was not normally one for cursing but she had never seen anything quite like it. The housekeeper raised a disapproving eyebrow.

She nodded a thank you and the housekeeper left. Once the woman was gone Marta turned the small key and locked the door. She unpacked her belongings, draping her dresses and stockings over the screen. A grey shift was entirely inappropriate for the opera but it was the finer of the two dresses she had packed and she

161

would at least be comfortable in it. She noticed the heels of her black shoes were dirty so she grabbed a pale pink hand towel from the sink top and dampened it under the tap. She rubbed it over her shoes, leaving brown and black stains all over the pretty cloth. Unsure what else to do, she hid it under the mattress of the bed and then placed her shoes back in her bag.

She slumped on the bed and tried to read. Returning to her studies proved harder than she had anticipated, the glare of the pink room contaminating the crisp white pages of her book. Her thoughts drifted to Elise and how disappointed she must have been to hear of her last minute withdrawal from the London trip. Right now, Marta knew where she would rather be and that was not in Budapest.

If she had gone on alone Elise would no doubt be preparing herself for the seminar. She would have packed properly and would be pulling on a nice dress and some elegant shoes, quite comfortable with courting her fellow professionals. She had planned their itinerary to the last detail. They would have arrived in England the evening before the seminar and filled their spare time with a visit to a theatre in the West End. Elise would have ensured they ended the evening in a jazz club. She might even have learned the Black Bottom by now! The next day would have been spent sightseeing before going back to the hotel to have dinner and attend the seminar. It would have been straightforward, fun even. She would not have to waste herself on trivial game playing. She would not have been curled up on a crinkled bunch of satin bedding with guilt and self-loathing rising up in her stomach.

Marta got up from the bed, went to her bag and took out the pouch containing her letter knife. What happened next was swift and well-rehearsed. She had long been a master at hiding all traces of the cuts and even now, away from home, she could still make the cut without losing a single drop of blood to her clothes or the carpet. Relief came quickly and helped to restore her concentration on her studies. She rinsed the blade at the vanity, dried it on the corner of her blouse and then after returning it to the pouch, tucked it back into her bag. As she did, she caught a glimpse of the buckle on her father's belt. She had forgotten she had packed it and was all the more delighted to discover it at this moment. She ran the length of leather under her nose and immediately she was home. Wrapping it tightly around her small waist, she fastened the buckle to hold herself in and went back to her books.

Leopold knocked the door just after six o'clock that evening. His disappointment was evident as soon as she emerged from behind it. Marta hadn't bothered to check her reflection in the mirror whilst she had been getting ready, but she knew she was clean, that her hair was combed and her shift dress was not too shabby.

He stopped her as she tried to pass him in the corridor. 'What are you thinking?'

'Whatever do you mean Leopold?' He was holding her by the forearm again.

'Look at you. Don't you think you might have forgotten something?'

'Oh yes of course.' Marta went back into her room and picked up her purse from the bedside table and the money that Leopold had given her earlier in the day.

'Ready.' She said, returning to the corridor with a wavering smile.

He stopped her a second time. 'Do you always have to be so incompetent at being a woman?'

'This is all I have. I'm sorry to disappoint you but nobody mentioned that I would need to pack for the opera.'

'I gave you money to buy something.' He snarled.

'I tried, honestly, but I couldn't find anything I liked. Here, take it.' She lied, returning the wad of cash.

'Herzl is my friend and business contact. Don't ruin this for me. You *will* participate fully this evening, have I made myself clear Marta?'

'Perfectly.' She stared back at him for a second too long.

Downstairs Marta felt embarrassed to see the effort Anna had made in getting dressed for the opera. Her gown was dripping with feathers and beads and the honey coloured silk panels coordinated with Herzl's pocket square and tie. She really was quite beautiful when draped with the trimmings of wealth.

They travelled to the opera together; the performance was Mozart's 'The Magic Flute'. Herzl said they had the finest seats in the house, a private box close to the stage. Marta couldn't have cared less, she just wanted to move unseen and avoid displeasing anyone else.

The opera was powerful. Marta was moved by it in a way she had not anticipated. She heard echoes of her father in the character of Sarastro, a man who could be perceived as an evil sorcerer or fierce protector keeping his precious Pamina safe. Her mother eventually banished to a life in hell.

During the interval, the men stepped out for whisky and a cigarette. 'Why don't you two get a little better acquainted while we are gone?' Leopold suggested.

'That charcoal dress is lovely against your pale complexion.' Marta could tell Anna was trying to sound affectionate but she found the comment patronising.

Marta turned away. If she could have run home right now she would have.

Anna tried to engage her again. 'I adore the Magic Flute; I've seen it three times now. Sarastro is my favourite, how about you?'

'The piper I suppose.' Marta struggled to fight her brewing inferiority. 'Excuse me.' She got up from her seat and made her way to the ladies room. Anna did not attempt to converse with Marta again for the rest of the evening.

Back at the country house, Herzl poured two liqueurs whilst Anna went upstairs to change out of her gown.

Eager to understand the proposed arrangement, Marta started the conversation. 'Thank you for a lovely evening Mr Aurel. If you don't mind my asking, may we discuss our future now?'

'I admire your ambition Marta I do. Please, join us for a nightcap and we can talk.' He poured another glass of liqueur and passed it to her. Before tonight, she had not drunk any alcohol other than Vin Mariani. It smelled sweet and made her cheeks and decollate glow after just a few sips.

Herzl took a seat on the upholstered Chesterfield sofa. 'Now, Leopold and I have been discussing your plans for the new children's facility in Vienna. I am interested in running a specific study on the soothing effects of different alcohol-based medicines for children. For example, if I can create my own brand of antitussive or perhaps a tuberculosis tonic that is a little more palatable than those opium alkaloid tinctures it would certainly help to stabilise my profits.' He loosened his bow tie and unbuttoned his collar. 'I mean, Laudanum and Papine just aren't popular with mothers anymore. If you ask me it's because of the tighter regulations and all the scaremongering about side effects, not to mention the bitter taste - a spoonful of honey does little to ease that.' Herzl's face was ruddy in the evening light.

'With respect, the regulatory controls are backed by some solid reasoning Mr Aurel.'

Leopold joined the conversation, taking a seat next to Herzl. 'I don't think Herzl is disputing that Marta. Alcohol is already being prescribed; we just want to prove that our remedy is more effective than others already out there and offers a viable alternative to the more controversial medical preparations.'

'But I am not interested in medicating the children in my care; I am interested in a more therapeutic approach. I want to collaborate with them and understand them.'

'Well, with the utmost respect for you too Marta, if I don't offer you any money you may not be able to help any children at all. I have already approached a colleague at the University of Vienna and asked him to run the research for me, but Leopold was insistent that you are one to watch. I like to follow my intuition and my intuition tells me to work with you but I am wondering if I am mistaken.' Herzl looked from Marta to Leopold, his face stiff and serious.

'What does your intuition tell you Marta?' asked Leopold, his stare widening with expectation.

Standing before them it was as though she was on trial. Realising she had come too far to back out now, she paused for a moment, choosing to resume the compliant role she often adopted with her father.

'It tells me that I should accept your gracious offer, I will need to maintain the physical health of the children in my care if I expect to gather accurate therapeutic data. I am sure I can find a way to make use of your preparations and record results whilst making my own observations. Your influence will, of course, add to my credibility too.' She replied, knowing that it was the only answer that would satisfy them.

'Then let's drink to that shall we?' Herzl stood, clinked his glass first against Leopold's and then against hers. Leopold did the same. After their toast, Herzl placed his arm around Leopold's shoulder and walked him out of earshot. The two men talked to each other in low mumbles then completed their quiet conversation with a smile and a handshake.

Marta sneaked another liqueur hoping it would suffocate the sinking feeling in her chest. She weaved around the room, her eyelids heavy and her head buzzing as she admired the art, hunting trophies and ornaments on display. It was late and she was woozy. A pewter carriage clock on the mantelpiece chimed midnight as Anna descended the staircase. Marta almost dropped her liqueur glass at the sight of her. She was wearing a floor-length chemise made of the sheerest white voile, which offered a full view of her bare breasts. The transparency of the fabric left little to the imagination, Anna's modesty barely covered by an intricate patch of pink and gold thread embroidery that fanned out across her pelvis like a peacock feather. How could this woman be so brazen, and in front of Leopold?

Leopold nodded a goodnight to Herzl and then to Marta as he crossed the room and took Anna's hand. It didn't take long for Marta to figure out what was happening. She remembered his order from earlier this evening '*you will participate fully*'. Marta watched in shock as he led Anna up the stairs, squeezing the back of her neck just as he had done to hers hours earlier. She did not dare to look up at Herzl for fear of what would happen next. The thought of Anna and Leopold together repulsed her, but the idea of being offered to Herzl in trade was even more unthinkable.

'Shall we seal our deal Marta?' Herzl walked towards her.

Marta looked up at the staircase just as Leopold and Anna disappeared behind a door she presumed must be a spare bedroom. Being with a man was still so new to her. Would a more experienced woman consider this liaison acceptable? Anna had certainly not made a fuss; rather she appeared eager and well-rehearsed. Marta was not ready to expose herself to anybody else. No, she would not do this, no matter how much they needed the funding.

Herzl drew closer, moving his hand to cradle her head as he secured her by a clump of her hair. He tried to pull her close and kiss her but she turned away. He slid his other hand around the back of her waist, pinching her skin as he pulled her to him and forced his lips against hers. She didn't want to jeopardise her facility but this could not happen. Unsure of what else to do, Marta pretended to faint, closing her eyes and collapsing her body in a slumping motion. Herzl attempted to keep her upright, gripping her with both arms but he was too late and she fell to the floor, knocking her head on a nest of tables as she dropped.

He knelt beside her, shaking her by the shoulders and looking for signs of consciousness he could mistake for permission. She kept her eyes closed firm, moaned a little and rolled onto her side but he pressed on, running one hand up the back of her thighs and under her dress, still trying to shake her awake with the other. Marta tried to remain still but he continued to molest her as though he was wholly entitled to get his money's worth from her. She panicked when Herzl began to unfasten the buttons at the back. As a last resort, she forced a retching

169

motion. He moved back in an instant. 'Oh hell, what is that? Are you sick now, or are you just teasing me perhaps? Leopold said you would like a bit of a tussle.'

Marta continued to retch and spit until it seemed apparent she would vomit. Frustrated at being unable to arouse her, Herzl whispered in her ear. 'You disgusting little vamp. You should be flattered that I would even attempt to touch a woman like you.' Then he called for the housekeeper.

'Fetch some smelling salts and get this woman to bed.' He ordered.

Through half sealed eyelids, she watched him pour himself another drink. He did not look at her as the housekeeper brought her round and escorted her back to her bedroom. In her room, she could not bring herself to undress. Instead she locked the door, kicked off her shoes and curled up into a ball on the bed. She tossed and turned all night, enveloped by clingy layers of cream satin, plugging her ears with her fingers and closing her eyes to block out the sounds and images she imagined of Leopold and Anna. It was irrational, why should she care? She and Leopold had not formally announced any kind of relationship so what right did she have to feel so hurt? As new lovers they had been intimate on just a few occasions, and he had only admitted to the possibility of almost loving her. Was he being gentle with Anna, or would he handle her as fiercely as he did Marta? It bothered her into the small hours until she gave in to sleep at around five o'clock in the morning.

CHAPTER EIGHTEEN

Marta woke with a start and immediately began looking around the room trying to remember where she was. Then flashes of the night before returned to her mind and her stomach lurched. She got up, tiptoed to the bedroom door, put her ear to it and listened; the house was quiet. She opened the door gently and peered out, to her relief there was nothing to see but her breakfast, which was waiting for her on a tray outside her room. A folded piece of notepaper was tucked into the toast rack. She took the tray inside, placed it on the bed and unfolded the note. It was from Leopold.

'You acted outside of our arrangement last night and now I must do the same. I am meeting Herzl at the Astoria this morning to try and smooth things over and then taking the early train back to Vienna tomorrow which is most inconvenient to me but entirely necessary. You will return alone. You clearly need time to reconsider your commitment to our project. If you decide you want to continue you can make contact with me when you get home. This did not go well. I thought you too intelligent to let such a rare opportunity pass you by.

Leopold'

Her return train ticket was tucked inside the note and some small change littered the tray. Marta put on clean underwear and the trousers and blouse she had arrived in, then packed up her belongings as quickly as she could. She did not have the appetite for breakfast this morning but forced herself to drink a cup of coffee and nibble on some toast. Her head was pounding from where she had hit it on the tables, and her heart – well her heart was about to shatter and now she could understand why. She was in love with Leopold. That is why it had disgusted her so, to see him with Anna. It was a new and miserable feeling and she did not like it at all. She had no control over the powerful pull in her chest. How she had got to this point she didn't know, she hadn't even liked Leopold at first. He had been a presence for most of her life and not once had she considered him appealing, at least not until the day he had found something appealing in her.

Marta wrapped some fruit pieces and two sweet buns from the breakfast tray in a napkin and put them in her bag. Without Leopold accompanying her she would not have enough money to dine on the train so she must take what she could.

Her stomach was doing somersaults as the car approached the railway station. Maybe Leopold would be waiting for her, his temper cooled and the deal with Herzl restored.

Nobody was there when they pulled up at the entrance. She allowed Lajos to help her with her bag this time; she was tired and defeated and did not have the patience for modesty.

'Thank you Lajos, you've been most kind.' She extended her hand and gave the driver a firm handshake.

'Have a safe journey back to Vienna madam.'

Inside the terminal, she examined the sea of faces bobbing along in front of her. He was not there. The train would depart in ten minutes and now she knew he would not join her on it. She really would be travelling alone.

Her train pulled to a standstill at the platform where she was waiting, suspended in isolation as passengers pushed past her chatting about the morning news and their plans for the day. Taking one last hopeful look around her she grudgingly picked up her travel bag and climbed aboard. Once in the carriage she took her books, pen and reading glasses from her bag before stowing it in the overhead rack above her seat. Minutes later a whistle signalled the train's departure from the platform. Marta put on her glasses, picked up her pen, and opened her journal.

'For the first time I am travelling home from Budapest to Vienna, and for the first time I feel so tragically alone. Both experiences new and unwelcome, and both I have brought upon myself. Self-inflicted wounds, the most painful kind I have ever delivered. How cruel is love? I had sworn I could live a lifetime without it. Solitude has been a faithful companion, but now thanks to love, I despair of loneliness. I miss the sound of his voice, the smell of the man, the meeting of our bodies. I wonder how I will ever exist without him.'

For the remainder of the journey, all Marta could do to distract herself was continue her study of the Institute for Child Guidance report. It was on consideration of the chapter on the child and its familial environment that she came to realise what she needed most right now. Her mother. Arnold had been a decisive and disciplinary parent and she valued his guidance in matters of the mind of course, but he had not been able to school her in matters of heart and soul. He had not talked to her of love or heartache though she was sure he must have felt them. There had been little talk of romance and affection. He could not teach her how to be a woman. How to recognise love and the ways to keep it. All the topics a mother should address.

Only a mother could understand the intricacies involved in coming of age and moving through life in a female skin. The physical milestones such as menstruation, sexual intercourse and giving birth, Marta had not been instructed in anything but basic anatomy and biology. Her tuition in matters of reproduction limited to that of frogs and their spawn. And there had been no mention of love and how one falls in or out of it. It was no wonder she felt so cast adrift, nobody had prepared her for this time in her life. She needed to see her mother.

Josefine Rosenblit, Marta was told, had at one time been an attentive and devoted caregiver. Her sisters had undoubtedly enjoyed the best of her attentions at a time when she was still of sound mind.

She could not remember much if anything of her mother, only photographic images came to mind when Marta tried to think of her. Two-dimensional moments arrested in black and white and offering little connection to the woman held within them.

Marta reached for those frozen memories now, the gentle movement of the train carriage rocking her like a lullaby. In one picture, Josefine stands barefoot in her bathing suit, belted modestly at her tiny waist. Taken in the summer before Marta was born, she is water side at the Strandbad Gänsehäufel. The light captures every wave of her pale hair, the length of which is braided on the top allowing loose tendrils to fall around her ears and shoulders. Her mother's head is tilted back and her face is animated with a smile that is breaking into a laugh. If only she could hear that laugh, be it gentle ripple or boisterous howl, at least Marta would have some idea of how happy she had been before darkness took her over - before Marta took her over.

In another photograph, Josefine stands alongside Arnold, looking towards him with wide, proud eyes. What colour were her eyes? Marta could not imagine. She assumed they must have been at a party. Josefine's dress is elegant and expensive looking, a long full skirt with a stiff satin bodice and an ornate silken sash just visible from behind an ostrich feather fan. Her father, sharp-suited as ever, is looking sternly at the camera, a slight squint creating a half grimace that hardens his face. It may well have been taken at one of the couple's own house parties. She had heard from her sisters that both of her parents had been quite the society darlings, keeping company with academics and artists including members of the Vienna Secession. Guests would revel into the small hours once the children were believed to be sleeping, though her sister Bertha had once told how she had witnessed a scene of such debauchery that she cried herself to sleep every night for three weeks. She had always been the most sensitive girl, however. Marta was sure she would not have been so shocked had she had the misfortune of coming across such a situation herself. Her tolerance for such things was, she felt, higher than the average. She knew she could, and had already been required to stomach things that others simply could not.

Her memories carried her into a light sleep for the next two hours, the images in her mind mingling with her dreams. As she slipped in and out of awareness she could have sworn Josefine was sitting in the carriage next to her holding her hand, then she would startle awake and realise it was her own hands intertwined and her mother was not at her side at all. When she was not sleeping she tried to stretch her limbs with a walk along the adjoining carriages, so insular in her mood that she jumped with alarm every time a guard or another passenger presented themselves. She had wanted to take out her letter knife but nowhere was sufficiently private to use it. When her urges grew too strong she had sufficed by rolling up her sleeve and scratching her arms instead. She sipped at a cup of lukewarm coffee now and then but found it hard to swallow. The fruit and sweet buns remained untouched.

Marta was surprised but somewhat relieved to see Elise waiting on the platform as the train pulled into Vienna Mitte Station. Since leaving for Budapest, she had been concerned that her friend would be angry with her, perhaps not even want to see her. As she gathered up her belongings she gave quiet thanks for the sight of a friendly face, though she was disappointed that Leopold was not there.

Elise rushed to greet her as she stepped off the train. 'Marta, Marta, over here!' She called, waving her arms.

'What a pleasant surprise to see you here. I was so worried you might not want to talk to me and yet here you are. You have no idea how pleased I am to see you, and again I am sorry for leaving you at the last minute.'

'Never mind that now; how was Budapest?' Elise put her arm around Marta, pulling her close as they walked along the platform and out into the main terminal.

Marta could have collapsed right into her friend but she was back in Vienna now, she must maintain some deportment. 'A lot like home. You'd be surprised at how you can travel hundreds of miles and yet so many things are exactly the same. What have you been doing whilst I have been away?'

'I went to London of course! Somebody had to go and find out what Matthias Biedermeier was up to if your absence was to go ahead without suspicion.'

'You went anyway? Oh, Elise I can't thank you enough.' Marta could have wept buckets of tears at the kindness of her friend. She hadn't even got around to thinking about how she might handle her father and his deluge of queries when she arrived home. She and Leopold had planned to come up with a cover story on their journey home together, but of course it had slipped her mind in the circumstances.

'Why else did you think I would be standing here waiting for you? I figured you and I would need to catch up on the details before you reported back to Arnold.'

'Always one step ahead Elise. Shall we go for coffee? We'll have to be quick as father is expecting me home soon.'

'Yes let's do that, there's a little café just around the corner. We can walk to it if your bag isn't too heavy.'

In the café, they ordered two espressos and Elise had a small cinnamon pastry. In spite of such a long journey home, Marta still couldn't rouse her appetite. The shot of strong black coffee, thick with sugar, was just what she needed to bring herself back to life ahead of her reunion with her father. He would expect her to be a buzz of news and ideas.

Elise took a sip of her espresso before she began. 'So, I have a copy here of the insulin therapy research notes. The headline is that Biedermeier wants to increase the use of aggressive physical treatments in the care of mentally ill patients. Whilst he didn't criticise your father specifically, he spent some time talking of how outdated some psychiatry methods have become. He believes a more invasive approach is needed to stamp out mental health problems. Broadly speaking, his treatment proposition involves giving excessive doses of insulin to patients in order to induce a daily coma. He said that during trials schizophrenics seemed to show the most measurable benefits. Personally I think it sounds a little brutal to leave someone unconscious for weeks at a time, maybe even years. It is ground-breaking but I am not sure it is a viable alternative to psychiatry. What do you think?'

Marta placed a careful hand on top of Elise's notes preventing her from reading on. 'Elise, can I ask you something?' A tiny tremble altered her tone.

'Anything, I'm positive the answers will all be here somewhere in my notes. I was thorough.'

Marta stared into her espresso, her head bowed. 'Will you help me meet my mother?'

Elise's spine quivered. She looked at Marta who had started absent-mindedly stirring a figure of eight into her tiny cup. 'Where did that idea come from?' She asked, wringing her hands.

'I don't know, I just… I have so many questions.'

'Whatever is the matter Marta? You haven't looked at all right since I saw you on the platform, I assumed it was just fatigue.'

'Nothing, nothing. I'm fine, really.' She insisted, still toying with her espresso.

Marta wished she could tell Elise about the sexual developments in her relationship with Leopold, but they had decided to keep it a secret. If word got out about the two of them it would cause such a disgrace, not to mention the damage it would do to their plans for the new facility. She wanted to share what had happened between Leopold and Anna in Budapest, she wanted to tell her friend about her lucky escape from Herzl and more than anything she wanted to ask her about love and how to make sense of it.

'I just feel as though it's time that's all.' She added looking nonchalantly around the cafe. 'The mysterious packages, the secrets meetings, plotting behind my father's back. I'm at the centre of so many lies when I feel I should be looking for some truth. You know what I mean?'

Elise did not respond, just nursed the remainder of her coffee as Marta continued to share her thoughts.

'Do you know that you are the first female companion I have ever had who does not have an obligation to spend time with me? I can't talk to my sisters, they have been gone for a long time and when they do visit I can't bring myself to converse with them. I cared little about it before, but knowing you has made me realise that I might have missed out on something important.'

'You understand that you can't just tap on the door of the Kreis des Wahnsinns and visit the patients don't you?' Elise reasoned.

Marta's eyes glassed. 'I know, I know. Why do you think I have lived this long without seeing her? But there must be a way in and trust in you to help me find it.'

'This is really important to you isn't it?'

'Yes Elise, it is. Please help me. You are the only friend I have right now.'

'What about Leopold?'

'He wouldn't understand and for the time being I don't want to bring him any more trouble.'

'Trouble? Why would you be trouble to the man? After all he is your business partner.'

'I just mean that he has gone to a lot of trouble to help me move things ahead with the facility. He's been glad to do it of course; it's just that I have become quite cautious about it all and have created enough delays and difficulties for him already. He would just see this as another distraction when I should be forging ahead.'

'I see. Well, if you are sure that is all it is. Leave it with me and I will see what I can come up with. If I can get you in to see your mother then I will.'

Elise finished her pastry whilst Marta reviewed the research notes. When she was done reading she spoke again. 'Now promise me that next time we meet, you will tell me all about your time in London?'

'I will look forward to it.' Elise pulled Marta into a hug she was unprepared for. Such a simple gesture but the newness of receiving it was arresting.

'Thank you for coming into my life Elise. I really don't know where I'd be without you.' Marta said, reluctant to let go of her. Emotions bubbled up from the pit of her stomach, but she must not let them spill over now. It would be too much to try and articulate it. She would see her mother soon and all of these feelings would be explained.

CHAPTER NINETEEN

On reflection, Elise was glad she had travelled to London alone. More street wise than Marta, as a child she had moved around quite frequently with her mother, a woman who was always impeccably groomed and could be mistaken for Gloria Swanson if it wasn't for her fair hair.

Once her father had gone her mother chose not to remarry but she remained popular with the opposite sex and often had men visit. Sometimes they would stay for a few hours and never be seen again. Other times her mother would introduce them to her and they would come and stay in their rented house for a few days or even a few weeks at a time. Sometimes an almighty argument would signal the end, but most often the men would leave as unceremoniously as they had arrived and without explanation.

Children cannot see the faults of their parents, but as a grown woman she had learned to take a closer look. In spite of dreams that her father might reappear one day, Elise soon realised what her mother had long since accepted. He was never going to return and so they would have to fend for themselves using whatever talents they had. Elise had always considered it fortunate that she had been gifted with more intelligence and ambition than her mother, so she was undeniably disappointed in herself when she woke in the arms of a practical stranger - Matthias Biedermeier.

The seminar had ended at nine o'clock and by ten she had already formulated a seduction plan to go back to his hotel room with him. It had been her intention to satisfy him just enough to get her hands on the research notes, but she had been so tired from a day spent walking around admiring London that she had fallen asleep next to him in bed. In the cold light of morning, she was pleased to remember that he was quite an attractive man. However, she was no longer intoxicated and full of bravado and so had made the decision to return to her own room before he woke.

Marta would be shocked to discover how elastic her morality was. Her friend had an endearing naivety that Elise wished she hadn't lost in herself. She couldn't remember how, at 19 years old, she ended up trading kisses for theatre tickets or why she had decided it was acceptable to have an affair with an engaged young banker just so that he could pay the rent on her apartment in Vienna. That was just the top and tail of it, there had been many more in between and now Matthias. She wasn't worried about her reputation. She had no children and did not see her mother much anymore. She moved from city to city with regularity and so nobody had ever kept track or passed judgement. Except now she had Marta.

It hadn't mattered to her in the beginning, she had just wanted to make a connection, but a friendship had developed and now she couldn't bear the thought of pure, sweet Marta knowing about her indiscretions. Her friend treated her as an equal, another bright career oriented woman, but she was quite sure that such a discovery would change things between them. She wasn't ready for that. In time maybe, depending on how things panned out, but not yet.

When he woke and realised Elise was missing, Matthias had knocked on the door of her hotel room. She decided not to answer. He had knocked again, louder, pleading with her to open up. She held her conviction once more. From the other side of the door, he told her how much he wanted to see her again, how he knew it sounded crazy but in just one night he had fallen for her completely. He had been charming, but she was too ashamed to let him see her a second time, especially after having thrown herself at him so brazenly.

He hadn't given up easily, sitting in the corridor outside for so long she had been concerned she might miss her train home. It must have been an hour before he retreated. When she went down to the hotel reception to check out, he was standing at the bar. Fortunately, she managed to give him the slip until the last minute when he spotted her as she was getting into her taxi. He had called after her, but she pretended not to hear, urging the driver to pull away.

Elise had thought about Matthias a lot on her return from England. He was attractive, intelligent and had been a kind and considerate lover. For a little while, she indulged the romantic fantasy that they could have a future together. How they might both move to London and marry in a small chapel overlooking the Thames River; it would not rain but she would carry a small ivory parasol just in case. After the wedding she would take a job as a paediatric consultant at St Thomas's Hospital and everyone there would respect her because her husband (who would be head of research and development at St Thomas's by then) would demand it. They would live in an elegant townhouse and Matthias would bring her English roses every day - yellow ones, her favourite colour. Holidays would be taken in his native America at his family's cottage by the lake in New Hampshire and they would return to Vienna every Christmas when the city was at its best.

But that was another life, for another woman. Elise had other obligations and she must not lose sight of what she had come to Vienna to do.

CHAPTER TWENTY

Marta returned home to find Arnold already pacing in the hallway. He did not offer to help her with her bag; he did not ask her about her journey, he did not even offer the common courtesy of a hello. Instead, he launched straight into an interrogation.

'Ah at last! I've been waiting here all morning. Quick, come to my study and tell me about this Biedermeier fellow.' Arnold demanded, pulling her by her hand before she had been able to release her grip on her travel bag.

It had not occurred to her until she looked at him now, just how angry she was that he had allowed her life to unfold the way it had. It was he who had brought catastrophe into her life, he who had opened the door to Leopold. He who was so driven by his own ego that he could not distinguish flattery from manipulation. The man her life had been entrusted to, who paid so much attention to the psychological adjustment of others, had squandered everything she was and could have been until she had become little more than a cadaver.

She realised all of a sudden how she had disguised an anger toward him that had existed inside her for so long it had become as unexceptional as the dimple in her right cheek, her wet footprint on the bathroom tiles, the scars on her thighs. She had been cognisant of it every day but paid it no real attention, veiling him with excuses and justifications until now. A light stronger than the sun itself burned through the gloom of his study as he sat before her, feet up on the desk awaiting her answers.

'How dare you demand so much of me!' She screeched, unsteadied by the ferocity of her tone.

For the first time in her life, she rendered Arnold speechless.

'You have no idea how difficult it is to live for you. No idea at all. Here you are, demanding your answers, and here I am withered with fatigue, my mind sapped of thoughts. But still you push, and you push. I cannot tolerate another second of this. I will not!' Still clutching her travel bag, Marta turned and walked out of the study slamming the door so hard behind her that the windows and front door rattled.

Pernilla had just entered the hallway, but on seeing Marta's face made a respectful about turn and headed back to the kitchen without saying a word.

Marta ran to her bedroom, closed the door and threw her bag into the corner. She took off her shoes one at a time and threw them at her vanity. Her aim was better than she had intended, the heel of one of her Oxfords causing a small fracture in her mirror. She stripped off her trousers and blouse, underwear and stockings and filled her basin with steaming water. Once full, she submerged a bar of soap and a washcloth, rubbed them against each other and squeezed out the excess water. Then, starting at her toes, she buffed her entire body all over moving the wet, slimy cloth in small circles until she was sure she was clean. After the task was complete she took herself straight to bed and did not step out of her room again until supper.

It was dark by the time she got up and sleet was pelting hard against her window. Her fire had diminished and so the room was chilly but not uncomfortable. She took her navy house dress from her bag and pulled it on. It was still wrinkled from travelling, but she didn't care. She removed a thick, oversized woollen jumper from her drawer and put it on over the top, more as a buffer from the verbal lashing she would now have to go downstairs and face than for warmth.

Marta gathered up Elise's notes from her travel bag and opened her bedroom door. The light of the landing made her blink, her eyes tender with stress and darkness. She was barefoot and the wooden floor was cold so she tried to place her soles on the runner. Suddenly she was five years old again, creeping to her father's bedroom in search of security in the middle of the night. Except she wasn't a child anymore and security could no longer be found clinging to Arnold's side. She was a woman now.

How would she explain her earlier outburst? *'Keep things simple, tell the truth.'* Arnold had always told her, and yet for Marta, the truth was fraught with complications right now. He would be furious at her, Leopold was furious at her and she was furious at herself, but she was surprised to admit that she did not wish to take any of it back.

Downstairs Arnold was half way through his supper, a plate of boiled grüne würstl and a slice of bread spread with a thick layer of spicy Liptauer cheese. A leberkäs loaf was sitting untouched on a plate to one side. The combination of ground beef, bacon, pork and onions did not appeal to her, nor the green sausage, but she knew she must eat something. She placed the notes on the table, took a plate and prepared herself some bread and cheese, and then she sat in the chair opposite Arnold. He made no attempt to break the silence, save for the occasional slopping and crunching coming from his mouth as he ate. Marta would have to talk first.

'It turns out that insulin shock treatment could be good for schizophrenics, maybe even psychopaths too.' No response.

'Biedermeier thinks talking therapies could soon be a thing of the past for patients suffering from those types of mental illness.'

'Hmph.' Arnold grunted.

Marta allowed a few seconds of breathing space to see if he might continue. Nothing.

'Putting insane patients into an insulin induced coma on a regular basis could all but eradicate even the acutest conditions. The figures are quite impressive; almost double the rate of remission in some cases.' She continued.

Arnold swallowed his last mouthful of sausage then mopped up the juices with a plain slice of bread.

Marta persisted. 'The man is a bit of a maverick and the research is in its infancy. I'm not sure I would see it as a comprehensive replacement for talking therapies but if the data continued to stack up then it could become a viable option for use in conjunction with psychoanalysis.'

He licked his fingers and pushed his plate aside then poured himself a glass of wheat beer.

'In essence the treatment is believed to affect the parasympathetic area of the nervous system, increasing anabolic force until normal function is restored.' His prolonged silence was harder to gauge than his booming temper, but she pressed on.

'Side effects include perspiration, restlessness, spasms and convulsions that sort of thing. Brain damage and death are a possibility but should be avoidable provided dosage is increased gradually and under strict supervision.'

Arnold continued to sip his beer without so much as a sigh of acknowledgment.

'I don't believe he is a threat to you at this point but it would be wise to monitor his presence in the medical journals and on the seminar circuit. What do you think?'

He drained the last of his drink and slammed his glass down on the table. Without a word, he stood up and left the room. There would be no discussion with Arnold tonight.

Sitting opposite his empty chair, Marta had nothing left to do but try to eat her meal. He couldn't ignore her forever, he was angry, she was angry. In time she was confident they would be able to talk it out. She would see her mother soon enough, and make contact with Leopold too. That's when everything would fall into place.

CHAPTER TWENTY ONE

She had committed to getting Marta in to see her mother
and that is what she would do. It was not the first time
Elise had used her connections to get her in or out of
places she was not supposed to be. She'd often taken
pride in her ability to wriggle her way into all sorts of
scenarios both illicit and benign. Her first success came
when she was a teenager back in Paris. Thanks to a brief
courtship with a delivery boy at the exclusive
chocolatiers Debauve et Gallais over on Rue des Saints-
Pères she gained unprecedented access to the company's
manufacturing facility. She even managed to secure a
free box of assorted luxury bonbons after telling the
factory manager that she was a junior reporter writing a
review for Le Petit Journal. Not one for sharing, she did
not offer her spoils to her mother or her friends, choosing
instead to consume all 22 chocolates and candied treats
by herself. With each one she devoured, she would pay
forensic attention to licking her fingertips clean of melted
chocolate or sugar sprinkles. Once she had emptied the
box she felt a mild sense of remorse, however, this was
largely brought on by the sickly stomach ache that comes
with an episode of wholehearted greed.

On her first day of University, she made it her
business to head for the library to introduce herself to a
middle-aged librarian with an achromatic complexion
called Alain Masson. After inviting him for coffee and
impressing him with her knowledge of the works of
Flaubert, Rolland and Proust, writers he fortunately

admired, she commented on how perfectly his chestnut coloured tie matched his herringbone pocket square. From that point on Alain ensured she was equipped with a steady supply of study books before any other students in her classes. If there was only one copy of *'Gazette Médicale de Paris'* he would see to it that it fell into her hands first. When Professor Séverin was unable to locate his own volume of *'Troubles Gastriques Dans l'Enfance'*, Elise made a pledge to replace it. The next morning the hefty 400-page book of childhood gastric disorders was on his desk, and Elise was ahead of the game having read it cover to cover overnight. Séverin was so impressed he took it upon himself to mention her talent at his next staff meeting and at many more thereafter.

She continued to utilise her understanding of manipulating relationships throughout her medical training. Elise made sure she was in the right place at the right time to initiate conversations with senior lecturers, picking up cues and ascertaining individual triggers in order to get ahead on forthcoming assessments and seminars. Her finest negotiation transpired as a direct result of her friendship with the Head of the Medical Sciences department. Dr Édouard Haroche was not an easy man to engage and casual flirting proved a waste of time. Instead Elise embarked on a deliberate and arduous campaign, researching him thoroughly and 'coincidentally' writing papers on topics she discovered he had a personal interest in. Uranium pitchblende and its role in modern medicine, the diagnosis and treatment of syphilis, the potential benefits of micronutrients and many more subjects not included in her syllabus but that she must understand and debate with him if she were to earn his respect. The more she learned the more she wrote. The more she wrote the more she interested him. The more papers she presented to him the more he wanted to talk to her, and so it went on until she had him hooked. In her final year of studying for her doctorate, she became the only female member of a student research panel to go on a six-month clinical placement at the University of Hamburg. The placement was quite dull, much of her time was spent watching male members of the panel participate in patient rounds, present clinical observations and experiment with laboratory testing whilst she was tasked with recording data and filing paperwork. However, she did manage to strike up firm friendships with Hilde, a botanist whom she met whilst on an errand at the terrarium, and a psychiatry student named Franz. The three of them would gather in Hilde's room at the top of a shared student house in the evenings to listen to music and discuss their hopes and dreams. Elise had considered a romance with Franz but nothing ever blossomed and so they stayed in touch as friends.

Now the head of his own psychiatric research team in Hamburg, it was Franz who had helped her arrange an appointment at the Kreis des Wahnsinns. It had been timely that Marta had reached out to her for help. Elise had wanted to see Josefine Rosenblit for some time but it was common knowledge that casual visitors were not permitted. Her friend had been only too happy to write in his professional capacity to the director of the facility – a psychiatrist named Julius with a double–

barrelled surname she couldn't quite recall. He requested access for Elise, under the pseudonym of Ms Vass, claiming she was an assessor on a fact-finding visit for a forthcoming study. A letter of invitation had arrived on the doormat of her apartment soon after. It was unfortunate that she had to meet with thirteen dangerously insane patients contained on the top floor of the building before she managed to see Josefine - particularly given that four of them had reeked of their own faeces and another two chanted to themselves in a way that made even pretend conversation impossible. Even she found it hard to chat her way through the taunting hum of 'Schlampe! Schlampe! Schlampe!' (Bitch! Bitch! Bitch!). It had also proved difficult to conduct a patient interview whilst avoiding a thrashing, but reassuringly shackled, pair of arms as they skimmed past her head with violent momentum. She was experienced in managing patients but her training had been in paediatric, not psychiatric, care. It was most fortunate that she had been able to make this visit alone.

Elise's nerves were quite rattled by the time she reached Josefine's cell but she remained determined. It was quiet on the other side of the cell door and after a quick peek through the spy hole she could see that Josefine was sitting on the edge of her bed glancing around, eyes like a lemur, wide and alert. A warden unlocked the door and pushed it hard, leaning into it with his hip and shoulder. The smell of the air in the room as it opened was refreshing, clinical and inoffensive. Relieved, she stepped in gently so as not to provoke any upset. They had met once before when Elise was a small child, but she did not like to think of that anymore and was unsure Josefine would recall it anyway. Sitting on the mattress she looked smaller than Elise remembered. Her fragile body perched almost as though it was floating, barely significant enough to make the slightest indentation. She did not look at Elise but the flinch of her right arm and shoulder, as she moved towards the chair in the corner of the cell, suggested that she had at least registered the presence of company. Some might have been afraid to meet with a mad woman but Elise knew enough about this one to understand that fear was unnecessary.

'Josefine Rosenblit?' She asked.

A hurried, almost apologetic nod of the head was all she offered to confirm her identity.

'Josefine?' Elise paused. Josefine remained impassive.

'Josefine, will you talk with me a while?'

Again, no response.

Elise would need some currency if she were to get her to collaborate after all this time.

'Josefine, I am a friend of your daughter's. Marta. Do you remember Marta?' She waited.

Josefine clenched her fists and began circling her hands at the wrists. Her feet began tapping the floor and for a moment Elise thought she might erupt from her position.

'I'm sorry. I didn't mean to upset you, but I did need to see you. Can you hear me? Josefine?' She asked, still trying to make eye contact.

No response.

'Forgive me, I should have introduced myself. We met once when I was a child. You might remember me...my name is Elise.'

Josefine's body softened into a rounded hunch, the intensity in her face was lost and replaced with something closer to human emotion. She turned to look at her visitor and for a moment the dynamic changed. The idea of talking to Josefine seemed overwhelming and Elise felt vulnerable. The flicker of recognition between them caught her by surprise. A lump rose in her throat and she choked a little before swallowing it down again. 'I'm here today under a false identity. No one must know I was here or the consequences could be dire for both of us. Do you understand?'

Another hurried nod confirmed that she was listening.

'I need to tell you about Marta and I need to ask you some questions. If you are honest and cooperative I can maybe help you too Josefine, but if you aren't I will have no choice but to walk away from here and never come back.'

She nodded again this time reaching her right hand up to her chest and letting it rest over her heart, and for the first time she spoke. 'It's good to see you again Elise.'

CHAPTER TWENTY TWO

'Ever Yours, Josefine.'

Whether her words had been cross or joyful, she would always sign off in the same way. Arnold folded the letter and placed it on the well-thumbed pile of correspondence he kept stowed in a shoe box at the top of his armoire. He had been in a reflective mood since hearing of the findings from Marta's trip to London. The world was changing, pioneers were making good ground and things could not stay the way they had always been. At one time he had been hailed as a pioneer, but he was acutely aware of his slowing wit. He struggled to retain new information, no wonder since he had developed a habit of falling asleep in his chair whilst reading his medical journals in the afternoons. Judging by her homecoming he suspected even his own daughter was beginning to nurture thoughts of leaving him behind.

Arnold missed his wife. Long before her mental illness had separated them, she had been his most encouraging and dependable friend - a head wind to his sails. It was Josefine who had enlisted the volunteers for his first hypnosis study; Arnold himself had been too arrogant in his approach and had driven a number of people away.

They had met in Germany; Arnold had been studying neurology there amongst other things. Josefine lived with her parents who, once satisfied with his ambitions and intentions, agreed to their engagement. Within weeks they had set a wedding date but not once had he regretted the haste of their union. Far from it, the whirlwind of a hurried romance had suited his impetuousness.

She had been the one to recommend he take up a job on a research team at the University of Vienna just a few months into their marriage. It would be good for him and after all, they had a lifetime to start a family she had said. He rented a small apartment in the Alsergrund district, leaving Josefine behind with her parents whilst he found them a permanent home and secured more stable employment.

Only she penned letters at first but, smitten as he was, Arnold quickly joined in the exchange. They would trade words of tenderness, tease each other with fantasies and at times even conduct arguments by mail. He would write to her with new ideas and request she trialled certain practices for him, a silent meditation technique he had picked up from a travelling artist in the city, a recipe for a consciousness altering tonic that a chemist friend had passed on. Sometimes even sexual experiments he would have considered it inappropriate to mention in person. On paper at least, no request seemed unreasonable. At times, receiving her musings by reply had been the only thing that kept his innovative spark ablaze and prevented him from being devoured by loneliness.

Even when they lived together again a year later, they continued to write to one another. Sometimes short love notes and at other times pages and pages. The letters did not detail the domesticities of raising a growing family, but instead became a sacred space for them to talk only of their feelings for each other. Theirs had been a special intimacy, the kind usually only found between the tightly pressed palms of the elderly couples waltzing in the Strauss Ballroom.

The letters stopped as soon as she was taken away from him, replaced then by a profoundly painful silence. But for a short time, amongst his shoe box of tatty pages, they were reunited and nothing was lost at all. If he focused all of his attention he could almost hear her narrating the lines as he reread the old ones, drawing him in like a Beethoven sonata until he realised with a stab that he couldn't even remember her voice anymore.

Amongst his regrets now, was that he had spent so little time at home with her. Each day consumed by the demands of his patients, his evenings devoted to further study and drafting research notes. A large chunk of their marriage fell away during his experimentation with cocaine and other stimulants but he persisted anyway, confident he might make another important breakthrough. Those were the moments he lived for then, the triumphs that reinforced his professional competence. Even he could admit that he had always been quite obsessed with his career, and as a result he had often wondered if he had failed to care for her in the way that she deserved. She had seemed so resilient and capable that he did not recognise her unhappiness.

Josefine had longed for a son, he had known that much, and yet she met the arrival of their daughters Bertha, Lotte, Carla and Nora with a grateful smile. However, in the five years following Christiane's birth he had noticed changes in her – an immediate detachment he had not witnessed before. They had thought for sure this time that Josefine would deliver a boy and had had to feminise the chosen name of Christian in recognition of their fifth daughter's arrival. Arnold had attributed his wife's drifting attention span and loosening behaviour to their increasingly busy lifestyle and rising social status. She was turning more of her attentions to the pursuit of wine and powder than the care of her brood, but he had encouraged her all the same. It was important to them both that she was seen in social circles; Vienna was such a fickle city where one could quickly be forgotten. Partying and playing hostess in the evenings seemed to return the warmth to her face that was often lost in the daylight. Fortunately Bertha was old enough by then to help with the care of the younger girls and her hard nature made her more resilient to the effects of Josefine's mood swings.

Whatever made her happy he reasoned, and he could not deny that the change was rewarding. The new Josefine was certainly more spontaneous and accepting than she had once been. She became quite unreserved in matters of intimacy, behaviour which certainly oiled the wheels for Arnold and his contemporaries. It was a frivolous time in high society and she was keen to share his indulgences for cocaine and alcohol, overtaking his own consumption now and then.

Sometimes they would spend leisurely evenings locked away in their bedroom, making love and pondering the problems of the universe. Josefine was once bright, vivacious, and though she believed that a woman should take a back seat to her husband, it was in these moments that she would coax her inner thoughts out to centre stage for Arnold to hear. When the morning came he would often find himself reflecting on her wisdom as he went about his own work.

It was the unexpected arrival of Marta that proved the tragic tipping point for Josefine. She was quite unstable throughout the pregnancy until eventually she plummeted head first into a disturbing hysteria. Arnold had come across many women in her condition suffering with ante natal and post natal maladies ranging from mild blues through to extreme puerperal psychosis. Intensive hypnosis aided by the right medication postpartum could resolve most cases adequately but not so for his wife.

Leopold had confirmed when consulted within his remit as GP, that it was quite common, predictable even, after bearing so many children. He had been adamant that she could overcome it with treatment and so Arnold had felt ratified. She would be hospitalised which was less than ideal, but Arnold had been concluding a prominent paper on individuality and character creation so he could put a small amount of time aside to oversee the care of the newborn with the support of a wet nurse until she returned.

During the first few months he had visited Josefine regularly at the Vienna General Hospital, but once there her condition appeared to deteriorate at an alarming rate and by the time she was committed to the asylum she was wild and incoherent. He could barely recognise the blank eyes and dull mind of the woman he had been so devoted to. He had taken Marta with him on a few occasions in the hope that the sight of the baby would help stimulate some kind of emotional or hormonal response but Josefine found it hard to look at her and would not respond to suggestions that she cradle her daughter.

When it was clear that recovery was impossible Arnold reluctantly consented to his wife's committal to the Kreis des Wahnsinns asylum, a secure facility some 60 miles away. All he could do after that was plough himself into his work. He turned the care of his daughters over to Bertha. A nanny would not be welcome at this point in time, privacy and discretion was essential if he was to minimise the professional and social impact of Josefine's absence, though he would consider employing external support in a year or two once things had settled down.

He kept Marta close; intrigued to see if the poor child would develop any negative effects from her experiences both in and out of the womb. He was not proud to admit that her complicated start to life provided a fascinating opportunity to study the thoughts, reactions and emotions of his new daughter; he was a psychiatrist first and foremost. It was the only sensible way to extract an advantageous outcome from such a personal disaster. He would nurture the girl psychologically and academically and note the differences in her development when compared to his other daughters who had been raised primarily by his wife. In order for his observations to have clinical relevance it became necessary to keep her quite separate from her sisters. Bertha would only be called upon for the most basic tasks of bathing, clothing and feeding her until a nanny could be employed.

And that was how he had dealt with the motherless Marta for the past 23 years.

Once a patient was deemed incurable, the Kreis des Wahnsinns did not permit them to have any contact with the outside world, but Arnold had continued to write to Josefine every few months for more than 20 years. By now he imagined she must have compiled volumes and volumes of his finest words, describing feelings he reserved only for her. Sitting at his bureau now, he filled his Shaeffer with ink while he wondered if she was ever lucid enough to read them.

'Ever mine, Josefine

The years thunder on like a freight train and yet my heart still trembles at the thought of you. So many things change with every passing day except for the grief I carry, which I fear will never leave me. I still see your face on the day they took you away from me, contorted and unrecognisable. It makes me so sad to remember how the pink apple blush of your cheeks turned to pale withered peach before my eyes.

I long for a loving companion once more, but we both know that can't be. Another hand on my forehead, so furrowed now, would feel too foreign. Do you miss me still? Do you imagine my face and how I might look in my older years? I believe I still cut a fine figure, my hair is now white and distinguished and suits me well – I'm quite sure you would like it. I imagine you often and even though you are not here, your kiss remains at my neck. I try to hold on tight to our memories but these days they are little more than tiny particles floating past as I lie awake in the half light of dawn. I curse my mind and yours for failing us both so gloriously. I miss you.

With love ever mine,

Arnold.

CHAPTER TWENTY THREE

The contents of the anonymous package Marta received today fit neatly into a small envelope. Inside were two pieces of paper. The first was a page torn from a novel entitled, *The Picture of Dorian Gray*. She had not read the book herself but had heard rumour of the outrageous and hedonistic tale of a double life had attracted.

On the page, a portion of the text was highlighted.

'With an evening coat and a white tie, anybody can gain a reputation for being civilized.'

The second piece of paper was a letter, but she did not recognise the handwriting as belonging to anyone she knew. The letter read:

'I never wanted for us to talk about this face to face, in fact I had hoped for both of us to live lives that would never prompt us to connect over such terrible circumstances. But sometimes the greedy are so hungry that they devour their prey in haste. Neither of us could have seen it coming and neither of us had a chance to defy such an indomitable force. Whatever happens next, hold on to the text enclosed and treasure the words and sentiment for they hold an important lesson.

Meet me at the Café Louvre at 11am today and I will tell you as much as I can. I am already sorry that I have allowed things to go so far.'

Marta folded the papers and slid them back into the envelope. She looked up at the clock. It was quarter to ten. She had arranged to meet Elise at the café at noon anyway so it would be easy enough to arrive a little earlier.

She ran back up to her bedroom and closed the door, then went to her chest of drawers to gather up the earlier packages she had received.

As she laid them out on the floor in front of her things started to make sense. The first clue, a receipt for the Café Louvre, must be of more significance than she had thought. That is after all, where the sender wanted to meet her. Or perhaps it was coincidence?

She still had no idea who had been sending the items. It was at that point that she remembered her first meeting with Elise at the same venue. Women generally frequented the place in the early evening, usually with children in tow. So why had Elise been there in the middle of the day? Could she have been sending things? If so, why would she? What was she trying to tell Marta, who was she trying to warn her against?

Elise had not been a fan of her partnership with Leopold but that was understandable given that they were both striving to make their mark as women without the need or influence of men. And he had stolen Marta away from the trip to London. She was also no fan of Arnold, which had been clear from their first meeting.

Leopold? She hadn't heard from him since Budapest. No, that made no sense. Who would he have been trying to steer her away from? He didn't even know of her friendship with Elise and she doubted he would be so underhand in his dealings.

Then it dawned on her. Of course. It would be Arnold. They hadn't spoken more than a few words since her return from the trip last week but she knew he wouldn't be able to keep it up much longer, particularly if this elaborate experiment of his was reaching its conclusion. Who else would have been able to access a picture of her mother, old receipts and even the page from the book? That is where she had heard the scandal of the novel; Arnold had a copy in his study and had gone to great lengths to talk to his friends about it at one of his dinners. Why hadn't she thought of it sooner? Perhaps the pendant was a trick, an attempt to see if she might give in to feminine things. If she had, he would deem her inadequate for the psychiatry profession.

Marta relaxed a little. She would go along with the game, meet with him and stroke his ego. Congratulate him on pulling off such trickery. He would like that. If he felt he had the upper hand he would be more likely to give permission for her to become independent. Yes, she would go along with it and then she would tell him about her plans for the facility. This was it, she would tell him today and then he would help her get Leopold back on side.

She had a spring in her step as she picked up her coat and made her way out into the city. The air was so fresh that she could smell the morning dew and a hint of soil, her senses buzzed. Traces of chimney smoke and roasted coffee beans took over as she stepped off the tram near the café. It was an impressive morning.

It was just before eleven when she arrived. She looked around but could not see Arnold. He enjoyed the theatrics of building suspense and this would be no exception. She tucked herself into a booth so that she wasn't easy to spot. For a second at least, she could have fun at his expense and make him think she hadn't come.

By quarter past eleven she was concerned. Arnold had not appeared. Had she got the time wrong perhaps? She took out the letter and re-read the closing line. She was not mistaken; it did indeed say to meet at 11am.

'Madam?' A voice from over her shoulder made her startle.

'Madam, can I get you anything?' It was just a waiter.

'Yes please, I'll take an espresso and a slice of nussbeugel.' Her hunger was revived today.

The waiter jotted her request on his order pad and retreated to the kitchen. Marta began nibbling and picking at the skin around her finger nails, unsure of where to put her hands. She was rummaging in her bag for her journal by the time a man approached her booth.

'Marta Rosenblit?'

She nodded as she looked up from her bag, instantly recognising the familiar figure in the Stetson.

'Allow me to introduce myself. My name is Frederick Beste. I am an acquaintance of Arnold's and I knew your mother Josefine many years ago too.'

Marta was impatient at the interruption. 'Oh yes, I know who you are. Pardon me for being rude but I really can't chat. I'm waiting for someone.' She looked past him.

'I know. You are waiting for me. That is why I am here Marta. I was once also a friend of Dr Leopold Kaposi.'

She looked past him again, still expecting to see Arnold walk through the door. Frederick spoke again. 'May I sit with you?' She did not answer but he wedged himself awkwardly into the booth anyway.

'I'm sorry we have had to meet like this.' He added, pulling a cigar from his coat pocket and lighting it.

'You! You were there outside the office building that day just a few months ago. I saw you getting into your car. Here at the café too, the day I met Elise. I didn't see your face, but your hat was on the table. I'd know it anywhere, and your cigars.' She rambled.

'Yes, that's right. I have wanted to meet with you for some time.'

'Have you been following me Mr Beste?' She asked, baffled by his presence.

'I suppose you might see it that way, but really I have been waiting for the right time to talk to you... about Leopold.'

Her blood turned to icicles that prodded at her veins. 'Leopold? Oh my, you haven't told my father that you have seen us together have you?' She asked.

He leant his elbows on the table, formed a bridge with his fingers and drew a heavy breath. 'The packages, I sent them. I have given you everything I can for now Marta. Leopold is not the man you think he is and I urge you to stay away from him.'

Her face flushed red and she glanced around the room searching it for any other familiar faces. He must be lying. What did he understand of her business with Leopold? His name had never come up in any of

Arnolds' or Leopolds' stories. She wasn't aware of him having any connection to the medical field; she had certainly not seen him at any recent conferences. From the little she knew his specialism was politics.

'I'm not sure I understand you Mr Beste. What do you know of Leopold and what do you mean, stay away from him?'

'Please, call me Frederick.'

'I'm sorry Frederick, but I don't think the odd sighting of me around town and a few dusty memories from your scrapbook entitles you to act as my advisor.'

'You are right. It is not my place to tell you anything else. You need to see your mother – soon.'

She studied him for a moment. His eyelids sagged and the rosacea to his skin suggested he enjoyed more than a couple of drinks, though he didn't smell of alcohol today.

'I think you need to leave. I do not appreciate the wild goose chase you have sent me on for the past few months and I am quite sure Leopold won't appreciate it either when he finds out.'

He reached across the table and gripped her hands between his. 'You mustn't tell him yet, please don't. It will give him more time and who knows what he might do with more time.'

She yanked her hands from his grasp and stood to leave.

He tugged at her sleeve as she tried to walk away. 'I'm trying to help you Marta. So much harm has been done, so many things are out of place. I have to put it right. You don't understand. I... I have to... it's just not right.' Frederick crumbled in front of her. His wide shoulders quaked with fragility under the weight of his raincoat.

CHAPTER TWENTY FOUR

MR BESTE, 1901

Frederick Beste carried the tray of boiled eggs, potato soup and green tea to his wife's room. He paused at the door, released a sigh, and altered his sombre expression to a smile. Marion had always liked his smile, lopsided as it was. She had told him it was one of the things that led to her falling in love with him all those years ago.

She was sleeping, as she did more and more these days, and so he set the tray on the nightstand. He hated to wake her, preferring the peace that replaced her pain, but it was time for her medication. If he left her longer she would wake with suffering in the next half hour or so. He ran his fingertips through her auburn hair, choking at how brittle it felt.

'You had the shiniest hair Marion, do you remember? You would sit at the dressing table brushing it over and over, and I would watch you from the bed.' He leaned in until his face was close to hers.

Marion slept on. Frederick lifted her gently, holding her to his shoulder as he rearranged her pillows. It would be easier to feed her if she were semi-prone.

He spoke a little louder this time. 'I've made potato soup and tea. Eggs too, but you don't have to eat them if you don't want to. We can share them or I can just take them away.'

She hadn't taken well to solid food for the last few weeks but he always prepared some anyway, ever hopeful that her condition might pick up. She had moments of lucidity sometimes and when she did she would be hungry, almost giving the impression that she was well again. The bad days came with increasing regularity, though the challenges varied.

Some days the biggest difficulty was managing her pain. She would cry out at the intensity of it, so bad it could keep her awake for hours through the night and into the morning. The only solution was more medication; barbiturates, opiates, anything that would garner more relief, but any increase in dosage was often followed by hallucinations and delusions. Tall tales and anecdotes of days that never were, Frederick could cope with those but if the delusions took a violent turn he could be forced to take cover as she threw ornaments, screamed at him and lashed out without warning. Remorse and regret would always follow once she regained her faculties.

'Marion darling, will you open your eyes for me?'

She stirred a little.

'Sweetheart, I've made soup.' He reached across to the nightstand and picked up the bowl.

'Will you eat for me?' Marion shook her head in defiance. She was going to battle with him today, but at least she was awake now.

Frederick did not know how many battles he had left inside him. Caring for a sick wife was not the natural order of things. Wives were the caregivers; born to the role of nurturing. It wasn't that he didn't want to do it, far from it. He would have walked on needles for her every day if he thought she would recover. It was more that he knew he did not have the strength of heart to watch her suffer for much longer. How much he wished he could rescue her from her plight.

All he could do for her now was feed and bathe her. The woman who had once been his flame-haired firecracker was now little more than a bag of bones.

'Marion you must eat for me. Please open your mouth.' She relented, parting her dry lips just enough for him to dribble soup into her mouth. She swallowed with a raspy choking sound. He would not try her with the eggs today.

When she had taken all of the soup she could manage, he offered her sips of green tea from a teaspoon. He had heard it could cure cancer but, after weeks of mixing and feeding her the tincture, his belief in it as a miracle remedy was wearing thin.

It had been nine months since the doctor had given her the diagnosis. Her abdomen had been swollen and they had hoped she might have been pregnant, but it was not a baby, only a tumour the size of a small watermelon. At just 39 years old, her age could be a curse or a blessing. The young recover well from the surgical removal of tumours they were told, but they are also more likely to harbour aggressive disease and can deteriorate rapidly if treatment is unsuccessful.

In the beginning, Frederick would take Marion to the surgery to discuss treatment options and clinical trials, but later when Marion had less energy he would come to the house. More than their GP, Leopold Kaposi had been a close personal friend for some years and would often visit two or three times a week. He had taken good care of Marion in the beginning and supported Frederick at his lowest moments, but as her illness advanced his suggestion of having her transferred to a nursing home was not well received.

'No, she would not want that all. We have never been apart and I will not abandon her now.' he had said when pushed on the matter.

When he couldn't cure Leopold knew he had a duty of care. 'We've exhausted all avenues Frederick, all we can do now is make her comfortable.'

'I'm sorry but it's out of the question. She can be comfortable here with me. I will take care of her until the end.' Frederick insisted.

'Look, it's your decision, but be realistic for Marion's sake. I have an alternative if things become too much and you need a way out, but it is a last resort.'

Frederick had thought a lot about Leopold's statement in recent weeks. In essence, all of this was too much. The idea of losing his wife had been more than he could handle from day one, but lately the stress of it had been cutting into him on a daily basis. He was ashamed to admit that he had dropped to his knees more than once and prayed for a way out.

Just three days ago he had asked Leopold what he had meant by an 'alternative option'.

'It's quite straightforward. I could give her an injection. Don't worry Frederick, Marion wouldn't feel anything. She would just sleep, as she does now, and eventually she would stop breathing.'

It all sounded so gentle and humane, but perhaps he was being hasty. After lunch it was time to help Marion to the toilet, and then put her in her chair whilst he changed the bed linen. The routine of caring for the dying.

He placed her arm carefully around his shoulder, encouraging her to hold on tight as he helped her to standing. Her legs wobbled as he lifted her from the bed and she found it difficult to stay upright. For such a slight woman she was surprisingly heavy to support. For the first time he had no choice but to scoop her up in his arms and carry her.

'It's okay, I've got you.' He reassured, and it was okay for a moment. They set off toward the bathroom. One foot placed cautiously in front of the other until he tripped on her slippers. How could he have forgotten to tuck them under the bed when he was undressing her last night?

Together they tumbled to the floor; Frederick heard a crack as his rib struck hard against the pointed oak bed post. Still holding her close, Marion landed slumped over on top of him. She was crying uncontrollably and yet, from what he could tell, his body had cushioned her from the fall.

'Are you alright?' He asked, ignoring the pain in his side. She did not answer but continued to cry.

'Marion, Marion, whatever's the matter?'

And then he knew. A warm, wet sensation spread across his lap and a pungent smell made him recoil. It was evident to both of them that she had soiled herself in his arms. This had not happened before. Until now she had been able to get to the bathroom and use the facilities with assistance. Keen to maintain her dignity for as long as possible she had always made Frederick turn his back on her whilst she used the commode.

'Don't cry my love. Please don't cry.' But Marion would not stop.

'Please Marion, please. We'll get cleaned up. Nobody will ever know.' His voice cracked as he tried to calm her. Frederick was defeated.

Between her tears, Marion murmured her first words of the day. 'Please Frederick, I can't continue. The pain is so overwhelming, and now this. I just can't.'

I can't continue. She had said it. The words he had been too afraid to say out loud himself, but intrinsically he knew she was right. This could not continue. He had to act; he would not let her suffer such an indignity again.

Holding her in his arms he remembered how he had carried Marion over the threshold on their wedding day. They had their whole lives ahead of them then.

They met when she was 17 years old. Frederick literally bumped into her whilst running along the street. He could remember it clearly even though it was more than 20 years ago. It had just gone nine o'clock and he was late for a Zionism lecture at the University. It was December. The air was frosty and the street slippery, causing him to skid as he turned the corner onto the Rathausplatz. Marion had been on her way to skate on the lake and was carrying her ice skating blades over her shoulder before he knocked her off her feet. He apologised profusely, reached for her hand and offered to help her up. He hadn't been looking for love, but he could not deny the electricity that ran up his arm and hit him in the heart as their hands touched. Just as soon as they were face to face he knew he had found her. She had freckles across the bridge of her nose and high, round cheeks. Though it had been tied back, her waist length hair now tumbled from beneath her beret laying a shock of red against her black velvet bodice. Theirs was not an ostentatious courtship; their first date happened just a week after meeting. They took a walk around the grounds of the University and then finished off with a hot bratwurst in the student refectory. One month and two carriage rides later and he had proposed, and six weeks after that they married. They could have waited, but it was clear to both of them that they were meant for each other.

Frederick took the first job he had been able to get after completing his journalism degree, working for the Bukowinaer Rundschau. Marion had cheered him up when he returned from his first day. He was expecting to work as a junior reporter so was despondent to find he had been placed in the advertising sales department instead. His disgruntlement was evident to his employers, who terminated his employment soon after. Marion did not scold him, neither did she fret or fuss. Instead, she held him close and reassured him that his time would come. It was not the only route into journalism; perhaps he could try his luck at being a stringer for the United Press she had said. With her encouragement he did just that, though the erratic pay made it hard for them to make ends meet. They rented a small flat above a barber's shop, furnishing it at first with just a large mattress propped on two wooden pallets, and one arm chair. On the weekends they liked to huddle under a blanket together in the chair and read the newspapers. Marion took it upon herself to help their situation and got her first job as a telephone operator at the central exchange. She was overjoyed when her first pay packet enabled her to buy them a small rug, then the next was spent on a second-hand bed frame. The pallets became a makeshift dining table, which suited them for another year before they felt the need to buy something permanent.

They had wanted children but after a few years of trying without success, they abandoned dreams of a family. Money was still tight for a while but as Frederick's career progressed he became a foreign correspondent, the regular salary preferable to the casual payment per story of his previous post. Travelling together became a welcome distraction from their apparent infertility. Marion loved to study other cultures and would often try to make the acquaintance of the locals and pick up a few phrases of a new language.

Back home in Vienna Frederick spent much of his time working from his regular table at the Café Louvre, always chasing the next story with local informants, politicians and diplomats. Marion would join him in the evenings when the day's business had simmered down. He would bring her up to date on the latest world news and she would listen attentively, always content to save the tales of her day for later.

Sometimes they would dine at the Louvre, cooking was not Marion's strongest talent. Though she did have talents; many of them. She was a beautiful dancer, knowing how to shape her long limbs and lean body in graceful lines. A musician too, she had taken piano lessons ever since she was a child and would play Beethoven or Chopin to Frederick in the evenings. Some nights she would play Brahms's Lullaby and she would weep for the babies she would never get to hold. To see her upset was the hardest thing of all. What he wanted most in the world was to make her happy, and that is why he decided to take the job as editor of the Wiener Zeitung. He did less frontline reporting, but the money was significant and so he could at last lavish her with all of the gifts and luxuries he felt she deserved.

They bought a bigger house, a villa in the Währing district and furnished it well. Frederick's had numerous connections and invitations came pouring in to join debutantes for dinner or attend lavish parties. That is where they had met the newly qualified Leopold, who moved in the same influential circles. He was introduced by the mayor, Konrad Schwarzenberg, who had appointed Leopold to treat his wife Vernette's pneumonia. She had recovered briefly under his care but died unexpectedly of heart failure a short time later.

Marion was always well received by everyone in their social circle, joining a group of women raising money for the new girl's grammar school in the city, hosting tea and even organising a ladies cycling group. Vienna was teeming with beautiful women, but Frederick only ever had eyes for Marion, as did many of the men. Whilst he felt jealous every time he saw another man looking at her, he knew she warranted the attention and had been so proud to have her on his arm.

To see her now it was as though the life they had, had never existed at all.

It was just after five o'clock on Wednesday and Leopold arrived to check on Marion as usual. Frederick had just poured himself a large brandy, his third since lunch, and was waiting for him in the entrance hall. The air in the house was suspended with a haze of stale cigar smoke. He had been so engrossed in his circumstance that it hadn't occurred to Frederick to open the windows for the past two days.

The men greeted one another with a quiet nod as had become customary given the circumstances. Leopold looked around at the house and then back to the glass in Frederick's hand.

'You want one?' he asked, remembering his duties as host.

'No thank you Frederick, I'm fine. I'll just go straight upstairs if you don't mind?'

'Of course. Of course.'

He followed Leopold up the staircase as per usual, but this time he stopped him on the landing before they reached Marion's room.

'Leopold I think we need your help.'

He turned to face his friend. 'Go on.'

'It's getting harder... too hard, for both of us.'

'It was always going to be Frederick. Cancer is a greedy beast and will take whatever it needs from her until she's got nothing left. That's just the way it is.'

Frederick sighed, his throat was tight but he knew the words that had to come next. 'It doesn't *have* to be though does it? You told me that yourself. Leopold, she wants out. You mentioned an injection that could end it, give her back some dignity.'

'You have to understand that it is not a legal procedure Frederick. If anyone ever found out about this we would both go to jail for many years.'

Frederick paused for a minute. 'Have you done this sort of thing before?'

Leopold shot him a glance that suggested it was a preposterous question.

'I mean, are you sure she won't suffer anymore? She won't feel any pain will she? I don't want her to hurt.' His doubts slithered wormlike to the surface.

'Do you think I would want Marion to suffer? I have always been fond of her, of both of you. I want to give you what you want, a swift and peaceful death.'

Frederick was hesitant, but how could they carry on like this? She had pleaded with him. He followed Leopold into the room, Marion was stirring.

'Marion my love. Leopold is here.'

She did not open her eyes fully, but she moved her lids enough to show she was listening.

'He has agreed to help us darling. He is going to stop your pain soon, just like we talked about.'

Marion looked at Leopold, who was unpacking his medical bag on the chair at the other side of the bed, and did her best to mouth the words *'thank you'*.

Nobody spoke again as Leopold carried out his usual check-up routine. Marion winced as he checked her blood pressure; even her eyeballs hurt as he shone a light on them. He made his notes, adjusted her morphine dosage and then packed his things away. He put his bag down on the floor and sat in the chair.

Frederick picked up Marion's hand placing it between his palms to warm her. It was time to discuss what would happen next.

Leopold leant forward. 'What do you want Marion?'

Her voice sounded distant as she spoke. 'I can't carry on Leopold. My body hurts so much and I am so tired.'

'And do you and Frederick understand the consequence if anyone finds out what we plan to do?'

She nodded. 'I don't want to take another day from my Frederick. He belongs out there in the sunshine not stuck in here watching me die.'

Leopold turned to Frederick. 'And you?'

'Yes, I understand.' Frederick confirmed.

'Leopold, I'm ready to go.' Marion winced again.

'Frederick has explained that I will give you an injection to bring on your death?'

'Yes.'

'You want me to help you die, is that what you are saying?'

'Yes.' She paused. It took everything she had to move her hand to her face and wipe her tears away. 'Yes, do it soon… please.'

He returned her words with a smile before speaking to his friend.

'I'll come back tomorrow evening with everything I need. Now I will give you two a little time together. I can see myself out.' He placed a reassuring hand on Frederick's shoulder, then picked up his bag and left.

Frederick climbed onto the bed and lay down next to Marion, cradling her in his arms. He was a stocky, well-built man and holding her now she looked like a child, a fraction of the woman she had once been. How had it come to this? They had travelled the world together, dined at the best restaurants, enjoyed beautiful music and made love under the moonlight. Now their world was confined to this one room, where homemade soups lay uneaten on the nightstand and the soundtrack was lowered to a whisper. Through the longest night they held each other, sometimes smiling at fond memories and sometimes crying quiet tears, the only tears left when hearts have been wrung out and the battle is lost.

CHAPTER TWENTY FIVE

The next day Frederick continued to lie with Marion whenever he was not taking care of her physical needs. As their final day together came to a close, he bathed and clothed his wife in a fresh cotton nightdress, breathing in her delicate floral scent as he pulled it over her head. It was a special nightdress for both of them, with French lace detailing at the neckline and sleeves, and a pale pink silk sash that tied in a small bow at her chest. She had bought it to wear on their wedding night and they had joked at the time that it could one day be turned into a christening gown. How he wished it could have been.

Having only woken half an hour before, she was exhausted again. He stayed with her, holding and kissing her hand over and over as she drifted off to sleep. Caring for himself had not crossed his mind today, he had not washed or changed since yesterday and he hadn't had the motivation to prepare himself anything to eat. He felt cold, weak and nauseous, but he dared not move for fear of missing a moment with her.

At six o'clock sharp there was a knock on the door. Leopold had returned. It would soon be over. It took all the strength he had to go downstairs and open the front door, each step moving him forward too quickly. The words '*go back to her, go back to her*' played on a loop in his head.

'Come in.' Frederick's voice that was half its usual volume. He led his wife's doctor to the bedroom.

He watched helplessly as Leopold repeated his bedside ritual, checking and recording Marion's pulse. Listening to her lungs and chest with his stethoscope then making a note of that too.

'Are you ready?' Leopold asked when he had completed his examination.

Frederick spoke with a bowed head. 'I will never be ready to let her go, but I have to don't I? Should I sit with her while you do it?' He was afraid to leave and afraid to stay.

'I think it would be better if you wait out on the landing.'

'I don't think I can.' His words almost inaudible.

Leopold was firm. 'It will not do you any good to stay. I urge you to leave the room. Really Frederick, this is not the time to fall apart, you must be strong for Marion. I will come out and tell you when it is over.'

Frederick understood what his friend was trying to say, and for a second was thankful that he would not have to endure the sight of Leopold taking his wife from him. 'My Marion' he murmured as he looked at her one last time. He kissed her tenderly on the lips before rising from the bed; he must allow Leopold to do his job. Outside on the landing, he felt as though the floor was falling away. His knees buckled beneath him. Sitting in a heap on the floor he fixed his head in his hands.

Once at Marion's bedside Leopold got to work, relieved to be alone with her as she slept. He took his equipment from his bag and set it on the nightstand, one vial, three small bottles of medicine and his black leather syringe case.

First he mixed the medicines together, a more generous dose of morphine enhanced by a dose of liquid he had obtained from a chemist friend at the Farbenfabriken Pharmaceutical Company in Germany. The liquid was labelled '*Heroin*', it was quite new and the medical scene was a buzz about it though he had not used it before. His friend had also sent him sample doses of a brand new and as yet untested substance called Benzedrine. He added a moderate amount for good measure.

He was unsure of the precise quantities required as he had not used this concoction before. Nobody had, this was Leopold's own creation and no research had been done to suggest what might happen if it didn't work. He looked down at Marion. She was practically dead anyway and so thin he was confident enough that it would do the job.

His excitement seemed inappropriate but developing an effective formula could significantly boost his career. He reckoned he might have a case to apply for a sizeable grant to fund further research into end of life care. He might even be able to convince the Farbenfabriken Company to invest in him, pay his way into the seminar circuit. It was a gap in the medical field that he would be only too pleased to dominate.

He corked the vial and shook it vigorously, causing small bubbles to turn in tornado swirls as he did so. Next he opened his syringe case, admiring the glint of the glass, silver and steel as he lifted it from the plush velvet lining. It was indeed a beautiful instrument, imported from Paris and his first gift to himself when he started earning good money working for the mayor. Leopold never tired of using it and watched with morbid fascination as the glossy brown liquid was drawn up into the syringe.

Perching himself on the shallow space at the edge of the bed next to Marion, he turned her head away from him until he could no longer see her face. Using the palm of his hand, he smoothed her waves of hair aside to expose the thin skin of her throat. Her vein was easy to locate and he was reassured to find that her pulse was already slow. A tiny pool of blood collected as he punctured her skin and pushed the sharp needle into her. Then he turned the screw with his forefinger and thumb to deliver the drugs. He kept on turning until he had emptied it into her bloodstream. She flinched a little, but he held steady, savouring every second of the procedure. He was pleased with the efficiency of his technique, not sparing a drop before he removed the needle.

His work done, he turned Marion's head back to the centre, pausing to look at her face. He had always found her thrillingly beautiful, and even as he watched her die he could still see it. He had tried to seduce her once, a couple of years ago at a masked ball. She refused him, but he had hoped to try his luck again just as soon as another opportunity had presented itself. It had been disappointing, but her illness had put paid to that.

All he could do now was watch and wait. Leopold gathered up the empty bottles and tossed them into the waste paper basket on the other side of the room. He replaced the cork in the top of the vial and put it back on the nightstand. Then he rinsed his syringe in hot water at the wash basin, drying it with a white flannel he had pulled from the drawer underneath.

Marion was still sleeping, but her face was now flushed. He checked her pulse; he was pleased to find it slowing, a sure sign that the opiates were taking effect. He looked at his pocket watch. It had been four minutes since the dose was administered. He hoped it wouldn't take much longer. He had promised Cecily he would be home in time for their dinner party this evening.

Leopold sat in the chair next to the bed, reached into his pocket for his cigarette case, took one out and lit it using his pocket lamp. He managed to take two drags on the cigarette before Marion started to make strange gurgling noises. He took another drag then exhaled a steady flow of smoke as he looked over to the bedroom door. Frederick might come and check on them. Things were not progressing in the way he had hoped.

Irritated at having to extinguish his cigarette, Leopold dropped it in the ashtray and returned to his equipment to mix up another vial. He had used up all of the Benzedrine in the first dose. He reached into his bag to see what else he had on him. Trimethylamine perhaps? No, wait this one would do it, propyl, perfect. He filled the syringe with the remains of the heroin and morphine and topped it up with the propyl.

He turned to Marion but as he was about to inject her for a second time she began to flail around on the bed. He set the syringe to one side. Her arms lashed wildly and the gurgling noise she had been making earlier had now turned into a loud grunt. Leopold did his best to restrain her body as it convulsed over and over, but she fought against him. He wouldn't be able to inject her like this.

As she moved her arms in protest she knocked his medical bag to the floor, sending a teacup with it which smashed as it hit the floor. He flicked a glance at the bedroom door again, he must stop her seizure.

On the other side of the door, Frederick was jolted from his daze by the sudden commotion.

He jumped to his feet and knocked the door. 'Is everything alright Leopold?'

'Just give me a moment will you?!'

He gritted his teeth, angry that things were not going to plan.

'Damn it Marion!' he muttered.

Leopold climbed onto the bed and straddled her torso in an attempt to steady her. Then he used his elbows to pin her arms down and placed his hands over her nose and mouth. Suffocating her seemed like the easiest option for him, of course, he would tell Frederick that the injection had worked. Unable to breathe now, Marion opened her eyes wide with fear and stared at him in search of mercy, but she could see in his face that he was not going to stop.

Frederick threw open the door and was shocked to see his wife convulsing and in distress, and Leopold on top of her. He looked into her open eyes, whatever was happening he could see the fear and pain in her. This was not the peaceful death she deserved.

Leopold clamped his hands over her face with even more force.

'What are you doing? No! No! Leopold stop, please. You are hurting her.' Frederick lunged at Leopold. His fists clenched, he began to pound on his back and head.

Leopold spun round on his heels and punched Frederick to the ground. 'Stop it you bloody-minded fool! You are making it worse. It's too late now. You have to help me or you will just prolong her suffering. Quick, grab the syringe.'

From his position on the floor Frederick paused to stare at them both, still in shock and unable to comprehend what he was witnessing.

'Move Frederick, now!' Leopold ordered.

With tears in his eyes and struggling to catch his breath, Frederick reached for the syringe which was surrounded by broken porcelain and medical paraphernalia.

'Just stab her where I tell you and this will all be over.' Leopold removed a hand from Marion's face and placed his index finger on her neck to indicate where the needle should go.

Frederick was numb, he couldn't think straight. He could see no other choice, her eyes rolled in her head and she was beginning to foam at the mouth. He positioned the needle, closed his eyes and pierced the perfect patch of skin he had once kissed so lovingly. Marion's body stilled as he delivered the final fatal dose. He dropped the syringe onto the pillow and both men watched as her eyes closed and her limbs went limp. Her breathing was shallow and intermittent until she let out a laboured breath. She did not attempt to inhale again.

It was over. Frederick folded in on himself, the pain in his heart unbearable.

Leopold climbed down from the bed and covered her face with the bed sheet, retrieving his prized syringe as he did so. Killing a woman was unpleasant but, he felt somewhat God like for his accomplishment. His technique had been all wrong, but one could always work on technique.

He returned to the sink, rinsing and drying the syringe again before washing his hands and smoothing them over his now dishevelled hair. The room was quiet once more.

Frederick rose to his feet. 'You killed her. You said it would be swift and peaceful, but you did not show compassion.'

Leopold protested. '*You* killed her Frederick. The final blow was dealt by your hand not mine.'

'She suffered to her end and you, our closest friend, made it happen. You must pay for what you did, you must!'

'If I must pay, then so must you.'

At that moment Frederick saw Leopold for everything he was. A cold hearted fraud. He was no doctor; he showed no duty of care to anyone but himself. He wanted to scream it from the rooftops, he was a journalist for Christ's sake, and he could print it on the front page if he wanted to. But the man was right. Any picture of Leopold would have to sit alongside his own. The truth was he had participated in his wife's demise. He hadn't meant for it to be this way. Marion had asked him for help, she had said she couldn't continue. They had both trusted Leopold and had no reason to think he was capable of such a mistake. What else could he have done?

'Frederick, you should bear in mind that you will need a death certificate if you want to bury her. As her GP and the doctor who pronounced her dead, only I can sign it off.'

Leopold straightened his tie and smoothed the lapels on his blazer. Frederick was powerless as he watched him packed up his bag. He wanted to kill the man for making his wife suffer to her last but his limbs were weighted by grief. With the loss of Marion, he had lost a part of himself forever. He had done a deal with the devil himself and in doing so had traded her freedom for his.

CHAPTER TWENTY SIX

Marta knew that gaining entry to her mother's asylum would not be easy, but Elise was about to explain how they would go about it. She arrived promptly at noon as arranged and took her seat in the booth across from Marta.

'I've managed to get hold of some research notes on Electroshock treatment. I think this is our way in Marta.' Elise stated in a triumphant tone, spreading a handful of files out on the table between them as she spoke.

Marta was unresponsive.

'Goodness, you look as though you've seen a ghost.' Elise clicked her fingers in front of her friends' eyes.

'Huh? Oh, sorry Elise.' She would not tell her friend of her meeting with Frederick just yet. She needed time to think and take it all in first. 'No, no I'm fine. What was that you said?'

'Electroshock therapy.'

'Electroshock?'

'Yes, it's a new treatment for psychiatric patients. Years away yet, but that's what makes it perfect. It's so new that nobody will be concerned that they have not heard of it, and it's a legitimate treatment idea so will sound convincing enough and is even traceable should anybody look into it. A contact of mine in Hamburg is testing and developing the method right now.'

'How will that help us Elise? I'm not electrocuting my own mother if that's what you mean?' Marta was puzzled but intrigued by her friend's ingenuity.

'No silly, of course not. I've already been in touch and have explained that as members of the development panel we need access to a cross section of patients, male and female, in order to make observations. I even told them that if they comply with our requests we might be able to help them secure funding for the place.'

The asylum was over in the small township of Liesing. They would go tomorrow morning, arriving by half past ten.

That night Marta struggled to settle into her bed. This would be the first time in her entire adult life that she would see her mother. Would Josefine recognise her? Would she recognise Josefine? Aside from the old photographs she had no images of her mother. In her mind's eye, she could see Josefine as the young beautiful woman she once was. She had no frame of reference for her now. She would be 20 years older, her skin and hair would have changed. The deranged face of a mad woman would undoubtedly have replaced her once soft expression.

Marta was afraid. This was it. The moment she had longed for her whole life and she did not know if she could go through with it. She wished she had questioned Frederick more about her mother; maybe he could have prepared her for the encounter. It was possible that he had known more about Josefine than he would let on.

She laid the papers Elise had given her out on the blankets, spacing them evenly until they covered a third of the bed before her. She was to read and memorise them one by one. Her name would be Dr Polgár and Elise would assume the identity of Ms Vass, a senior assessor. The electroshock treatment sounded brutal. Electrodes placed on either side of the patient's head are used to conduct a high-voltage electric current which is discharged from a machine nearby. The method was thought to 'jump start' the brain into normal activity, or as Marta suspected, it probably damaged the brain to such an extent that the problem areas of the cortex were irrevocably impaired. As a psychiatrist, she could not see herself subscribing to such invasive treatment, but as a daughter desperate to see her mother she was willing to go along with the pretence.

Marta and Elise were to advise the staff at the Kreis des Wahnsinns that they were looking for patients suitable for testing the method on. The patients would be split into two groups, conscious and unconscious. Treatment would be carried out on both to ascertain the impact of anaesthesia on patient recovery. It was a lot to take on board. Understanding the treatment was quite straightforward to Marta, but thinking of her mother as a patient or 'inmate' seemed outrageous. Even if her mother were insane she could have benefited from psychological care. She could not understand why her father had failed to do this; surely he knew better than anyone the benefits of such therapy? Was she too crazy, beyond help?

Sleep was elusive that night as vivid dreams punctuated the darkness leaving Marta in a state of perpetual unrest that visited her so often these days it had started to feel normal.

In one dream she was a little girl, running towards her mother's outstretched arms. Her mother was smiling and calling to her. Arnold was not there, but an unidentified man stood looming in the shadows, his domineering frame seeming to lurch forward just as she reached Josefine.

In another she imagined her mother seated on the floor, her limbs pulled tight rounding her into a ball at the centre of a grey concrete room. No windows, no walls. She was sobbing uncontrollably and rocking herself to and fro. Marta did nothing to help her but stood tall at her side. Small drops of blood at her feet grew to form large pools of blood that covered the entire floor surrounding her mother like an island. She looked down at herself and realised the blood was pouring from her wrists, trailing across her palms and coating her fingertips before hitting the hard floor. She did not try to stop it, she just let it drip and drip until eventually she collapsed into a heap next to her mother.

One final dream woke Marta just before dawn. In it she lay on her bed being devoured by snakes, hundreds of them, all different colours and sizes. They slithered all over her body, sinking their sharp fangs into her legs and wrapping themselves around her chest and neck. In the corner of the room a lion was pacing, licking its lips and watching her battle with the snakes intently. Just as the lion leapt at her she startled awake. Her breathing laboured and her heart raced. Perspiration had soaked through her nightdress and wet the bed linen. Her hair had come loose from its top knot and was clinging limply to the side of her face and jaw.

She jumped up from the bed and pulled off her nightdress, throwing it to the floor and stamping on it as if putting out a fire. Then she began pulling at the bedding, grabbing layer after layer of sheets and blankets and tossing them all over the room.

Naked now and surrounded by white linens, she looked down and caught sight of herself. Marta did not turn away as she normally would. Instead she reviewed every inch of her body out of sheer curiosity, shocked at the sight of herself in the early morning light. She had not fully appreciated how much harm she had inflicted over the years. On the most superficial level her arms were speckled with small bruises, some new and some faded to little more than yellow stains. She had angry red welts on both of her hip bones, which jutted out at angles from her flesh just like her collar bone and shoulder blades. Her scarred inner thighs read like a timeline of her mutilations. The first cut she had ever made, at just 13 years old, was now a thin silvery white half-moon. The more adept she had become the neater and more orderly her scars were, she could read them like a timeline of her episodes. This pleased her, she was almost proud to see how far she had come in mastering the cuts so that they would be less noticeable once healed.

She moved toward the full-length mirror in the corner. Widening her attention she noticed three large ugly marks amidst her well-tended collection. Not the work of her hands, Leopold had inflicted those. The first was a reddish brown bite mark to the side of her neck. Marta had been wearing a high collar blouse and a teal silk scarf for two weeks now in an attempt to hide it from view whilst it healed, and yet it was still quite visible when exposed. Leopold had called it a love bite, he had sucked the skin so hard that the blood vessels popped underneath it and tiny impressions of his teeth encircled it.

During another frantic encounter, Leopold had restrained her with a ligature that had cut into her wrist. When he noticed the damage it had caused to her skin he said that scars were ugly and that the sight of it might put him off looking at her at all. It was probably because she was so rake thin, he had said. Her skin was not as tough as it should be because there was so little flesh between it and her bones. She wept for almost an hour after he had gone that day.

She swivelled her hips to look at her bottom, which was peppered with bruises, some small circles, others hard lines. She had not looked at herself from this angle before.

At that moment, Marta was overcome with nausea and her mouth flooded with saliva. She rushed to her waste paper basket, crouched down and vomited into it. Then, sitting back on her knees for a moment, the bile began to rise again. She vomited for a second time, emptying her whole self into the basket before discarding it.

Her face was chalky white, her papery skin clammy and sore all over. She did not want to participate in the day. Elise had tried to make it sound fun but Marta knew it would be horror and heartache.

First she ran cold water into her basin. Plunging her face into it, she held herself below the surface until she could not hold her breath any longer and bubbles of air forced their way out of her mouth and nostrils. She pulled her head up and grabbed a towel. As she patted her skin dry she ran the hot tap until steam rose in plumes and the mirror was obscured by condensation. It felt like a thousand bee stings as she moved her icy cold hands under the scorching flow. When she couldn't stand it any longer she pressed her palms against her cheeks, bringing a temporary flush that made her complexion look healthy. She did her best to smother the acrid aftertaste of vomit with lots of toothpaste.

Opening her dresser, she pulled out the warmest undergarments she could find and put them on. She pushed the top drawer back into place with such force that it jolted the bottom drawer open a fraction. Marta knew that the blade of her letter knife was waiting for her. She could use it to relieve her anxiety right now, just a quick press of the sharp metal and she could go on her way. She would feel better for it, she always did. As she bent down to remove the drawer, Pernilla knocked at her bedroom door.

'Ms Rosenblit. I'm coming in.'

'Damn it Pernilla, you will not enter my room without permission! Do you hear me? What do you want at this hour?'

'But Ms Rosenblit, you asked me to wake you at this time. I have your breakfast on a tray and it is very heavy.' Pernilla mumbled from the landing.

Marta had forgotten her instruction to the housekeeper before she turned in last night. She had indeed asked her for a wake-up call, and that she would be taking breakfast in her room having been certain she would not want to face her fathers' questions at the table on such a momentous morning. They weren't quite on speaking terms yet and so she had taken to avoiding him. She would tell him of her plans when she returned from the Kreis des Wahnsinns later.

Marta shut the drawer and bundled all of the bedding and her nightdress into a pile.

'Come in Pernilla, come in.'

Pernilla entered, and was alarmed by the chaotic sight before her. She could see the bed was bare, and that the lamp on the nightstand was lying on its side. The single stem Cala lily that she placed in a crystal vase just yesterday was withered on the floor, the vase was missing. An empty water glass was wedged between the mattress and the bed post; she hoped the wet patch on the floor beside the bed was attributable to its spilt contents.

'Pernilla, I am sick and tired of sleeping on unstarched sheets. You must try harder to keep this house in shape. I have removed everything for you. I want you to take them down to the laundry right away and have them washed, starched heavily and returned to my bed before I return this evening.'

Pernilla was confused, she always took great care over the laundry and Ms Rosenblit had never complained before. However, she did as she was instructed without question and scooped up the pile of cotton, pulling the corners of the largest sheet around it to create a kind of sack for carrying it down to the laundry room at the back of the kitchen.

As soon as she heard Pernilla's footsteps descend the stairs Marta checked the clock on her mantle. No time to make a cut today; she must try to eat a little breakfast before making her way to the station to meet Elise. Her mouth was too dry to tackle the pastries, so Marta took a few sips of her mélange before breaking open the soft boiled egg. The yolk felt slimy and unpleasant on her tongue but she was able to swallow it with relative ease so she persisted in spite of her queasy stomach. She replaced her napkin on the tray and finished dressing herself before heading downstairs. On the way out, she stopped off at her father's study to take a swig of Vin Mariani from the bottle he kept stowed in his drinks cabinet. It would be locked but Arnold often left the key hanging out of the lock, especially if he had indulged in a few too many whiskies the night before.

By the time she boarded the train, the effects of the drink had kicked in. When she reached Elise she was in a much more alert and accepting state, all evidence of her earlier undoing was now banished from her face.

'Are you excited? Elise questioned fervently.

'Nervous, but I have done as you asked and have learned my part to the letter. In fact, I am beginning to wonder if I might be wasted in psychiatry and should perhaps take to the acting profession. I have even worked on my accent. From the moment we arrive Marta

Rosenblit will cease to exist until I enter that cell and greet my mother.'

Not wanting to unnerve her friend further, Elise made idle chit chat throughout their short journey. She talked about the weather, a new dress she had seen at the House of Drécoll, where they might take lunch later. The meeting with Josefine was important to both of them, she would not jeopardise it now. It was crucial to reunite mother and daughter. They had to catch up on all that had been missed.

CHAPTER TWENTY SEVEN

The asylum was a cylindrical building housing a significant majority of Vienna's mentally ill population. A psychiatric nurse who had introduced herself as Hannah walked them up several flights of stairs and along the curved corridors 'We have a modern facility here. No corners see? It makes sense when you think about it. Kreis des Wahnsinns - the circle of madness.' she explained, 'Corners interrupt the patients who like to wander; it unsettles them when they have to change course. Stops them hurting themselves too, the worst ones get a real kick from running their heads into a sharply angled wall.'

The five floors were categorised by level of disturbance, 32 cells per floor, most dangerous at the top down to the depressed, demented and downright disobedient at the bottom - a sort of filing cabinet for the clinically insane. On the upper two floors prison style iron bars replaced doors, doing little to shield patients or staff from the sights, sounds and smells that emanated from the deranged. In those cells, furniture was screwed to the floor and patients displaying violent or delusional behaviour were cuffed and chained to the walls.

A central courtyard was a welcome outdoor space for exercise though it offered only a tunnel view of the sky which Marta thought must be as bleak as seeing no sky at all. A view without the context of a horizon was not a view. No wind ruffled trees, no prancing wildlife, no green lawn or babbling stream; just blue sky, white sky or grey sky.

Hannah paused at the door of a cell on the third floor and peered in through the small spy hole. Josefine was sitting upright in a straight-backed metal chair reading a book today. Hannah unlocked the door and pushed it wide open. Josefine put the book to one side just as soon as Marta and Elise came into view.

'You look like you are expecting company Josefine.' Hannah said before turning to Marta 'You wouldn't think it to look at her but this one's got a reputation for clawing out your eyes given half a chance. We move her up to the top floor when she gets out of hand.'

Josefine wrapped her arms around her body, hiding her small trembling hands in the folds of her armpits. Her long cotton smock concealed her bare feet which tapped the ground in a nervous tic. Her hair was more strawberry blonde than Marta had imagined, plaited and with a subtle sheen that offered the impression of good physical health. However, a coin-sized bald patch behind her left ear replaced the loose tendrils that once curled there. Josefine maintained a downward stare as they entered the cell. Marta was disappointed that she was not yet able to meet her mother's eye.

'We'd be grateful if you could leave us alone with this woman Hannah. It is crucial we are not interrupted if we are to assess her suitability for treatment. Ms Vass will call for you should we need anything.'

'I'll be just at the end of the corridor.' Hannah left the women to talk.

Marta's stomach lurched as she took in the full-length image of the woman sitting before her. Josefine was everything she expected, and nothing like she hoped. Her vapid expression did not offer any flicker of recognition. She was a submissive shell bearing the vaguely familiar features of someone who, to Marta, was little more than a character from a storybook.

She had rehearsed her cover story well, but she had not paid enough attention to what she might want to say at this moment. So much had gone unsaid and yet so little came to mind as she sat across from the woman whose existence had haunted her all these years.

Checking over her shoulder to see that Hannah was out of sight, she spoke.

'Mother?'

Josefine did not look up but her lips began to quiver.

'Mother, it's me, Marta. Do you remember me? I... I didn't expect...' She floundered as she tried to summon the right words.

Josefine looked first to Elise and then to Marta. All three women sat suspended in the silence.

Elise reached across and squeezed Marta's hand. 'We don't have much time, don't lose this opportunity Marta.'

'Mother, I don't know where to start.'

Elise urged her on. 'Both of you must feel as though you have an enormous mountain to climb. Why don't you start with just one step at a time?'

On hearing those words Marta let a single tear escape down her cheek. She blinked hard to prevent the further flood of tears that might follow and overwhelm her if she allowed them. It was no use. Pools formed at the corners of her eyes before running down her face and dropping into her lap.

When she spoke she directed her words to the floor. 'Why mother? I just want to know why I was not enough for you.'

Josefine began to shake her head in denial.

Dissatisfied, Marta pressed on. 'Why was the burden of my birth too hard to bear? I was just an infant. How could I have displeased you so soon?'

Her questions seemed to drift like fallen cherry blossom. How much she wanted her mother to restore the blooms with soft words and loving explanations.

'And father? What of father? How could you turn away from us?'

Josefine's shoulders begin to quake, followed by her arms and legs, until her entire body seemed to have lost control. Her face creased and her mouth opened wide as if she was trying to scream but no sound came. What was this? Madness? Sadness? Was there a difference? Marta was unsure. She dropped to her knees before her mother, took hold of her hands and laid her head in Josefine's lap. Her shaking subsided until slowly, she moved her hands to cradle Marta's head and began to rock with her.

'Of course I remember you. Of course I do. For more than twenty years I have thought of you, more than anything else.' Josefine said.

'Then explain yourself, tell me why?'

'I cannot explain those days away with ease my darling girl; to tell of the events that led me here will bring more questions. But you do deserve your answers Marta, you do.' Josefine looked over at Elise.

'What do you mean mother, what events? You had me and the sight of me sent you mad. Still as I sit here at your feet you are unable to meet my eyes with pleasure or pride.'

'We went to parties Marta, we hosted parties. Many influential people, lots of them drinking and taking things. Doing things too, and I didn't want to at first, but the more I indulged in the drink and cocaine the more I went along with it, enjoyed it even.   Arnold was so persuasive... and everyone was...'

Though she could see her lips moving and hear her words, Marta could not make sense of what her mother was saying.

'Then we... well, I thought he loved me and I thought I loved him back. I could never have imagined Marta. And to think of him now, so close to you. I could not protect us back then, but I will now. I will, you'll see.'

'Protect us from what mother? If you were in any kind of danger why didn't you...'

Josefine interrupted, taking Marta's face in her hands as though it were a precious painting. 'You have taken on more of Arnold's gestures and attitudes than I had expected. I am so pleased and proud to see that.'

'Then give me what I deserve. Give me my answers. You make no sense rambling like a crazy woman. No wonder they left you here!' Marta regretted her vitriol as she watched her mother's smile diminish.

Hannah banged on the cell door. 'Five minutes then we must move on to the next patient.'

Silence fell for a second time. Josefine broke the stalemate this time, her earlier smile now replaced by a look of foreboding.

'Marta, crazy is not always as obvious as you might have been led to believe. One thing I have learned during my time here is that things are rarely as they first appear. I hear you are working with Leopold Kaposi now.'

'How do you know about Leopold?'

'I know that he has visited me frequently over the years Marta. I know that he is not the man you think he is. You must not put your trust in him, I forbid it.'

'Forbid it? How dare you forbid me now! Where were you to forbid me when I was climbing trees at five years old, or when I raced my bicycle off track at ten years old?'

'I wish I could say more but we have such limited time.' Josefine paused. 'Marta, you must listen to me, is the Karlsplatz Stadtbahn still open?'

'I don't know. The railway line and station were closed to civilians during the war.'

'Oh dear, yes of course. I forget so much has changed since I have been in here.'

Elise interrupted, 'I know about the Karlsplatz.' The other two women looked at her. 'I travel a lot.' She said by way of explanation. 'The line reopened three years ago, though I believe the old terminal building

249

remains closed to the public. It is still standing but is only used for freight now.'

'Good. Thank you Elise.'

Marta looked from her mother to Elise. Josefine continued. 'There used to be a run of lockers just inside the main entrance. Do you think you could gain access to the building?' Josefine asked.

'I don't know mother! I'm here now, just tell me for heaven's sake!'

Hannah knocked again.

'I wish I could but this is not the place for such a discussion and there's not enough time. Just go to the station, once inside find locker number 24 and open it. It's all there Marta.'

With a jiggle of her keys, Hannah opened the door and entered the room.

'They took everything from me when I came here, but they never knew about that. Once you understand everything, if you still want to know me then come back here. I will be waiting for you.'

'You'll be waiting alright.' Hannah laughed. 'It's a shame really; poor thing must think you've come to assess her for her annual case review. All of the reviews are being carried out next week, but Josefine's been here for a lifetime. I can't see any reason why they'd let her out now.' She added to Marta and Elise.

Elise and Hannah made their way out to the corridor. Marta stood up to leave, as she did Josefine rose from her chair and reached out to pull her close. Marta was reluctant to give in to the embrace but she knew she needed it as much as her mother.

'I'm so sorry my darling girl. I'm so sorry. I'm getting better Marta, even more so for seeing you here today. With your help I'm positive I could leave this place, we could start again. I don't belong here, I never did. You'll see.'

Looking at her now Marta could see no traces of insanity, she did not look at all deranged. Lost yes, but gripped by madness? Not at all. She wondered what could have happened to her that resigned her to a life in an asylum.

CHAPTER TWENTY EIGHT

Parents are not perfect people; of that much Marta was now sure. She had invested many years rationalising her father's casual sexism, his reluctance to credit her talents and his absolute refusal to discuss her mother. But the more she was beginning to understand about life, the harder it was to continue making excuses for him.

She had been glad to watch her sisters leave home but she had not intended to become the sole focus of his suffocating attention. She was tired of being guarded like an ancient relic that might crumble if touched. She was tired of being dissected by him; he knew more of her than she knew of herself.

Of course she had lived to please him too. At times she had tried to substitute the wife he had lost because of her. Whatever debt she owed him, it did not justify what he had taken from her in withholding her independence. Women her age danced the Black Bottom in jazz clubs, kissed strangers in alleyways and drank alcohol until they passed out – many of them capable of being studious and responsible as well. She might not have chosen to do the same, but she should have had the choice.

Leopold had filled the growing space between her and Arnold, not to mention her desire to know more of carnal relations. She depended on him. He offered her hope. She had been happy to take his affirmations wherever she could find them. If that happened most often in the throes of his passion then so be it. Any flattery was graciously received. But what if he was not the man she wanted him to be?

Until she had visited her mother, Marta had not stopped to consider whether or not Leopold was trustworthy, she just accepted he must be. To consider such things would have required a degree of fortitude that she was too inexperienced to apply to matters of the heart.

Marta was unsure whether or not to heed her mothers' warnings about him. Leopold might be furious at her if she started throwing around unfounded accusations. He had only just resumed contact after their disastrous trip to Budapest. She did not want to jeopardise everything at such an unpredictable time.

She would find out soon enough. Her stomach was still sick and she struggled to stand still as she waited outside the office building for him. Before long he was striding up the path to join her at the entrance. He placed his hands on her hips and moved in to kiss her.

'Leopold! What are you doing? Somebody will see.' she asked, spinning away from him.

He looked offended. 'Are you too good for me now?'

'No, no. You frightened me that's all. I was lost in my own thoughts.'

'You mustn't fear me Marta; I'm all you have to rely on when you are sneaking about on this side of town.' He quipped.

Upstairs in the office Marta reached to open the shutters, but Leopold approached her from behind and pulled her into a kiss. His tongue entered her mouth, a new sensation she was unsure of.

'Leave the shutters closed Marta, we don't want the whole world to see the scandal we are creating in here.' He kissed her again but as he did, her mother's words echoed in her ears.

'Leopold stop.'

'You know that when you say stop, it makes me want to take you even more don't you? Come on, it's been too long since I had you all to myself and soon I will have to rush off and do my rounds.' He was already fiddling with the buttons on her trousers.

'No, I mean it. I need to talk to you.' Marta pushed him away.

Leopold stepped back and looked at her with some suspicion.

'Go on.' He said.

'I went to see my mother yesterday. At the Kreis des Wahnsinns.' She hadn't meant to come straight out with it, but the information was there now. Marta watched for a reaction in his face but his expression remained fixed and cool.

'Was she as crazy as ever?' He asked dismissively.

'She didn't look as crazy as I had anticipated but she was saying some rather outlandish things.'

Leopold stepped away from Marta and walked across to the other side of the office. He pulled a cigarette from the silver holder in his jacket pocket and lit it. He turned to look at Marta, sucking hard on the filter then controlling the trail of smoke from his lips so that it writhed upwards like a python.

Marta continued. 'She told me not to trust you. That you have been visiting her for years and that I was forbidden from seeing you.'

'Forbidden you say? And what do you think about that Marta?'

She felt uneasy but she was still unable to find fault in his expression so she persisted.

'I think she must be talking nonsense on account of the medication they give her to keep her stable.'

'And do you think that perhaps these *visits* as she called them are scheduled medical consultations, a requirement of her detainment? I am still her GP you understand?'

'Yes, of course. I understand that.'

'Did you tell her that you are my lover Marta?'

'No.'

'Did you tell her how you let me bite and scratch you, tie your hands behind your back and pull your hair?'

'No, of course I didn't.' She was humiliated by the memory of the things she allowed Leopold to do to her.

'Of course you didn't! Perhaps if you had, she would have thought you crazy too. Then maybe you would have been locked up right next to her. Ha! Imagine that, mother and daughter side by side in the asylum.' Leopold roared with laughter.

He quietened himself down with a few more tugs on his cigarette and then, without warning, he became stern and serious. 'You must not tell your father about your visit. He didn't want you to know, but he is in poor health right now. Your mother hurt him irreparably and I fear such news might kill him. It is your fault that your mother was institutionalised, I'm quite sure you wouldn't want the death of your own father on your conscience too would you?'

'Poor health, whatever's the matter with him?'

'A man has a right to his privacy Marta, and as a doctor I am bound to keep my patients medical information in the strictest confidence. You are not to talk to him about any of this, no matter what.'

Marta looked at him, her thoughts beginning to drift.

'Do you understand what I have just said? No matter what.' He repeated.

'Okay Leopold, I won't say anything but will you also swear not to tell him I visited my mother?'

'You have my word Marta.'

He stubbed his cigarette into the ashtray on the desk and reached for his briefcase which was on the floor by the door. He pulled out a wad of papers and a bound document.

'I have these for you. Make sure you sign your name wherever you see an X and keep hold of them until I ask for them back.' He instructed, dropping them on top of the filing cabinet.

'What are they?'

'Provisional plans, work schedules, title deeds that sort of thing. You really don't need to bother yourself with the details, but you do need to sign them. I will take care of everything else.' He opened the door.

Marta didn't want to be left alone. 'Wait, where are you going?'

'We've wasted so much time talking about this nonsense Marta, I haven't got all day to sit around here listening to you prattle on.'

'Can't you just sit with me for a while?' She pleaded. 'I'll join you for another cigarette and we can go through this pile of paper together.'

'It sounds as though you could do with some time to yourself, free of any further distractions. It is best that I leave you to it and get on with my appointments.' Then he left.

CHAPTER TWENTY NINE

Pernilla knocked on the door of the study.

'Come in.'

'Excuse me for interrupting you Mr Rosenblit but I have an urgent message for you from Dr Kaposi. He needs to see you urgently and suggests you cancel your afternoon study group and meet with him at his house right away.'

Arnold did not like interruptions. He did not like being told what to do or when to do it, but he had been friends with Leopold for more than 25 years and not once in all that time had he known the man to act irrationally. He was a model of composure, quite incapable of being ruffled by anything much at all. It must be serious so he must go.

'Pernilla will you make contact with my student group and tell them I will not be available today?'

'Yes of course, what excuse should I offer?'

'Excuse? You will offer no such thing. Young lady I do not make, nor do I accept excuses. I do not feel the need to apologise or explain myself to anybody. You will tell them that I will not be available and they will just have to accept the certainty of it.'

'Yes of course Mr Rosenblit, right away.'

It was rare for Leopold to invite Arnold to his own home but he felt that the gravity of the situation required him to do so. He did not want to embarrass such a prominent fellow in a public place. That would not reflect well on him at all.

He idled away his time as he waited by wandering around his house admiring his collections including his latest acquisition, a glass medical slide featuring a detailed sketch of a two-headed infant. Holding it up to the light of the window he could see the image, dissected in the middle to display the subject's internal organs in all their glory. Two hearts, two pairs of lungs but only one liver and shared intestine, quite fascinating.

He changed his cufflinks; winter blue enamel was not at all fitting for a business meeting. 'Dress for the life you deserve.' he told himself as he swapped them for a jade green pair with a small square diamond inset. He checked his outfit one more time before he was satisfied. 'Yes, yes, much better.'

The sound of Arnold's taxi pulling up in the driveway alerted Leopold to redress his demeanour. He mustn't appear quite so nonchalant; it would not gel with his script at all. He was in the entrance hall when Arnold knocked at the front door but he did not rush to answer it. Instead, he counted quietly to himself. 'One, breathe in and breathe out. Two, breathe in and breathe out. Three, breathe in and breathe out. Four, breathe in and breathe out. Five, breathe in and breathe out.' Arnold knocked a second time, more insistent now. Leopold continued to count until he reached ten, and then he opened the door.

'Leopold, I got here just as quickly as I could my man. Whatever is the matter?' He stepped inside the house without waiting for a reply.

'Ah, yes. I should probably apologise for my insistence, it's just that...'

Arnold interrupted him. 'No need to explain. You know me well enough to know that I do not like being ordered around so I will assume your need is as important as you implied.'

'Oh it is. I'm afraid it is not good news, but it was my duty to tell you first hand.'

'Well, if it's that bad I do hope there's a whisky with my name on it somewhere around here.' There was a hint of trepidation in his voice.

'Far be it from me to neglect your needs Arnold. I always keep some handy, you know that. I'll pour you a glass and then we must sit.'

Arnold followed Leopold into the study, a large but dimly lit space lined with bookshelves. The majority of them were crammed haphazardly with documents and magazines, loose papers wilted amongst books with broken spines and there was no obvious filing system. It had the appearance of a storeroom rather than a functional working space. Leopold did not apologise for the mess and Arnold did not attempt to question his practices. It was not for either of them to judge another man's workplace.

'I need to talk to you about Marta.' Leopold said, picking up a decanter and two glasses from his drinks table.

Arnold watched as he poured a generous measure into one of the glasses, then reached out an eager hand to claim it. Leopold replaced the crystal stopper without pouring a drink for himself.

'Marta you say?' Arnold raised his glass to his lips and took a sip. He felt his stomach sicken a little. It was not the first time his friend had delivered bad news about a woman he had dedicated himself to.

'There's really no easy way to say it Arnold, she is plotting against you.'

'Plotting what?' He took a second sip of whisky, then a large gulp.

'To branch out on her own, she has some egotistical notion that she can work in the psychiatry field without you, open her own facility no less.'

'And how do you know this?' Arnold was alarmed but not surprised. He had noticed the shift in his daughter's attitude, an aloofness that now made perfect sense.

'She came to talk to me about it, asked me to help her. Quite why she felt it appropriate to try and draw me into all of this I will never know. I can honestly say I have never invited her to approach me about anything.' Leopold shrugged his shoulders in repudiation.

'Of course Leopold, of course, you barely have any contact with her.' He nodded as if understanding the impossibility of it all.

'That's exactly right. As you said, I don't even see her all that much and when I do I can tell you that conversation with her is the furthest thing from my mind.'

'Do you think she's okay?'

'How do you mean?' Leopold asked even though he knew what Arnold was getting at.

'In the head.' Arnold tapped at the right side of his temple. 'I've noticed some changes in her over the last few months; do you think it could be happening again? You know, what happened to Josefine, do you think Marta is suffering too?'

'I suppose it's possible. These things can be in the family you know. I think it depends on how far she has got with it. I mean, when she came to me she was all big ideas and fantasy, no hard facts. If she is losing herself in a world of make-believe and you are suggesting she has displayed other symptoms at home then maybe we should bring her in for a formal clinical assessment.'

Arnold drained his whisky glass, placed it on the desk and planted his face in his hands. 'I was so afraid this might happen.'

'Let's not jump to conclusions. Marta might surprise you, she might have solid plans. Either way is fraught with difficulties, but I felt you had to know.'

'You're right, difficult days ahead. Thank you for being here for me again Leopold. Where would I be without you my friend?'

'Have you considered what you will do if this is not just in her head? What will your colleagues say if they find out she has turned on you? And your students? I hate to state the obvious,' he lied, 'but she could ruin your reputation Arnold.'

'She is mad or she is devious. Whichever she is I will not allow another woman to destroy me like this, not now. It took everything I had not to let my life fall apart after Josefine. My career is all I have left and I will not sacrifice that for her whether she is a conspiratorial sycophant or just another hysterical woman!'

Arnold was angry. How dare this happen again. He was the best psychiatrist in Vienna, one of the most notable in the world. For one woman in his life to fall foul of mental illness was unfortunate, for a second to suffer the same fate or worse to be plotting against him, would be downright negligent. He would be a laughing stock.

'I'm so sorry about all of this Arnold. Just take it easy, and please, don't rush into anything.' Leopold said, aware that his friend preferred to be oppositional whenever he was given advice.

He stood and offered his hand. Arnold stood too and returned a firm shake. 'Marta and I are the ones who should be sorry. I'll see you soon Leopold.'

'Would you like me to arrange a car for you?'

'No, I'd prefer to walk. I need time to think about how I am going to handle this.' Arnold made his way to the front door in silence.

'Goodbye Arnold.'

He did not respond, he had no words, only venomous thoughts and a heart sagging with questions.

Arnold was gone and Leopold was hungry. It was half past four. He poured himself a whisky, knocked it back with a buoyant swig and headed out for an early dinner.

CHAPTER THIRTY

Marta had signed her name three times already and she was only six pages into the paperwork Leopold had left her with. After Leopold had left the office she had decided to take the files home with her. It was indiscreet of her but she hated being alone in that building.

Arnold hadn't come home last night so she had got to work categorising the papers into piles and laying them out on his desk in the study. She knew he had a morning appointment with the Medical Council and would usually eat lunch out so she had plenty of time to work through them all.

As she signed her name for the fourth time, the telephone rang in the hallway. It was Elise.

'I've arranged for you to have access to the Karlsplatz Stadtbahn. You can go over there now if you hurry.'

'How did you manage that? And so quickly too.' Marta enquired.

'Oh you know me; I have contacts all over the place. When you get there, go around to the side entrance and knock. The station master Max will be expecting you.'

This was it, time to see what Josefine was hiding. 'Will you come with me?' She asked.

Elise had anticipated the invitation. 'I'm sorry but I can't. I have to complete a job application, the deadline is today. You know I would if I could. Perhaps this is something you need to do alone anyway.'

'Yes, I think you're right. Well, I'd better go then.' Marta said, preparing to hang up. 'Will you wish me luck?' She added, in need of a little courage.

'Marta?'

'Yes.'

'I love you.'

'And I love you Elise.'

How beautiful it was to know that whatever she discovered today, she would always have the love of Elise. Marta went straight to the coat stand and grabbed the moufflon fur trim coat Elise had donated to her. It was over the top and not to her taste but snow was forecast for later, it wouldn't hurt to wrap up. Her house keys, purse and gloves were still on the table by the door from when she had returned home yesterday. She put the keys and purse into the deep coat pocket and began pulling on her gloves as she ran up the garden path.

'Damn it!' She turned back to the house, let herself in and paced the stairs up to her room two at a time. Once there, she took her purse from her pocket, fetched out her letter knife and pushed it inside. She tucked the purse back into her pocket and headed downstairs and outside.

On the street, the weather was harsh and blustery so she hailed a taxi. 'Karlsplatz Stadtbahn please.' She ordered the driver.

'Is that the one over by Resselpark?' He asked.

'I believe so.'

'You know it's closed now don't you?'

'Not to me it isn't. Now stop your questions and hurry up, please.' She ordered again.

Marta had never visited this station before. It may have been out of use, but the gilded mouldings that braced the archways of the entrance pavilion were still exquisite. The wrought iron gates had begun to rust and the emptiness of the   walkway that surrounded it was eerie when compared to the hubbub she had seen at the Mitte or Keleti stations.

As she approached the pavilion a uniformed man emerged from the side of the building. He was not wearing a coat or hat and his breath was condensing in the air.

'You must be Marta.' He came closer.

'And you must be Max. Aren't you cold?' She asked, not knowing what else to say.

'I'm used to it. All part of the job.' He replied.

'I appreciate you helping me out like this.'

'You know Elise. She could charm a bag of snakes into submission.'

'It would appear so.' She added, following him through the side door and into the pavilion. It was tranquil inside, like a church. The electricity no longer worked, but the double height glass frontage allowed light to reach into most corners of the building. Everything there looked remarkably intact.

Max led her to the locker area. 'You can help yourself to whatever you want from here. I don't have any keys but if you can open any of them you are welcome to keep what you find.'

'Thank you. Would you be able to leave me alone for a while?'

'Take as long as you need. My shift is over and I don't have anyone to rush home for. It's warmer in here than at my apartment anyway.' He shrugged.

He took himself off toward the rear of the building then vanished behind a doorway marked 'Lost & Found'.

Marta walked along the rows of lockers. Some were already open; doors hanging loose, others were sealed shut. She counted along the brass numerals, 18, 20, 22, 24. Number 24, just like Josefine had said. She looked around the empty pavilion then took her purse from her pocket. She opened it and lifted out the letter knife. For a second the glint of daylight on the blade made her think somebody was standing at her shoulder, but nobody was there.

Marta inserted the knife into the small gap that ran the length of the locker door. With a bit of leverage, she managed to pop the pin from the frame, catching her knuckles against the small door as it came undone. She hid the knife away again and looked inside, her heartbeat was erratic.

The first thing she noticed amongst the contents of the locker was a journal. The cover featured a painting of lupins and the date 1903 was stamped on the top right-hand side. She lifted it out, the pages felt damp but it was otherwise in pristine condition. Underneath the journal was a small velour box. She opened it to find a pair of earrings. She recognised the image on the small oval enamel droppers, and the pretty tourmaline stones. They matched the pendant she had received in the most recent of the packages. Unsure if she was ready to know the truth, Marta collected together the items and moved herself into the station waiting room and closed the door. She made her way to the far side of the room and took her place on a bench facing the door. She set the velour box to one side and opened up the journal. A folded piece of paper covered in cerulean handwriting slipped out onto her lap. She unfolded it. It was a letter and it was addressed to her.

December 7th, 1904

Dear Marta my darling,

You are just born and I am afraid. I am afraid for both of us and so I feel I must write to you now or fear losing the truth forever. I am not sure when you might find this letter, perhaps you never will, but it is the only way I can think of to tell you of my dishonour.

I imagine one day that I will be well, that we are reading this together and that you will already know everything but love me anyway. I fear that they will find me dead, or worse that I will live a lifetime without knowing you. I have so much to explain, it is all here within the pages of my journal. I am not proud of myself, but I am proud of you.

I want you to understand that Arnold had passions and I didn't want to disappoint him. He is a charming and persuasive man and I would have done anything for him at one time. And so I did. I shared myself with his friends as he wished, at times I am ashamed to admit that I enjoyed being shared, but then it got so out of hand and for that I will always be sorry.

It was not my intention to fall for Leopold so fast and so hard, but I can assure you that I was in love with

268

him. I have made many mistakes in the past few months, but the biggest by far was to believe that he loved me too.

Marta blinked hard and read the sentence again.

It was not my intention to fall for Leopold so fast and so hard.

A sour taste of bile crept from the back of her throat and into her mouth. She continued reading, searching for a correction in every line. She turned over the paper and read on, struggling to focus her vision.

Arnold did not know about my growing infatuation for Leopold. Is it possible to love two men at the same time? I still don't know the answer to that Marta.

When I told Leopold that I had fallen pregnant with you, he was not at all elated. He had a daughter and he did not want a child by his mistress. My heart was broken Marta, I had nowhere to turn. I could not hide a pregnancy from Arnold, and to masquerade you as his was unthinkable. I pleaded with Leopold, unaware of the extent he would go to in order to protect his high profile career and social connections.

I was debilitated by sickness through my pregnancy. Leopold gave me medication and still trusting, I took it. How did I not see the greed and manipulation he was capable of? I wish I could explain that. The medication stopped my sickness Marta, but it caused such horrid hallucinations. I felt tired all of the time and slept for hours every day.

During my period of incapacitation, Arnold came to me. He said Leopold had told him everything. I was frightened but relieved Marta. I foolishly thought

Leopold had done the right thing. Instead, he led Arnold to believe I had been stealing prescription drugs from his office. That I had become hysterical when he had tried to stop me, and that I had tried to seduce him. He told Arnold I was pregnant but suffering from psychotic delusions which led me to make false accusations. He forged test papers to prove to Arnold that you were his baby. He gave him false blood results that confirmed high levels of cocaine, opium and amphetamines in my system. Marta you must believe me when I tell you that I never had any tests.

None of this is true Marta. Not one word. For a while Leopold continued to stupefy me with medication, but he has grown lazy over the last few weeks and no longer watches me take my tablets. He does not know, but I have been free of those toxic drugs for quite some time now. I needed a clear head so that I could write this for you.

I don't know what will happen from here, but I do know that Dr. Leopold Kaposi wields more power than I had ever imagined. In case I am unable to write again, please know that as I sit here cradling you I am telling you I love you Marta.

Forever yours, Mother

It was too much to take. This could not be true. Josefine was crazy; this letter proved it by its every word. Marta picked up the journal, her hands shaking so violently that it tumbled to the floor. That's when she saw it, Leopold's face peering out from an old photograph. It was an almost exact copy of the one she

270

had received in the first package; only his face was not scratched away this time and Josefine was standing at his side holding his hand. There he was, his familiar face looking back at her, defiant. She thumbed frantically through the pages of the journal.

February 22nd

Shlomo and Issac joined us for dinner and drinks. Arnold introduced us at the premiere of Buckner's Symphony a week or so ago. Isaac was charming but Shlomo was a brackish brute and I have refused to entertain him.

May 11th

Today was reserved for sewing and tending to home chores. Arnold says the house has become an unruly hellfire and I can't continue to ignore it. He's right I know, but I do not have the motivation for it. Already I long for Thursday evening, dining, drinking and dancing with the most wonderful man is all I can think about.

July 6th

We are going to the river today for a picnic, and if we can find a quiet place to make love then today will be the most idyllic of days. The change in my heart has lifted me from my unrest, and Posey has become the reason for my every breath.

September 24th

It is becoming difficult to hide my feelings for Posey. At home I am sullen and rude almost all of the time, Arnold is finding my behaviour insufferable but I no longer care. Bertha is quite able to cope with the children, they don't need me. If only I could spend all of my spare hours with my love. I have decided to leave. Posey is so unhappy with Cecily, I know I can serve him better.

The more she read, the harder it was to deny. She thought back to the name that had been written on the back of the photograph she had received. *'Posey, 1903, Karlsplatz Stadtbahn'.*

Posey. Kaposi. It must have been her nickname for him. She could not stomach another word of this.

Was this really happening? The only man who had ever noticed her apart from Arnold, was actually her biological father? The man who forced himself so brutally on her, was of her flesh and blood? Marta's head began to spin out of control. Her synapses clanged and rattled inside her head, the sparks so ferocious she thought she might just burst into flames right there in the waiting room.

Leopold had known of her all along. He had destroyed her mother and now he was trying to destroy her too.

She dropped from the bench to her knees, tucking her legs underneath her and assuming the posture of a cowering animal as she began to sob. Her stomach rolled in a continuous wave of heaving but nothing would come out. She had been vomiting at regular intervals since yesterday and she was empty. Only now it began to dawn on her that she had not had her period this month. She and Leopold had been so busy finalising proposals for the facility, and she had been so lost in her deepening love for him, that she had not paid it any mind.

Panic took her over. She ruffled her hands through her hair, pulling it from its tightly wound bun as if trying to claw the facts from her brain. She wanted to cut herself open and climb out of the skin she was crouched in. Reject her sin-ridden carcass; go back to the unblemished child she once was and start again.

By the time her sobbing quietened, her face was blotchy red and her eyes swollen. She looked fresh from combat. Holding the velour box, journal and letter close to her chest she did her best to pull herself to her feet.

The waiting room door felt heavy in her hands as she opened it. Stepping gingerly into the pavilion she could see that the previously frosted walkway was now covered with a sheet of freshly fallen snow.

****

Arnold arrived home relieved to find an empty house. He was too tired and hungover to face the prospect of a discussion with Marta. An evening spent swaying alone in a bar with a brandy glass had not calmed him. Neither had his fumbling with the waitress cum prostitute he had spent the last few hours with. It had been his first encounter with a woman other than his wife since Josefine had been taken from him.

He went straight to his study; he needed to ground himself in everything he knew before he became entrenched in what was to come. Piles of paperwork were arranged on his desk, but none of them belonged to him. As he sorted through them he was defeated to see that everything Leopold had alleged was true. Architects

273

drawings, legal documents, even a research and analysis model – it was all here, and some of it even had Marta's signature on. What more proof did he need? This could not be an absent-minded mistake; she wanted him to see it. She was taunting him with it.

'How dare she double cross me?!' He shouted, clutching handfuls of paper and tossing them to the ceiling. 'How dare she?! I shared a lifetime of insights with the wretched girl and she has the audacity to try and outfox me? Me, the grand master of psychiatry in Vienna?!' Pieces of paper fluttered to his feet, tattered and disorganised.

He took a decanter from his drinks cabinet, poured himself a drink, then picked up a hand full of paper from the floor and tossed into the fireplace with some splinters of kindling.

'Time to light a fire.'

CHAPTER THIRTY ONE

The day after he met with Arnold, Leopold finished his morning rounds then took a taxi straight to Liesing. As he approached the familiar round brickwork of the Kreis des Wahnsinns he remained quite calm. It was not an act. On the contrary, Leopold was not fazed by the storm that was mounting; always confident he would come out on top. He regarded this situation as no different from any other, a minor crease that would be ironed out, smoothed over. It wasn't as though he hadn't expected such a mishap at some point.

He passed the front desk, it was lunchtime and it was unstaffed so he did not bother to sign in. In the storeroom off the main corridor, he gave a courteous smile to Hannah and a second nurse Emely, who were busy preparing the medication trolley. 'Just doing my rounds.' He said striding right past them.

'Of course Dr Kaposi.' Hannah called after him.

'Good day doctor.' Emely added.

Leopold made his way to the third floor and followed the curved wall around until he reached Josefine's cell. He looked through the spy hole. She was sitting on the edge of her bed doing nothing at all, beautiful in her stillness, just as she had always been. It was a shame it had all turned out this way, but he could never have built a life with her. Not the life she would have wanted and certainly not the life he had spent years working for. He took his keys from his pocket and opened the door.

Once inside, he closed it carefully behind him and crossed the room to pick up the metal chair in the corner. He placed it in front of her and sat down.

Josefine spoke first. 'I knew you would come.'

'Did you now?' He was amused by her certainty.

'Marta will find out about you. She and Elise visited me, just last week.'

'Elise?' He asked sternly. 'What do you mean Elise visited you?'

'She is here in Vienna. She helped bring Marta to me.'

'Is that so?' He was surprised but curious. 'Well I'm afraid to say you are one step behind yet again Josefine. Don't you get it? Marta sent me here today; she doesn't want to see you.'

Josefine hoped he was lying. She had been so sure that Marta would understand.

'Of course I was happy to bear the bad news.' He continued, 'I don't know what you said to her but she is now convinced that you are insane and is quite sure that she does not care to see you ever again.'

'What did you do? What did you do?!' Josefine screeched at Leopold before throwing herself onto him, arms flailing as she clawed at his face and tried to yank at his neck tie.

Leopold gripped her by the wrists, smirking at her loss of control. 'It is *you* who did everything.' He pushed his face into hers. 'An act of genius on your part, telling her to stay away from me, you did me a favour. If you knew anything about your daughter you'd know that she has a rebellious side. She's a good girl who likes to do bad things; it's quite funny when you think about it.' He laughed.

Josefine continued to fight, but he held her firm leaving her thrashing around like a tantrum ridden toddler - her thin limbs flapping and her body too small to accomplish any real harm.

He whispered in her ear 'I will have your case review overturned for this and ensure your detainment is indefinite.' before shouting out for help.

'Nurse! Nurse!'

'I will kill you.' Josefine screamed and she continued to struggle free of him. The veins at her temples protruded and she was crying uncontrollably, her voice fading to a croak as she shouted 'I hate you, I will kill you. Do you hear me? I hate you and I will kill you.'

Leopold heard Hannah come running along the corridor. As she entered, accompanied by a thick-necked warden, he forced himself back on his chair, toppling it to the floor and pulling Josefine on top of him as he fell. He released her wrists and she began pounding at his chest and face.

The warden reacted, pulling Josefine's arms behind her back until she squealed like a piglet. He dragged her body from Leopold's and threw her face down to the ground. Then he knelt in the small of her back as Hannah tied her wrists together. The nurse took out a syringe and pushed a sedative into her arm before pulling her onto her back.

'Thank you nurse, let me have a moment to calm her.'

'Are you sure you aren't hurt Dr Kaposi? She really should be chained up in one of the cells on the top floor. She seems to have the most difficulty restraining herself around men.'

'I'll be fine; the poor woman is having some kind of psychotic episode. Terribly sad isn't it?' He flashed his best concerned face at Hannah. 'Now, let me just finish up my assessment of her physical health and then I will leave her to recover.'

'Very well doctor.' Hannah turned to leave, gesturing for the warden to follow.

Josefine stared up at Leopold, her eyelids dropping as she tried fervidly to remain awake. It was no use, the sedative was pulling her under and she was powerless to stop it. As she faded out of consciousness she heard Leopold's voice close by.

'Marta and I are lovers. Just like you, she was too weak to stop my advances. Like mother, like daughter eh Josefine? She doesn't want you, she wants me. You failed and you will rot in here. I don't know why you ever thought you could change anything from inside a lunatic cell. Perhaps you should accept that you are deluded after all.'

He pulled off his loosened tie and placed it in Josefine's deep pocket. 'Here you are my darling; why don't you put yourself out of your misery and leave us all to get on with our lives. There's nothing left for you in this life but to eke out your days chained to a wall.'

She looked at his triumphant face one last time before everything went black. Once she was unconscious Leopold lifted her from the floor and carried her to the bed. He lay her limp body on the mattress, rolling her over so that she was facing away from him. He ran his hand from her shoulder, down her arm and followed the line of her body along the sink of her waist and up over the curve of her hip. 'Terribly sad.' He mumbled to himself, and then he left.

He located Hannah in a cell down on the first floor. 'She's all settled down now Hannah. Listen, I hate to say it, but I can't approve her case review whilst she is in such a state. I will call her psychiatrist and have her moved upstairs as a matter of urgency. Can you cancel the rest of my consultations this afternoon? I've had quite enough for today!'

'Right away Dr Kaposi, whatever you need.' She nodded.

'Oh and by the way, Josefine mentioned that she had visitors here last week. Two women I believe?'

Hannah thought for a moment. 'Oh yes, Dr Polgár and Ms Vass from the electroshock research project in Hamburg.'

'Right, of course, yes, the Hamburg people. Can you give me their postal address please; I think it would be beneficial to update them on Josefine's condition.'

'Of course doctor, I'll fetch it for you now.' She shuffled off in the direction of the administration office.

CHAPTER THIRTY TWO

Elise had been telling the truth when she told Marta she was unable to come to the Karlsplatz. She did have a job application to complete for a post at a private children's hospital. However, she had also been grappling with feelings about her own family situation since she and Marta had visited Josefine at the asylum. She had been going over and over the details of the night her father left her mother.

Just four years old at the time, Elise had been nestled in the small dark space beneath the stairs waiting for her father to come home. She had been planning to jump out and surprise him. He was often away from home for days at a time and she missed him so much that it could make her stomach ache. Her mother had been preoccupied with something and had spent the whole of supper and bath time crying in her room.

When he came home Elise had decided to stay where she was. Looking out from the darkness she could see the back of his head and his shoulders as her mother screamed and screamed about some other woman. She could see her mother clearly, the lamp shining harshly on her face which was as pale as white lead and streaked with glistening black.

Her eyes looked strange and her prettiness was squashed and contorted as she asked him – *'It's true isn't it? Admit it, go on! Admit that what Josefine told me is true.'*

Her mother was holding a collection of scrunched up papers in the clenched fist of her left hand, tickets or notepaper or something she couldn't quite make out. Some sort of trinket dangled from between the thumb and forefingers of her right hand, and her mother was waving it in his face. '*The photographs, the jewellery, mementoes from your little dalliances - all the evidence I need is right here. I just want to hear you admit it!*'

Her father did not offer much protest.

'*And she tells me she is having your baby! The shame of it punches holes in my heart.*'

Elise had not heard her mother use such an angry tone before.

The other woman – Josefine – had visited Elise and her mother a couple of hours before. Elise was scolded for opening the door to her, a child has no right to meet and greet she was told. The other woman had not minded, in fact she had thanked her, stroking a wisp of blonde hair from her face and whispering something under her breath that she quickly choked back as though someone had pulled the air from her lungs. She was tall and more sinewy than Elise's mother, with exotic eyes and shiny hair. However, her face was also bleakly pale and within a short time her cheeks were wet and streaked with black too. It had been a perplexing scene to witness.

Neither Elise nor her mother could have anticipated what was going to happen after Josefine entered the house. The day had started out as an ordinary one; the sky had been a predictable shade of mineral blue and lunch had been served in the garden under a high noon scorch. By supper she had been huddled in the armchair in the sitting room, her mother had fallen asleep next to her whilst reading her a story of an Emperor and his new clothes.

It was only after Josefine arrived that the sated peace of day was taken over by a fractious night.

'Cecily, I'm so sorry.' Josefine had said, over and over. Her mother, the actress in her preferring to take a dramatic stance, was *'blown apart'* she had said before calling her *'a despicable witch!'* over and over.

Elise watched her mother drop to her knees when her father called her a *'neurotic fool'*, turned away and told her he was leaving. She did not know what neurotic meant, but it was like a magic word. A word that stopped her mother from ordering him out and instead had her begging him to stay.

It was his last words that made Elise's ribs crack with an emotion her tiny body had never known before. Her mother was wailing and incomprehensible but from the shadows she could read every word as it fell from his lips.

'I never wanted a child. Elise is the reason you lost interest in me. You took what you wanted and now you've got what you deserve. I don't want either of you.'

Even in the dim light, Elise was sure he looked right at her when he said that last bit. Until that moment she had believed she was the apple of her father's eye, but no, he thought her rotten to the core.

After he left the house Elise remained paralysed under the stairs, unable to move discreetly back to her room, her only option to listen to the whimpering of her mother. She tried to block it all out, making shadow puppets with her hands, counting her toes repeatedly, from the little toe of her left foot over to the little toe of her right foot and back again. Her feet were so cold; she wished she had worn her slippers but she hadn't meant to stay in her spot for so long. She watched a spider make its web in the nook above her head, and she tried to pretend she wasn't scared when it dropped for a second before shimmying back up its silken line.

Elise was still waiting under the stairs when the clock in the hallway chimed 11pm. She was curled up in a ball and had almost drifted off to sleep, but she awoke to see the hem of Cecily's housedress trailing over the edge of the bottom stair. Her shoulders were still hunched over, but she was quivering silently now having calmed herself with a few sips of liquor from the cabinet. She jumped out of her skin when she heard a bang at the front door, and so did Elise. Cecily rushed to answer it, but appeared disappointed to see a tall portly fellow on the other side.

It was Mr Beste. He looked as though he had been drinking lots of liquor too. Elise had thought it so strange that adults sought solutions in glass bottles. Far from giving them answers, the drinking seemed to make them more confused, talking over each other in riddles and rants. Elise had watched, still silent, as he stumbled into the hallway without invitation. He was looking for her father; apparently her mother wasn't the only one he had angered.

Mr Beste shouted a lot. Her mother cried a lot. And in between, she caught more snippets of conversation as they were spat into the air. She juggled phrases such as 'He killed her!' and 'Not to be trusted.', and 'He must pay.'. Then more words she didn't understand. Revenge. Despicable. Charlatan. With every word he shouted, her mother cried some more. Elise began to wonder if she might cry her eyes dry and force her lids to turn inside out. At times Cecily would hold her hand to her mouth, and then she would wrap her arms around herself as though she had a stomach ache.

Eventually she wiped her tears from her cheeks and straightened herself and her dress. The air changed then, stiffening just as she did. All the messiness that had spilled out of them all seemed swept away. The broken doll she had been just moments before now mended, albeit not quite as she was before but good enough for now.

It was at that point that Mr Beste saw Elise. She tried to slip out of sight, tucking herself into the blackest corner, but she was too slow.

'It's okay, don't be afraid. I'm so sorry for all my shouting.' He had reached out his hand to her.

She clambered to her feet and stepped forward, obedient but anxious. Elise looked at her mother. She wasn't sad or angry anymore. She wasn't anything in particular, just sort of, hollow.

'Come on out Elise and say good evening to Mr Beste.'

He took her hand and squatted down to her level. His breath smelled like aniseed and his overcoat smelled damp like the rain outside.

'I don't know how long you have been hiding back there, but I guess you may have heard some harsh words.'

She nodded, looking at her mother for signs of reassurance. Cecily remained distant.

Mr Beste continued. 'I'm sorry. I was upset. Not all men are bad, but those who are must pay for their mistakes.'

'Did you make a mistake Mr Beste?' She had asked, curious to know if it was just her father who got everything wrong.

'I did, and I pay for it every day.' His eyes were still red-rimmed, but they were softer now than when he had arrived. 'We always wanted children. A little girl would have been so precious.' He added, though she didn't know why.

Then he let go of her hand, turned to Cecily and apologised. He asked her what she would do now and she told him that she and Elise would be leaving in the morning. She would return to her parent's home in Paris. She didn't consult Elise about that or anything else she decided that night, but that is what happened and she never saw or heard from her father again.

Standing in her apartment, now a 27-year-old woman, she knew it was time to move on. She had to let go of her acrimonious ideas, settle into a sensible life. She was ready to cast off the bitter convictions of her past and start again. Elise sat at her small dining table and began to fill the blank pages of the application form with details of her aspirations for the future.

CHAPTER THIRTY THREE

Elise was not expecting visitors. She was reviewing her application when she heard a knock on the door. For a moment she thought she might not answer it, but then a second knock came even louder than the first.

'I'm coming!' She shouted down from the top of the stairs in the hope of preventing a third knock that might just take the door off its hinges.

Her door did not have a window in it so she was unable to see who was so impatient, but a familiar sound of whistling coming from the other side made her shiver. As soon as she opened it she recognised the tall frame of the man in front of her. She had not seen him in 23 years but she knew it was him. Everything was the same even though he looked much older. His distinctive posture, head always held high, his hair, wiry and golden, and the faint smell of Brilliantine took her right back to her childhood.

She shouldn't have been surprised to see him. It was only a matter of time before he heard of her presence in the city, even though she had used a false surname. She was more surprised that it had taken him so long to find her; after all, befriending Marta had been quite a risky move on her part.

'Well look at how you've grown. You are the image of your mother.' He was as arrogant as ever.

'You'll have to excuse me; I have no idea how I am supposed to address you. Dr Kaposi? Leopold? Father?' She turned her back on him and made her way up the stairs to her sitting room. 'Do come in.' she added coolly.

Leopold surveyed the street outside before stepping across the threshold, it was late afternoon and the murky daylight was already giving way. Once inside he slammed the door with a force that made Elise shudder. She looked over her shoulder to see him racing up the stairs towards her, his eyes wild. As he reached the top he yanked her upper arm and rushed her into the sitting room before throwing her down on the sofa.

Elise was not afraid. She jumped back to her feet at once, stepping forward until she was toe to toe with the man she had once adored out of childish innocence.

'What are you going to do Father, discipline me?' She snarled.

'I should have denounced you the day you were born. Your mother had so many lovers I wasn't even sure you were mine, but to see you now all feisty and venomous, it's quite clear that you, my little apple, did not fall far from my tree after all.'

'I am nothing like you. I have spent a lifetime trying to forget you ever existed at all. It's so typical that you left when I needed you, and now you reappear just as I had decided I didn't need you at all.'

'It is you who reappeared; I never left Vienna just you and your worthless mother. I've been right here all this time.'

'Yes, taking care of your other daughter.'

Leopold was taken aback. 'What do you know of that?'

'I know that you left because mother found out Josefine Rosenblit was carrying your baby. I know that you are helping Marta now, that you chose her instead of me. I know that you secured her a life of privilege with Arnold, but left mother and I to starve in Paris.'

'Is that it? Is that what you think you know?' Leopold started to laugh. 'Oh you silly, silly girl you don't know the half of it.'

'I'm going to tell her.' Elise threatened.

'Tell her what?'

'I will tell her who you really are. I will tell all of them. Arnold, Marta, your colleagues, your patients. I will shout it from every street corner in the city until your name is as sullied and putrid as you are.'

Leopold grabbed a fistful of her blouse and pulled her face close to his. 'You think any of my esteemed friends and contacts will believe some crackpot junior doctor, a woman so ruthlessly ambitious she would do anything to get ahead including trying to discredit one of the city's most prominent doctors? You are nobody here. Nobody.'

'People know you had a wife and a daughter, they'll believe me when I tell them all about mother in Paris and how you left us.'

'Had. I had a wife and a daughter, but you see your mother made it remarkably easy for me to move on. When she left for Paris without a trace I was able to tell people that she left me, and that you had both died in a fire in some squalid little flat soon after. Everyone thought it quite tragic. I'm the first to admit I thoroughly enjoyed the sympathy and comfort extended to me by so many of the women here.'

Elise raised her hand like a talon ready to swipe her father's face, but as she moved Leopold blocked her. He moved closer still until the tips of their noses touched. 'You see my darling girl; you are dead to me and everyone else in this city too.'

Her eyes burned but she refused to give in to tears. Leopold was a liar of the highest order. She could see now that it was pointless trying to get him to surrender to her. She was smarter than that. If she had inherited anything from him it was the power of manipulation. To win, she would have to resort to behaving just like him.

Leopold released his grip on her blouse and began strolling around the sitting room. He picked up the tambour clock on her sideboard. 'Is that a mahogany or walnut casing?'

She did not answer.

'What's this now? A job application?' He asked, picking up the partially completed form from the dining table.

'I'm a paediatrician now.' In spite of her feelings towards him, Elise still wanted him to know that she had grown into a successful woman.

'You won't need that anymore.' He smiled at her as he ripped the paper into long strips and dropped them to the floor.

'If I don't have a job I might just find myself with too much spare time. I'm sure you wouldn't want me to sit around with idle hands, you never know what I might do.'

'I wouldn't hear of it. I will find you a job. I suppose I owe you that much at least. You will not get a job in Vienna I will see to that, but I can arrange something in Paris if you want to be close to your mother or maybe Hamburg – I hear you are well connected there. I wouldn't want you thinking I'd let you starve again now would I?' He scoffed.

'Don't you want to know anything about mother?'

'Is she still alive and well?' He asked.

'Yes.'

'Then no, thank you but I don't care to know anything more about her at all.'

'Right.'

'Quite right.' He confirmed sharply.

'So you will find me a job if I leave here?'

'If you swear you will not make any further contact with Marta, Arnold or anybody else of importance to me. Nobody is ever to know of you as my daughter. Do you understand?'

'Perfectly.'

'I will make some calls and have something arranged for you by the end of the week, after which time I will not expect to see you or hear from you again.'

'I promise, after this week your life will be exactly as it should be. I will not be a part of it. Oh, and make it Hamburg. I don't think I want to go back to Paris.'

'Very good. You know, if the job doesn't work out you could always trade on your looks, you are a pretty little thing.' He looked her up and down then turned to leave. 'Yes, every inch your mother.'

Marta ran past the Lost & Found office at the back of the station and made her way to the side door.

Max came out from behind the office door. 'Hey, where are you going? Is everything alright?' He called.

She could not bring herself to answer or even look back at him as she pushed open the door. Outside the snow was still powdery under foot but she was already so numb that she did not register the icy temperatures stabbing at the bones of her hands and feet.

She must get to Elise and tell her what she had found out. She must admit to the full extent of her relationship with Leopold. Elise would understand everything, she hoped. They had so much in common and had grown so close.

She took the tram as far as possible then continued on foot. She started to run the rest of the route in a bid to keep warm, though she had to pause from time to time to retch again. As she turned the corner off the Ringstrasse Marta was sure she saw Leopold stepping out from the door of her friend's small apartment. It was misty and growing dark but as he crossed the road under the street lamp she could see that it was him. She did not know how he could have found out about her friend, but Marta had to warn her.

What if Elise didn't believe her? Surely she would be disgusted by the truth? This was not the time for doubts, Marta had to tell somebody and right now it appeared that she and Elise only had each other.

She hammered her fist on the door. Elise shouted from inside. 'How dare you come back here! I have said all I need to say to you.'

'Elise? Elise, it's me Marta.' She cried, too cold to consider what she had just heard.

The rattle of a chain was followed by the sound of a key turning in the lock. Elise opened the door dragging up a flurry of snow at their feet.

'For heaven's sake Marta, what has happened to you? You look utterly bereft and what is all that in your hands?' Elise glanced up and down the street before pulling Marta in from the pavement. 'Quick, come inside.' They climbed the stairs without talking.

Inside, the apartment smelled of freshly baked pastry that wafted in through the vents from the bakery downstairs. Elise grabbed a colourful crochet blanket from the back of the armchair and wrapped it around her shoulders, rubbing her arms vigorously in an effort to warm herself.

'It's cold out there, you must be cold through. Let me fix you something to eat.' Elise went to the kitchen to fetch a bowl of goulash that had been warming on the stove. Marta was too exhausted to complain.

'Here. You must eat if you want to put some colour back in your face.' Elise handed her the bowl and a spoon.

Marta was sure she could not stomach even the tiniest of morsels, but she pretended to sip the rich liquid from the spoon so as not to offend her friend.

'Elise, I opened the locker at the Karlsplatz. I know things, about Leopold. I saw him leaving here just now and I know you must think him charming and trustworthy but he isn't. Josefine was right about him, but there's more. More than that and I am so afraid you will abandon me if I tell you everything.'

Elise did not look as shocked as Marta had anticipated. She pulled the blanket tighter around her shoulders, an excess of adrenalin sparking small spasms in her arms and legs.

Marta continued, 'I have made a terrible mistake, the kind which could not have been foreseen and cannot be undone. Leopold had an affair with my mother, but he did not return the love she felt for him. He had been using her until she fell pregnant with me. She wanted to start a new life with him, but he refused. He drugged her until she turned quite mad and then saw to it that she was admitted to the Kreis des Wahnsinns. He tricked everyone Elise, made everyone believe that my mother was crazy, but it was all a lie!'

Marta broke down, more tears forcing their way out with her words.

Elise interrupted. 'And now I too need to stop telling lies Marta. You deserve the truth. I'm afraid to say that I have long known more than I let on. I have known about your mother for some time.'

'You knew? But... how...? What are you saying?'

'Do you remember how I told you my father had left when I was a young girl?'

'Yes, but what does that have to...'

'We have been estranged for many years. I have been using my mother's maiden name Saloman instead of Kaposi.'

'Kaposi? But that's Leopold's name.'

'Yes, I know.' She lowered her head.

Marta's world was spinning again.

'My father always spent so much time with Arnold and his marriage to my mother fell apart as a result of you being conceived. He chose to live his life here in Vienna watching you grow up rather than come to Paris looking for me. I thought I had lost everything because of you Marta. In the beginning I wanted my revenge on all of you. The more I got to know you the more I began to regret my decisions and my motivations.'

'But you were at the Café Louvre? Our meeting was a coincidence.'

'No, it wasn't Marta. I knew you would come in time and so I waited there day after day.'

'That's ridiculous! How could you know? I only went there because of the packages and they had nothing to do with you. I found out who was sending them.'

'Frederick Beste.'

'Yes, but how…'

'I gave him the receipts, the photograph, all of it. I scratched away the face on the photograph when I was a girl. I cut Josefine out of it too, but I never threw it away. I couldn't let him get away with it. Frederick has known me since I was a child; I made contact with him when I moved back to Vienna. Neither of us knew you and so we came up with a way to warn you about Leopold.

Frederick has as many reasons as I do to see him strung up.'

'But you've been so kind. You are my friend. You told me that you loved me.' Marta said.

'And I realise now that I do. Once I got to know you I began to feel so differently about so many things. I grew to like you and then I grew to love you as my half-sister. That is, after all, what we are. Sisters. When you asked me to help you visit your mother I saw it as an opportunity to put things right.'

Marta was furious now. 'Why Elise? Why? How could you not tell me? Do you realise what you have done? Do you have any idea of the consequences? Leopold and I were not just business partners. We were lovers Elise, lovers! He took advantage of me in a most unforgiveable way. And now during all of this horrific catastrophe I fear I am carrying his child too. The unfortunate result of an incestuous union. Do you see what you have allowed to happen? You knew all along that he was my father. You knew and you did nothing!'

Elise was in shock. She had been so driven by revenge that she had allowed her own sister to be used in such a despicable way. Perhaps she was more like Leopold than she had dared to recognise.

'Oh my. Oh God Marta, what have I done to you? I... I had no idea... I love you, I do. How could I know that? In the end I just wanted you to find your mother again, that's what you wanted isn't it? I'm so sorry.'

'I can't hear any more of this, it is unbearable. I have to get away from here, from all of you. My world is crashing down and you are all staying to watch as I disappear under the rubble!'

'What will you do? Where will you go? Let me help you, I'll do anything. We will fix this Marta, together.'

'Together? What do you know of togetherness?' She snapped. 'You got your revenge and I congratulate you.'

'Everything is lost if we are divided. Together we might stand a chance, please Marta, please?'

Marta pushed the bowl of goulash away from her, took off the coat Elise had given her back when she had thought they were friends, and threw it to the floor. She took her keys and purse from her pockets, gathered up her remaining belongings and descended the stairs. As she opened the front door the chill sliced the warmth of the flat and caused her to catch her breath.

She turned to look back at Elise who was clinging to the bannister, her grief-stricken face staring down into the dark lobby. 'I have a knife in my back and your fingerprints are all over the handle.'

Marta stepped out into the night, slamming the door as hard as she could behind her. She was nauseous. She wanted to go home to her own bed, and to sleep, forever.

CHAPTER THIRTY FIVE

It was almost midnight when Marta reached home. Pernilla opened the door before she managed to knock.

'I've been watching out for you. Your father is not here. Come inside and get warm.'

Her lips had turned violet-blue and her skin was translucent as fish bones. Something was wrong; Arnold was always in his study or in his bedroom at this time of night. It had been his routine for as long as she could remember. For him to stay out last night was out of character, going missing for a second night was unprecedented.

Pernilla took off her cardigan, twisted it into a length and wrapped it around Marta's neck like a scarf. 'I have a message for you Ms Rosenblit; I think you might want to sit down.'

Still clinging to her purse and the collection of her mother's secrets, Marta allowed Pernilla to lead her to the drawing room, where she dropped into a wingback armchair.

Pernilla continued. 'Dr Rosenblit has gone to the Kreis des Wahnsinns. I'm sorry but it's your mother. I don't know how else to say it. She was found hanging in her cell this evening.'

An explosion erupted in Marta's heart, ripping her apart with such ferocity that she pressed her hands to her chest in a futile attempt to contain it. Her eyes searched, disbelieving.

'Your father will return in the morning, he and Dr Kaposi are tying up the loose ends.'

Pernilla knelt in front of Marta. 'Will you be okay?'

She had no words. She waved Pernilla away.

All at once she was consumed by a creeping black cloud. Marta was certain she could see it enveloping her, starting at her toes and moving in swirls up her legs. It curled around her stomach and pulled tight around her ribs. She felt the blackness rise up to her face like two black oiled hands, slippery fingers probing her mouth and nose until the slick seeped into her throat. Up again it moved, slithering in circles around her head and neck until she was absorbed by it. Unlike the treacherous thoughts she had succumbed to before, this darkness was different, irrepressible. It shrouded her with grief and loss. She had no desire to release it and no strength to fight it.

'This is too much.' She whispered, helpless.

As she moved from the chair and made her way into the hallway she felt heavy. With every laboured step, she felt as though tiny pieces of her flesh were falling away until she believed she had no physical body at all.

She paused at Arnold's study to fetch a decanter of whisky and the remains of a bottle of Vin Mariani. As she entered the room she could see that all of her paperwork for the facility was strewn around the floor, some of it screwed up into little balls, some of it torn apart and some of it still in relatively good order. He had seen it all and she did not care. Marta reached into the drinks cabinet. The decanter and bottle clinked together as she tucked them between her body and forearm. Then she went around to his desk drawer and took out a small bottle containing a reasonable quantity of Hysocine pills he kept there.

When she got to the stairs she could have sworn they collapsed beneath her as she climbed. It was only the sensation of the soles of her feet pressing against each tread that reassured her of their existence. She kept going; she needed the safety of her room. Again she whispered to herself. 'This is too much.'

She made it to her bedroom. Inside, the room was dark but for the silvery strip of moonlight that seemed to divide the room in two as it entered through the window. A dwindling fire in the hearth left a nip in the air, the coals now reduced to a dim glow of tangerine embers and white ash. She went straight to her chest of drawers, placing the drinks and pill bottle on the top next to the items she had retrieved from the locker. Her fingers were nimble again as they warmed to the moderate temperature of the house. She opened her purse and reached inside.

Removing her knife, Marta untucked her blouse lifted it up and over her head and used it to polish the blade to a shine. She let the blouse fall to the floor and held the knife up to the moonlight to admire it. Her hand was still unsteady, causing the reflection to break into glittering illuminations that refracted around the walls and ceiling. She watched as the light jostled for her attention in the darkness.

Glad to find the blade sharp, she sliced into her left forearm. The letter knife sunk into her again and again as though she was warm butter, but she felt nothing. Pools of her blood collected at the site of her fresh wounds. She lifted and turned her arms so that the crimson flow trickled down in a pattern that reminded her of candy stripes, but the relief was not enough.

Next she removed her skirt and step-ins and cut again, this time at the top of her thigh. She did not care about creating orderly lines now, but instead lashed out at herself with abandon. Cutting this way and that, she surrounded her old scars until she came to the one left by Leopold. Her stomach curdled at the thought of how it came to be there. He had bitten her hard, breaking the skin and causing a large blood blister to form. How stupid that she had mistaken his violence for lustful affection.

Marta turned to look at the fireplace. She staggered over to it, putting her hand out to feel for heat. It was still hot. Pushing her knife into the centre of the ember stack she held it steady until the blade turned red hot like a searing poker. Returning to Leopold's mark on her, she pressed the metal against it until her skin was burning and she cried out in pain. Still she didn't remove it, just pressed it harder and held it for longer. She cried out again and tears flowed down her cheeks.

When the metal had cooled she returned it to the embers, and then set about branding herself over and over until even her healthy skin was ravaged.

The initial intensity was no longer enough. Her numbness returned. Why couldn't she replace her heartache with physical pain? Was she now dead outside as well as inside? She must keep pushing herself.

She went to fetch the bottles and pills still perched on top of the chest of drawers, and as she did she thought of how she might be carrying Leopold's child. If it were true she knew that it would never be her child, it would always be his. Everything belonged to him now, she had nothing and she was nothing but a vessel. She loathed the idea of a child inside her, especially one who held no attachment for her. Marta unscrewed the cap from the pill bottle and shook the remaining pills into her open palm.

She removed the stopper from the decanter and dropped it to the floor, sucked a number of pills into her mouth and pressed her cold dry lips to the decorative spout. Swallowing the pills made her gag, but she kept drinking, scooped up the last few with her tongue and drank again. As the warm whisky tumbled into her she wished for Leopold. She hated to admit that she had grown to love him. He had a power over her that no man had ever had. She had enjoyed it, she had. She had craved it. But she could see now that he had not loved or craved her. He had controlled and manipulated her. If he were here now she would make him see that whilst she may be bleeding and dying, this time she was in control of her suffering. She would force him to watch as she erased the scars he left behind and tried to abort the child he may have planted inside her. She would make him see that she could scrub him out of her life, even if she had to strip herself to broken bones to do it.

The Vin Mariani went down with ease and did not make her shudder quite as much as the whisky.

Swift and powerful sensations consumed her body as the two liquids washed together. Marta had not eaten properly for a couple of days and the emptiness of her stomach allowed the effects to hit her hard. She scooped up the letter knife once more and took her sore tired body over to her bed, where she collapsed on her side.

'How could she have a child when somewhere inside of her she remained a child?' she thought.

As she ran the blade of her letter knife across her abdomen, she cried out longingly for Arnold and Josefine.

'Where are you? Why don't you come to me? I need you now... I need you, please.'

If only they could cradle her. It was a thought that rattled around her head like a runaway train until she slipped into unconsciousness, her torment finally drowned.

She did not know that Pernilla had come to her bedroom some time after to check on her. Marta did not have to bear the sight of her tortured body lying on blood-soaked sheets. She did not have to scrub the stained rug that was stretched out in front of the hearth, or mop up the vomit from the polished wood floor. And she did not hear the two men standing at her bedside, discussing her fate with solemnity.

Had she been able to pull herself from her catatonic state, she would have protested as Leopold convinced Arnold that she was plagued with insanity just like her mother. She would have fought. She would have prevented him from approving her committal to the Kreis des Wahnsinns. She would have shown him the letter, the clues, the jewellery, all of it.

But she had not been fit to do any of those things and so the events of that evening rumbled on without her consciousness or consent.

She did not register her unfamiliar surroundings when she awoke, but she was grateful to see that Elise was keeping vigil at her bedside. Marta tried to sit up but her body felt brittle and she was overcome by nausea.

Elise raised her hands to offer support, helping her lie back down on the bed. 'Shhhh. You need to rest.'

'But Elise, I've said and done so many terrible things.' Marta surveyed the room, her head began to pound. 'Where am I?'

'You are in the medical wing of the Kreis des Wahnsinns.'

Marta shrieked in fear.

'Do not be concerned Marta, just rest. You will be leaving here by the very doors you entered, and soon.'

She shrieked again, unable to calm herself. 'But, how and what...' Her breathing was erratic and shallow, her heartbeat irregular.

'Shh Marta please. Don't be afraid. Pernilla brought the contents of your mother's locker to me. She may not be the best housekeeper, but she was smart enough to realise that it should not be left lying around for Leopold to discover. I have it hidden away for safe keeping.'

'What will you do with it?' Marta was struggling to make sense of Elise's words.

'I got us in here once remember? I will get us out of here again. Our German cover story came in handy once more. I have been able to access the office here and review your mother's case notes going as far back as the year you were born. I have learned many important things Marta.'

'I don't understand.'

'You don't need to at the moment. I will explain everything just as soon as I get you out of here. Don't worry; I will not let you down again. I will repair the abuses of our father if you will only forgive me.'

Elise ran her soft fingertips across Marta's brow and for the first time she felt as though she might like to accept the care of her half-sister. Comforted, she realised she was no longer alone in her battle.

As the hours passed she reflected on the events of the last few days. How could so much have changed in such a short space of time? Why had she poured herself into the idea of a future with Leopold? She had been so sure that this was her time and that she deserved to carve her own niche, yet all she had done was fall under the control of another man.

With the fading morphine she became aware of an immense pain in her uterus. She moved her hand down instinctively and as she did she felt the wound dressings. Instantly she remembered what she had done the night before.

Marta was unsure whether she had induced the abortion of her unborn child through drink and drugs and trauma, whether the foetus had chosen to abandon its unwelcoming home inside her, or whether there had perhaps never been a pregnancy at all. Either way, she was aware that she was bleeding now as her body emptied itself of all it had been holding on to.

She had gone further than she ever thought she was capable of and it frightened her. Perhaps she belonged here in the asylum, destined to share her mother's fate. At once she was overcome with sadness at the loss of a mother whom she now understood had loved her for a lifetime, but that she had only just come to know.

CHAPTER THIRTY SIX

Arnold had not left the drawing room of his home since Marta had been taken away. The green velvet drapes had remained closed for days. A sprinkling of dust now dulled the wings of the hummingbirds that decorated the frosted glass lamp shades. The air in the room was fusty and still, and the temperature so low it was sure to bring on influenza.

Pernilla had tried to rouse her employer once, but had been dismissed and ordered not to return under any circumstances. Leopold had visited the household three times in as many days and had failed to gain access on every occasion.

Arnold had so many questions touring his mind that he struggled to contain them all. When he dozed off in the darkness they would come to him in dreams, sometimes narrated by his wife, and he would startle awake still unclear of the answers. How could Marta betray him? Why had Josefine chosen to end her life now? What would Leopold make of all this? Louder and louder they grew until his only security could be found sitting in the wing back chair Josefine had bought for him as a wedding present all those years ago. It held him like her arms once did and muffled the questions to the background until one question remained.

Had he failed them both?

No, no, he must not entertain it. The fact that both his beloved wife and once trusted daughter should lose themselves to mental illness was a cruel irony of course, but he could not help everybody. They were adults. In the end they could only have helped themselves, and he too could only help himself.

But what would become of him now? Marta had been his legacy. His link to immortalising his work long after his time was done. What would his peers make of that; of him? This sorry state would not do. He must return to his practice where his colleagues and patients depended on him. He must lead from the front and share his learning from this experience. Maybe even publish it in the form of a research paper or case study one day.

Whatever he felt about it, both Josefine and Marta were gone now and he had no choice but to continue or suffer the dissipation of his life's work. He had sacrificed too much to let it all fall away now and he reasoned that neither woman would want that for him.

Closure, that's what was required if he wanted to rid himself of this melancholy. Rising from his chair he opened the drapes. It was late in the afternoon and the light was not as bright and warming as he hoped, offering little more than a gentle gloom of coal wash grey. He switched on the table lamps. No, that wouldn't do at all. The room was still too dim to achieve anything significant or precise. He would go to his desk in the study and work under his writing lamp.

He startled Pernilla who was in the hallway polishing the brass as he emerged from the drawing room.

'Fetch me some tea and bring a tray of bread and jam please Pernilla.'

She nodded obediently, still wearing an expression of surprise to see him in the flesh after such notable absence.

When he reached his study he was relieved to find that Pernilla had tidied away the evidence of Marta's betrayal. All of the remaining papers were in a pile on the floor next to the log basket. He would burn what was left later on. Taking out his writing instruments and headed notepaper, he drafted identical letters to each of his five daughters notifying them of their mother's demise and sister's confinement. He included a postal order for 50 Krone, instructed them to spend it on ensuring their on-going stability in whatever way they deemed appropriate. He added that he would not be in touch again and that he would appreciate it if they could return the courtesy. His daughters drained his personal and professional resources and so it was best if they each got on with their lives independent of him.

Next he wrote to Marta.

'Dear Marta,

I do not apologise for failing to visit you after your episode. I'm sure you can appreciate the sensitivities such a visit could have disturbed in me and I must protect my sanity. It is for the good of my own survival and indeed yours that I will now continue on my path alone. I'm unsure of your fate and have decided not to take further interest in it.

Before you bleat or wallow at this you should note that I am being neither cruel nor unfair. I have informed your sisters of your mother's passing, and your own situation, and I have despatched of my duties to them, just as I am despatching of you now. You are not the pitiful victim, I urge you not to submit to the martyrdom you seem to love so much. You are a grown woman and you should take on that role with purpose and determination.

I wish you well, but I no longer wish to carry your burdens.

Goodbye Marta.

He did not sign off with the care of a loving parent or even an approving mentor. Instead, he ended his letter only with his signature.

'*Dr. A Rosenblit, Chairman of the Vienna Psychiatric Council.*'

Feeling satisfied, he placed each letter in a pristine white envelope and added his daughters' names. He plucked the last slice of bread from his plate and pushed it into his mouth whole before licking the sticky remnants of jam from his fingers. A memory of Marta bringing similar treats on a tray for him tried to slip into an unlocked corner of his mind but he was quick to banish it. 'Closure', he said, pushing the memory away and reclining in his chair.

He called out for Pernilla. 'Add the addresses to these envelopes for me and post them today, second class. Oh, and will you bring me more tea?' He ordered as she stood in the doorway of his study.

'Of course Dr Rosenblit, as you wish.' Pernilla took the six envelopes from Arnold and placed them on the tea tray, which she then hurried away. When she returned she placed the refilled teapot on his desk and lit the two candles he had perched on elephant shaped candlesticks on either side of his desk. He had one more instruction for her.

'Pernilla I would like you to call Dr Kaposi for me. Tell him that I apologise for my absence and that I should like for him to join me this evening for drinks and to discuss a new project I have in mind.'

She considered objecting. She had wanted to alert him to the items she had found in Marta's room but she knew it was not her place. Pernilla needed her job and she was sure he would not have believed the word of an incompetent housekeeper over that of his old friend and colleague. Reluctantly she agreed and retreated from the study in order to go about her obligations.

Alone again, Arnold thought for a while before pulling out a final sheet of paper. The feather edged parchment he reserved for his letters to Josefine. It featured a fine line botanical illustration of her favourite magnolia flowers. For a second he imagined their soft perfume. The smell of magnolia was familiar,comforting. A small tear crept out from the corner of his eye.He let it roll, inhaled deeply and let out a sigh. It was time to move on.

Ever mine, Josefine,

My heart is broken. I do not care to repair it for I fear that it will never beat the same again. I know now that the time has come to bring an end to us. So with the words of this letter I stamp upon the shards of my heart until they are only dust. You are swept away and my heart will not beat for you again.

I will not write to you again. You are not here. I have nothing left to say.

Your Arnold.

He folded the paper and pressed it to his lips. Then he reached forward and hovered the paper over the candle flame until it caught light. Arnold stared through bleary eyes as his words crumbled to the ashtray.

CHAPTER THIRTY SEVEN

By the following Friday, Marta was feeling stronger and had been able to keep down small amounts of food. The more she brightened, the more she became aware of the whispered chatter of the staff as they debated her suitability for transfer to the Kreis des Wahnsinns. Elise had not visited since that first morning, but she had faith in her new sibling. The spaces left by Leopold and Arnold were notable, neither had visited. Marta was not surprised, but it did not hurt any less to think of them out there living life without her.

As for Leopold, she had dedicated herself to him and tolerated his demands in the hope that one day she might earn his love and respect. She was not proud to realise that she would miss him, and now she knew he was her real father she found it hard to sever her bond with him.

Perhaps he genuinely did want her to succeed and that Arnold had been tormenting her all of these years. But wait, no, *that* was madness. She should be locked away in an asylum for thinking such things. More harmful than any of the physical afflictions she had endured.

Leopold Kaposi was a manipulative abuser of people and no good could ever come of a familial relationship and most certainly not a romantic one. She must hold on to that no matter what.

That afternoon Elise returned. She was carrying the large embroidered bag Marta had used for her trip to Budapest. Elise opened it in front of her.

'Look inside.' She invited.

Marta inspected the contents and saw that the bag was full of folders, envelopes and documents. She looked back at Elise for explanation.

'It's evidence. Against Leopold. You and I are leaving here today and taking this straight to the police.'

'What kind of evidence?'

'Case notes, prescriptions, review documents and more. All relating to the detainment of Josefine Rosenblit; all forgeries and all signed by Dr Leopold Kaposi.'

'How do you know they are forgeries?'

'Because I have the real test results and I have the original psychiatric assessment documents.'

'Wherever did you find them?' Marta was stunned.

'That is a story I may never fully tell you about, but I can tell you that I have been all over Vienna and beyond, tracking down anyone who may have come into contact with your mother over the last 23 years. It's been quite the task.'

'But how do you know that is enough to stop him from practising?'

'We can do more than stop him practising Marta. According to the rules of the General Practitioner's Council, all detainments must be countersigned by a second doctor if they are to continue for more than six weeks. The countersignatories on your mother's case notes and review documents were all fakes penned by Leopold himself. It's a clear case of fraud if nothing else.'

'But fraud is a criminal charge.'

Elise hurried Marta through the rest of the evidence. 'There's more. Leopold visited your mother the day before she committed suicide. After spending some time alone with her, she became uncontrollable and violent and so he had her sedated. He filed a letter of recommendation that she was not fit for a review and should remain at the Kreis des Wahnsinns indefinitely. I don't know what he said to your mother but Hannah, the nurse we met when we visited that day, told me that the neck tie she hung herself with was the same as the one Leopold was wearing during his visit. He practically goaded her into doing it and left behind a ready-made noose.'

'That's not possible. You can't just lock people away for life without question.' Marta resisted.

'By law, any recommendation for permanent detainment must be approved by the Chairman of the Psychiatric Council of Vienna.'

'Arnold signed my mother away?' Marta was horrified.

'No, he didn't. I checked the signature and it does not match Arnold's. He had no idea that Leopold had even been in to see her. Leopold was careless with this final forgery.'

Marta knew she should be relieved to have confirmation of the truth, but she found it all so hard to comprehend. Her sadness was all encompassing. Leopold had given her life then took it back just when she had felt capable of living it.

Elise slowed and softened her voice. She mustn't forget that whilst she had long suspected her father a fraud, this was all still so new to Marta.

'He must have intended to return and destroy the document but forgot to do so when he got caught up in arranging for your admittance. Josefine wasn't crazy; she was telling everyone the truth Marta. Leopold kept your mother here under false pretences, and he has tried to do the same to you.'

'But how was he not discovered?'

'Shortly after your mother's initial transfer to the asylum, Leopold became a generous benefactor. He supports a number of other institutions across the city in a similar way. He arranged funding for research projects, new equipment, and bonuses for staff who carried out his recommendations. He effectively bought your mother's imprisonment. I'm sorry to tell you of this, you have been through so much but I hope you will see that this is the only way we can stop him from ruining other lives.'

Marta did see, of course she did. The realisation that she deserved justice brought her a sense of peace.

'How am I ever going to get out of here?'

Elise had a glint in her eye. 'We are going to stand up, our heads held high, and we are going to walk right out the front door. I have shared my evidence with the director general of the Kreis des Wahnsinns and he has agreed that further treatment is unlawful. You are being released into my care.'

With that she handed Marta a change of clothes and her gardening boots.

'Elise? You should know that I am not pregnant.'

'Well...' she hesitated. 'That's one less thing to concern ourselves with. Now, get dressed and let's go and put Leopold in jail.'

'I am so sorry Elise. For a while now everything has been about me. I know that you have lost a father too and this must be hard for you.'

Elise smiled, holding the swell that had formed in her throat.

Marta pulled her clothes on with care, feeling unsteady on her feet at first having been confined to a hospital bed for a week. They held on to each other with linked arms, made their way out of the room, along the corridor, and through the front entrance of the asylum. As they walked through the grounds Marta noticed the landscape for the first time in months. The clear sky, the busyness of the wildlife and flashes of emerald emerging from beneath the thawing snow, brought context to the horizon once more. She needed that. Nobody should lose sight of the horizon.

'Will we be okay?' She said to Elise.

Her sister squeezed her hand. 'We will be better than okay, we will be outstanding. Now let's go home.'

'Where is home for me now? I can't go back to Arnold, not now.'

'Of course you can't. You're coming to live with me. We are family.'

Marta leaned close. 'Home.'

317

CHAPTER THIRTY EIGHT

On the other side of the city, Leopold was striding along the Paradisgasse in the wealthy suburb of Döbling. He was pleased with himself. Josefine was gone, Marta was locked away and he was as sure as he could be that after the threats he made at their last meeting, Elise was most likely packing for her new life in Hamburg.

He had received word from Arnold that he was ready to pick up their friendship where they had left off. They would drink together this evening and he would be sure to make all the right noises of encouragement and support.

He had come closer to being exposed than he might have liked, but overall he was satisfied that things had turned out as well as he could have expected. Maybe better than he had expected. After all, he had imagined that he would have to endure a few years of Marta before getting to the pinnacle of his career. It would have been tiresome, but he had seen how having her around had boosted Arnold's professional status. The majority of their peers could acknowledge that the girl had all the brains and his old pal was little more than a showman nowadays. Leopold had decided long ago that he would one day take back what was rightfully his. Any intellect she possessed was inherited from him and he would not have allowed Arnold to continue to reap the rewards of his own loins. Becoming a romantic partner, as well as her business partner, was the only way to get what he wanted and have a little fun along the way.

It was unfortunate that she had fallen apart so spectacularly, Marta would have helped him lubricate many a closed door long after Arnold's star had waned. He would have to work harder and faster now to glean any benefits from the old chap, but it was the best opportunity he had for the time being and so be it.

It was gone midday and already his voracious appetite was getting the best of him. He had one more house call to make and then he would stop off for lunch and a coffee.

He rapped his knuckles on the door of an imposing modern villa. He had always liked the pungency of new money. The polished silver number 38 on the front door glittered as it opened to reveal an equally sparkling woman.

'Ah, you must be Ms Miller.' The woman returned a smile framed by a shiny ebony crop, the sharp edges of which seemed to lick at her jawline as they peeked out from beneath her earlobes.

'I'm Dr Kaposi; we spoke on the phone yesterday.'

'Of course, come on in. Oh and it's Elena.' Her distinctive New York accent was as distracting as her enormous hazel eyes.

'I've seen your revue posters all around the city. Vienna is excited to have you, and so am I.'

He extended his hand and flashed a smile at the young Follie girl, who offered out her hand before inviting him inside.

'It seems the silver linings will keep on coming.' He thought to himself as he stepped over the threshold.

He had set his sights on his next prize and she was a beauty.

'I'm not sure how you do things here in Vienna doctor, but I guess you will need to give me a complete check-up in order to register me with your practice?'

'From where I'm sitting you look very healthy, but of course it would be unprofessional of me not to check you over thoroughly.'

'Glad to hear it. As you can imagine, I'm used to undressing in front of strangers as part of my work.' She laughed.

Leopold was delighted to detect a little flirtation; it would make her more malleable in the long run. He loved his job and all the advantages that came with it. If only those school boys who had once ridiculed him and thrown stones at his head could see him now. He was no longer a gawky little stripling and girls did not squirm away from him anymore.

'Would you like to join me for lunch?' he asked once the consultation was over.

'I had a little bite to eat earlier and I'm none too keen on some of the food you have here, but some coffee or a gin would be great.'

'Ok, then give me an hour to dine and join me at the Café Sacher for coffee. While we've been talking I've been thinking about how I might be able to help you make it on your own in Vienna. It's great that you are part of such successful ensemble but don't you think it's time you stepped out of the shadows?'

'Sure, I'd love that. If we get along we could always drink gin after.' Elena was flattered and excited at the prospect of becoming better acquainted with such an influential gentleman.

'Absolutely.' He picked up his coat and hat and made his way to the door. 'See you in an hour.'

He went straight from Elena Miller's house to the Café Sacher. After feasting like a royal, Leopold ordered two coffees and waited for his new companion.

He was sipping his espresso when the federal officer entered the café. Outside, two police officers stood guard, their impressive Alsatians tugging at their leads. Immediately he knew why the police had come. He had to admit he didn't think his girls were quite so talented. Elise had warned him that he would not get away with any of his discrepancies, but he had thought her no more than a foolish child. He now wished he cleared his office at the Kreis des Wahnsinns.

How dare she and Marta turn on him in this way? His own flesh and blood had come to finish him off, and whilst he was furious at them he was also impressed that they had inherited his cunning.

'Dr Leopold Kaposi?'

Leopold nodded once in confirmation but kept his gaze fixed on Elena Miller, who had just walked in through the double doors. He watched her scan the café tables looking for him.

'I am arresting you on suspicion of fraud and money laundering.'

'That's fine officer, but if you could wait a moment I must continue with my coffee break. This espresso is one of the finest in Vienna and who knows when I might get chance to enjoy another.' He took a sip, swilling it around in his mouth before swallowing.

As the officer leant forwards in readiness to handcuff him, Leopold raised his index finger toward the man.

'Wait. There's still a drop left.'

Just as Elena thought she had caught sight of him, he stood up and turned his back to her as he was led away.

CHAPTER THIRTY NINE

The case of Dr Leopold Kaposi was heard at the Constitutional Court of Austria, beginning on Friday 3rd February 1928. The trial lasted six weeks.

It came as something of a surprise to Leopold that such matters had even made it to trial, but he had not been too concerned about the evidence submitted by Marta and Elise. He was confident that his friends, including judicial executives and members of the Supreme Court of Vienna would resolve matters.

He had passed a list of contacts to his lawyer Wolf Kipperman. 'These fine fellows will help you tidy away all of this nonsense. Members of the upper class take care of each other you know.'

What he hadn't reckoned on was the outcome of a detailed investigation into his personal activities and business interests which uncovered a further 15 criminal offences and incidents of malpractice. Fraud, theft, extortion, medical negligence and other abuses all read out in court. As it turned out, Frederick Beste had friends in high places too. Many of them only too willing to distance themselves from the scandal - particularly when the final charge, the murder of Marion Beste, became common knowledge.

Frederick was relieved to give his testimony, and though he was implicated, he had felt that any sentence he received would be a small price to pay to get justice for Marion. She would have been proud of him.

Leopold's numerous convictions resulted in a custodial sentence totalling nine years and indefinite removal from the GP register of the American Medical Association of Vienna.

He maintained his composure throughout the trial and during its conclusion; the court had to appear to follow procedure and so a guilty verdict was inevitable. Nine years seemed quite fair, the murder charge could easily have resulted in an execution had it not been reduced to manslaughter on account of the lack of hard evidence. He would smooth out the issues with the GP register in good time.

As he was led from the courtroom Leopold smiled at Marta and Elise, who looked down on him from the public gallery. He had already instructed Wolf to appeal. After all, he had only done what his clients and colleagues had wanted him to do. Even Frederick had had to admit that in court. Far from being punished, he believed he should be celebrated. He had made some remarkable things possible for the city's most respected professionals and often in the face of impossible odds.

Wolf Kipperman visited Leopold one week into his detainment at the Justizanstalt Graz-Karlau. They met in a small side room away from the main visiting area. It was too noisy to talk out there. Prison noises irritated Leopold the most, guards yelling, doors slamming, shouting and fighting. He couldn't even hear himself whistle. He was looking forward to returning to the peace and solitude of his own home.

'Ah, Kipperman. A little late perhaps, but it's good to see you all the same. So come on then, how long do they need me to play the game before they let me out of here?'

Wolf put his briefcase on the floor without opening it, pulled out a chair and sat down. 'I'm afraid it's not been quite as simple as that.'

'I feared as much. They want more money don't they? Greed is a terrible trait indeed, but if they weren't greedy they wouldn't be so successful, and then where would I be?'

'I don't think the money is…'

'Fine! Have it your way. I have a deposit account in Geneva. I have been setting some aside for a new car, a Locomobile. Did you know you can get seven people in the Model 48?' He paused. 'I tell you what, offer double my usual gratuity and tell them I will take them all out for a ride in it just as soon as I get out. Have somebody diary something for next Sunday afternoon will you?'

'Leopold, you won't be getting out next Sunday.'

'Okay, the week after then.'

'Nobody will help you Leopold. Not the judge, the Chief of police, nobody. Even Arnold Rosenblit has refused to see you. And you have no assets. All of your accounts have been seized, including the one in Geneva. I'm sorry but there is nothing more I can do.'

'There is always something that can be done for someone. You know that as well as I do.'

Wolf Kipperman stood to leave.

'Wait, let's make a deal. We can shake on it; you know I'll take care of you.' Leopold stuck out his hand. 'We go back a long way you and I, remember?'

'Not this time. It's over. You are nobody now, you might as well consider yourself ostracised.' Wolf did not return the handshake, just turned and walked away.

Leopold was stunned. 'I'd have been better off going to the gallows.' he thought to himself as the guard took him back to his cell.

His daughters were relieved but not triumphant when informed that his appeal had been withdrawn. They had both felt love and compassion for Leopold at different points in their lives though neither could explain it rationally.

By July things had moved on at a pace. Marta had released her debut research paper entitled *'Childhood Attachments: A Break in the Bond'* and was being well received by her peers. She and Elise planned to move to London later in the summer. With the help of Pernilla, they had managed to get hold of much of the original paperwork and had resurrected the plans for the child analysis facility. Elise had finally agreed to start dating Matthias Biedermeier, who had harangued her since they had met in England. He was now based full time in London and had helped them secure a small flat and a delightful country property where they could base the facility. Work was underway on the renovation and they were on track to open in October. Elise would join the organisation as Head of Paediatric Care, her first job in medicine since she qualified.

That year was the year of firsts. Amelia Earhart became the first woman to fly across the Atlantic. The first colour television broadcast took place in England. Marta Rosenblit became the first female child psychiatrist in the world to open a facility for children, and for the first time in his life Leopold Kaposi was being held accountable for a lifetime of manipulation and dishonesty.

ONE YEAR LATER, LONDON, ENGLAND

19ᵗʰ October 1929

Dear Father,

I will not write again, it seems that you might not appreciate receiving my letters though I like to send them even so.

In spite of everything you now know of Leopold, I shall always regard you as that man, my father. I wonder if you are still able to feel the same love for me, if you remember me as your daughter, the girl that used to light your eyes with pride. Perhaps you prefer not to remember me at all?

The Marta Rosenblit Centre for Childhood Analysis celebrates its one year anniversary next month, and tonight Elise and I shall attend a dinner and prize giving ceremony. Father, the Centre has been hailed as a pioneering facility for children, and I have been nominated for the most prestigious award. World leading experts in child psychology have made their way to London to hear me give a presentation after the ceremony.

If only you and my mother could be here to share my joys. About that, I have many regrets. I hope that I am not alone and that you hold as much compunction as I do, maybe more? Do you wish that you had done better, fought harder and listened more? If only you could have seen the diffidence, rather than the defiance in me.

When all is said and done, you are the man to whom I owe my life, with all of its pleasure and pain.

I used to imagine that living without you would not be living at all, but I see now that whilst I was at your side I was, in reality, living through you. Now I must live for myself, a life underpinned by enormous gratitude for everything you are and everything you were unable to be for me.

Goodbye my beloved Father.
Forever yours, Marta.

Marta set her pen down on the inkwell; the one Pernilla had obtained from Arnold's study for her before she left Vienna. She folded the paper and slipped it into a crisp white envelope before replacing the front leaf of her writing bureau. Pausing to hold the envelope to her chest, she felt a palpable sadness. He might not have been the most predictable of men, but she missed him all the same and a part of her ached for him every day.

She placed the letter on top of the bureau and turned to look at the evening dress she had chosen for this special occasion. It was time to get ready.

Marta removed her robe and pulled on the simple cotton camisole she had already prepared. Next her stockings and suspender belt, followed by the petal edged knickers she had chosen at a department store in Knightsbridge the previous week.

This would be the first time she had ever worn such a special gown. She had found it quite difficult to shop for and had gone to great lengths to find something stylish but modest. Not wanting to make an overstatement but needing something worthy of the honour she was to receive.

She held the dress out in front of her, admiring it before pulling it over her head. The pale green beading made a gentle rustling sound as it dropped down her body, loosely skimming her narrow hips. The waterfall skirt sat softly at differing lengths between her shin and ankle. She watched it move in swirls and catch the light as she twisted her waist from side to side.

Her shoes were pewter satin, with a T-bar and a delicate ankle strap. Out of habit she pulled the straps until they pinched then corrected herself, loosening them a little before fastening the tiny buckle.

She had decided against make-up, still unaccustomed to it. However, she and Elise had been to the salon to have their hair set. Marta had chosen waves set and styled close to her head and tucked neatly into a low bun at the back.

Elise tapped on the door and peeped inside. She had chosen pin curls to match her more elaborate gown which was plum coloured taffeta embellished with frills and a corsage. She was the more beautiful but, for the first time in her life; Marta didn't feel any less of a lady.

'Are you ready to go?'

As she stepped into the bedroom Marta thought of how thankful she was that her half-sister had helped her to get to this moment.

'I don't know how I made it Elise. At times like this I feel like such an imposter. I dropped so low into a black hole that I wonder how I deserve to see the sky at all.'

'You can only lead the charge if you have identified your enemies, and you did even more than that. You left them slain, and now you stand taller because of it. You fought hard, and you deserve your glory.'

'You fought too Elise.'

'Yes, I did, and I have my rewards. Leopold is dead to both of us. You are standing before me glowing with possibilities. Matthias is waiting for me downstairs. Life is good Marta, so let's get on and live it. Now, before we go, I have something for you.'

Elise handed Marta a small box. Inside were Josefine's earrings and necklace.

'I hope you don't mind, but I invested in a new chain for the pendant and had the whole set cleaned and polished. I just knew they would look beautiful with your dress.'

Marta's eyes welled as her face broke first into a smile, and then into a soft laugh that cushioned her tears of joy. She hugged Elise tightly before walking to the mirror and putting the earrings on. She turned her left cheek and raised her chin, delighting in the droppers as they dangled at her jawline. Next she took out the necklace.

'Elise, will you help me with the clasp?'

'I'd be delighted.' Elise stood behind her, joining her reflection as she fastened the chain and straightened the pendant.

The pair paused as they stared at their image held in the oval surround. Marta raised her hand to her shoulder where she found Elise's, squeezing it gently in a thankful gesture.

'I'm ready.'

THE END

Did you enjoy this book? If so, please tell your friends and family, share on your social media networks and leave a review on Amazon.co.uk, CompletelyNovel.com or Goodreads.com

Follow Vanessa on Twitter @VanessaMatthews or Facebook at facebook.com/VanessaMatthewsWriter to find out more about her latest projects and forthcoming book releases. You can also subscribe to her blog ordinarylifelessordinary.wordpress.com